The Valley of Dragons Book 4: The Basilisk's Revenge

Fanny Garstang

GLOABTONA
MORONLAND
DUNTORN
DRUKGANG
RIVER SENS
KEYTEL
LINYEE
THE HOUSE
KEYTELIA
VILLAGE
VILLAGE

SENSPANTA
JUKIR
JUKIRLA
N

Part One: One

The three youths stood at the mine's entrance, breaths misting in front of them. It was boarded up apart from one corner where the wood had rotted, and the leader of the group had kicked it in.

Behind them was an abandoned mining village. Most of the roofs had caved in on the buildings from years of snow settling on them. Some buildings were blackened skeletons burnt in a mountain lightning storm. The long wooden troughs that had moved water around to filter and clean the ore were filled with ice or had icicles hanging off them from where water had overflowed.

No one visited as it was rumoured to be haunted by ghouls and spirits from the disaster that had caused the inhabitants to flee on mass.

The youths turned as two more joined them, crunching through the snow in fur lined boots. Their bodies were wrapped up in fine wool lined caped coats with deep rabbit fur lined hoods, "we can't find the old galoot anywhere."

"Maybe he's actually dead."

"He was around last week, half frightened me to death when he appeared behind me." The leader remarked.

"What are we doing here anyway?"
The leader, brushed black hair out of his eyes grinned,

"there's got to be something special in here if they have a guard on site, don't you think?"

The rest of the group glanced at each other. This was the riskiest think their Crown Prince had done in a while. Did they try to deter him? None of them knew what condition the mine was in.

There was a howl of wind and someone made a decision, "if we are doing this let's do it. I don't fancy meeting a ghoul or that grumpy guard. He looks like one of them and it's got to be warmer in there than out here." He stamped his feet and crossed his arms against the cold. The Crown Prince ducked down and entered the mine through the hole followed by the other four youths.

The last one to enter glanced nervously around. He had a bad feeling about this expedition of theirs. This was more dangerous than anything else they had done and he felt sure it wasn't going to end well.

Inside the Crown Prince said, "Dota, have you got the lamps? Get them lit."

"Yes sir."

With a flash of sparks and then the brightening of the flames the mine's tunnel was revealed. Ice lined the walls, glinting in the lamplight. Water could be heard dripping somewhere further in. Wooden posts held the roof up and in some places the sides had collapsed in where the wood had rotted. One of them asked, "What did they use to mine here? Why did they leave?"

"Don't know. I think it was silver and it was said they found something terrible in here and just fled." Dota said with a shiver of excitement. This was the most thrilling thing they had done in a while apart from finding the remains of a dragon skeleton. He was so ready to freak the others out when the opportunity came.

"How far are we going to go in?" The last in line asked, glancing back at the boarded entrance as they had started walking, the Crown Prince in the lead.

"Don't be such a coward Guang-fu." The Crown Prince called back, "keep up and then you won't get lost. We are going as far as we can. Come on." He waved a hand forward.

The tunnel gently sloped down and they came to a junction where one route was blocked. The Crown Prince turned to the others and grinned, "our way is obvious." The others rolled their eyes and followed their leader down the new tunnel.

They decided to keep to the main tunnels rather than going down the smaller, narrower ones where silver seams had been chased and dug out. Hearing eerie sounds from some tunnel entrances they skirted round those while others they peered down with curiosity.

It got warmer the deeper they went, the tunnel continuing to slope down. At another junction they looked down both tunnels to decide which way to go. There was a pulsing glow in the distance in one of them and the Crown Prince decreed, "this one. It looks like there is something this way."

Guang-fu froze when he heard, *"it's so cold in here."*
He nervously asked, "what was that? Let's go back. They'll be starting to wonder where we have got to." He took a step backwards and bumped into something soft but it wasn't any of them as he was the last in the line. He span round but couldn't see anything

"What was what?" The second in the line asked.

"Keep up Guang-fu." The Crown Prince called up the line.

"It was probably a ghoul, come to eat you." Dota teased.

The young men continued on, determined to see what was causing the glow before turning back. The tunnel came to an abrupt end, opening out on to a ledge. Ahead of them was pitch black and it felt as if it would suck them in. On either side of the ledge were two fire bowls, the cause of the glow, eternal flames burning in them, flickering. As a group they cautiously approached the edge that could just about be discerned in the firelight. They peered down and got a sense that it was a bottomless pit straight to Hell. There was a flash of movement in the darkness and they quickly retreated back to the tunnel. One of them whispered, "what was that?"

"Help me."
They all heard it and Guang-fu said, "that's what I heard earlier. That's definitely words, not sounds."

"Help me." The voice changed languages.

"Who's there?! Show yourself!" The Crown Prince demanded, hand going to the knife tucked into the belt of his tunic under his coat, "I am the Crown Prince and I order you to reveal yourself."

"I'm trapped. I'm sooo cold and hunnngryyy." It whined.

"How long have you been here?" Dota asked, thinking it must be another person, maybe the guard, who had come in and got lost, "have you a lamp, we can't see you."

"Bring your lamps closer to the edge." It called out. Cautiously they approached the edge again.

They felt something probing their minds, seeking out their deepest darkest thoughts, as the two lamp holders held up their lights. None of them could see a thing beyond their lamps. There was movement again and what looked like black scales reflected the lamplight.

It chuckled as it found something suitable in one of them and whispered into his mind, "you want power, I can give you power."
The chosen young man remained cautiously silent, wondering what the voice was about to suggest.

"To your right, him, push him in and feeeed me."

Guang-fu froze, not believing what was being

suggested. He couldn't push his cousin, the Crown Prince in…. or could he? He sent a question to the voice in his mind, "what sort of power?"

"More than what that boy will ever have. Take his country and then move on to the next and the next and the next." It laughed, "rule them all with me behind you." It paused as it analysed the young man's thoughts before sneering, "fine, keep him as a puppet king. What about the gnat to your left? He used to beat you up didn't he? Mocks you still?"

Guang-fu's eyes widened, he thought and then he nodded. Out loud he said, "Dota?"

The young man to his left turned, "yes?"

"Could you shine the lamp over here?" Guang-fu pointed to his right.

"Have you seen something?" The lamp holder shuffled and then before he knew it he was stumbling and then falling. He let go of the lamp and sprayed out his arms in the hope of landing on something solid.

Three young men turned and fled as they heard something solid grating against the hidden rockface and uncoiling.

Guang-fu stayed, staring as the blackness formed into a nose and open mouth filled with teeth and watched as his rival and bully screamed all the way down the throat of whatever was being held prisoner deep into the mine. He couldn't help laughing as he watched the jaws snap shut.

"Now, push those fire bowls in. Then leave and wait for me. I will come to you."

Guang-fu put all of his weight behind the shallow bowls of burning oil and flipped it into the hole. The oil and flames revealed more of the monster in the pit. He stared in wonder at the huge black scales that were revealed by the fire. What was about to be unleashed on the world?

The other three were already out of the mine, gasping for breath. One exclaimed, "what was that?!"

"How do we explain Dota's absence?! Where's Guang-fu?" The two looked to the Crown Prince for guidance as their leader.

"He must have slipped, it was greasy." The Crown Prince stuttered, still in shock at what had happened.

"We can't go back without him, perhaps we should go back and find him."

"Guang-fu, thank the Gods!"
Guang-fu appeared, crawling out of the hole.

"We thought we had lost you too. What happened to Dota?"

"He is gone, it was a deep hole." Guang-fu remarked calmly but the others weren't listening as they were looking at each other.

"I'll have father give the family compensation. Come on, let's get going." The Crown Prince declared and led them away from the mine trying not to think about what he had seen in the lamplight. He felt sure he had smelt the sour sulphuric breath as it had inhaled his friend. He decided there would be no more adventures, he would stick to just hunting from now on which would please his father.

Two

Deep within the mine the monster stirred, the flames were warming him and the blood from the chosen sacrifice was fueling him. He needed more to reach full strength but for now it would be enough to get him out of his prison. The invisible chains were breaking as he flexed his muscles. Using his coiled body as a spring he pushed himself upwards and out of the mine, straight through the rock into the dull evening light.

Black clouds quickly gathered, hiding him from the stars and moon but he couldn't resist testing his voice and roared so loud that the palace thought there was an avalanche happening nearby. Wrapping itself round the mountain was a huge black scaled serpentine dragon, black mane wisping in the wind behind an open hood which had a silver crown imprint in it. There were scars on its body and his mouth was full of blood stained sharp teeth with bone stuck between them. One claw was a stump, all its toes gone from it. Short sharp spines ran down his long back.

The call was heeded throughout the known world. A wind rose up and swept through the lands fast and strong, pulling over trees, disturbing all the animals, tearing roofs from buildings until it arrived at its caller and whispered all that had been happening in the world since its master had been imprisoned. A lot had changed in the world it seemed but not completely. He chuckled to himself. He was sure he would be able to make use of his new knowledge.

Far away in the mountains between Moronland and Keytel Ozanus felt fear envelope him and he blacked out and crumpled to the floor. Arno, Ozanus' servant, could only stand in shock, trying not to let his mouth drop open. His master and Nejus had not shown any signs of fainting moments before.

Five minutes later Ozanus stirred and vomited, emptying his stomach. He felt a horrendous headache forming with no idea what had just happened. The War God that lingered in him had, for the moment, shrunk to nothing.

"Sir, what happened?" Arno helped Ozanus into a chair, trying not to look at the vomit he was going to have to clean up.

"Arno… Just help me to bed." Ozanus whispered. Anything louder was making his head pulse painfully.

"Yes sir."

He had heard the young men talking of guards around the mine. That would be enough to give him the strength to seek out his human puppet. He slid down the side of the mountain while calling out for his prey, seeking out their location.

The two old men were huddled by their ceramic corner stove in their two roomed shelter. Warm bowls of stew were clutched in their liver spotted hands. They were the last of a long line of guards for the old mining village. Their king had decided no more money should be wasted on guarding a ghost village for no obvious reason. The reason had got lost through the decades. The wind whipped up the snow and howled through the crumbling ruins. One remarked to the other, "think there is a storm coming?"

"That wind has definitely come up sudden, wonder what is agitating the Gods?"

The first sat up straighter and looked towards the tiny windows with panes of thin horn, "did you hear that?"

"What?"

"Oh, nothing." His head shrunk back into his worn fur collar, "thought I heard someone calling for help. It was probably the wind."

The other lifted his head, "no, I heard it then. Fetch the spears and we'll go look." He stood with a heavy sigh and reached for the lamp.

Warily they headed out. No one ever visited. The locals herded their hardy sheep and yaks at a safe distance. There had been the occasional visit from bored youths from the palace but not recently. They pulled up their hoods and pulled on their padded gloves before stepping out of the door. They waited and listened.

"Over there."

The two men glanced at each other, gripped their spears tighter and headed off into the ruined village, snow lying thigh deep against crumbling walls. They stuck to the tracks they had made in the snow, following the same route they always took.

Close to the mine entrance they paused. One asked, "can you hear breathing?"

Above their heads the monstrous dragon's mouth opened wide. One of the men looked up, feeling the hot breath and let out a scream that was quickly swallowed as the demonic dragon clamped his jaws over them both and swallowed them whole.

Now it needed to find more heat. It began to shrink and change into the form of a black skinned man, scars white on his skin. It followed its senses to the guards' two rooms. It threw more wood and dry yak pats in the stove and found the men's spare clothes and pulled them on before wrapping its new human body around the ceramic stove with a sigh. He had been too long in that cold pit. Once warm he would start plotting his revenge on the dragons that had locked him away, including his own kin.

He remained hidden throughout the short winter day, feeding the fire and warming himself up. Snow fell outside but he didn't care. With the new night he emerged to start walking, following the scent of fear left by the young men the previous day. The veil of black clouds continued to keep him hidden from the stars and waning moon. Every step he took, the little grass there was underfoot, perished.

After several hours he saw ahead of him his destination. The palace was built upon the mountainside, tiered up it, each courtyard on a higher level to the one below it. The lower ones had graveled yards and the higher ones had enclosed gardens. Snow covered curved tiled roofs with the exposed ends of eaves carved into the shape of dragons. Covered corridors ran round the accommodation courtyards with doors to rooms coming off them. At the top was the Great Audience Pavilion, rarely used at this time of year. The snows kept travelers and visitors away. Only a few lamps were lit, at the closed doors that partitioned the individual courtyards.

One corner of the entrance gates had a watch tower whitewashed like all of the walls marking the perimeter of the palace. Marks, painted as a thick line, on the outside corner showed how high previous snows had reached. None of the lower courtyards had any windows looking out.

There weren't any guards on duty but chained to the wall on long chains were six large thick furred dogs sheltering in a long low kennel against the outside wall. As a group, sensing His presence, they uncurled themselves and stood, sniffing the air with curled tails high. Then they began to bark, pulling at their chains. Then the barking became howls which quickly became snarls until they were whining and whimpering. No longer were they straining at their chains to attack the unwanted visitor but pulling sideways to escape, tails between their hind legs. Then there was silence as the chains broke and the six of them fled.

Next to announce the stranger's arrival were the rats and mice who fled the warmth of the storerooms, preferring to risk the ice cold night rather than stay. The cats yowled, hair up on end and arched backs. They hissed and spat before fleeing as well. In the stables the stocky mountain ponies were rearing and neighing, trying to break out of their pens.

The whole palace was waking up, even the captain of the guard who normally slept like the dead. He woke up grumbling and pulled on warm clothes as a soldier came running into his room without even knocking. The captain demanded, "What is going on? What is causing all this noise?"

"The animals sir, they are all afraid. I've just seen the vermin leaving as well."

"What is out there?"

Another soldier appeared, "sir, you've got to come see this."

The captain stared at the soldier, wrapped against the cold, his skin drained of colour. There was a wild look of fear in the man's eyes.

"I'm coming." He grabbed his sword and the three of them hurried to the main gate and its watchtower.

Soldiers hung around the barred double gates and looked to their captain for guidance. He shouted, "well, open it then."

"Have you looked sir?"

"What do you mean?" The captain frowned.
The man stepped out of the way to let the officer peer through the square peephole at eye height in the gate. The captain opened the little door and looked out. Coming towards them was what he could only describe as a black void. The stars and moon had disappeared in the fog that surrounded it. He shouted, "don't open the gates."
He stepped away from the peephole as pale as the soldier who had fetched him. He ordered, "get men up to the top courtyard. We must protect the family."

"What is out there sir?" Another soldier asked with fear. The captain gulped, "our worst nightmare." He would be having words with the boys when he next saw them together for some how they had unleashed something terrible.

The heavy wooden gates bulged, and they turned as a group. The captain shouted, as he felt the sense of terror growing, "keep those gates shut!"

"Nothing can stop me."
The men against the gates were flung back as the wooden bar cracked, broke and the gates flew open.

They stared out through the gates from where they had fallen. In front of them stood a tall black skinned man with an angular face and sharp nose. Only one hand hung out of the sleeve of the coat that was clearly too small for him. He pushed the hood back revealing black hair tied in a plait that ran down his back. He smiled, his eyes staring into the soldier's eyes, "are you going to let me in?"
The captain stepped back, hypnotised, "come in."

"Take me to your king."
The captain turned to one of his men, "go let him know he has an important guest."

The king was not happy to be dragged out of his bed by the palace guards. He was still angry at his son for going on a foolish and dangerous adventure and coming back with one of them dead. He had had to pay the family compensation and now his son and his friends were banned from leaving the palace for the rest of the winter. Strangely they were happy to accept the punishment. All had looked shaken from whatever escapade they had gotten themselves into. Hopefully it would make his son grow up and start to take more of an interest in the admin involved in running their mountain kingdom.

He made his way to the Audience Pavilion when he got the message there was a visitor, an important visitor. When asked who no name could be given. He settled on the dais and adjusted his padded coat and silk undercoat around him. He pulled his padded trousers down to cover his silk slippers. In his anger he shouted, "get these stoves working, it's freezing in here and where is Tobden and Mengma. They should be here as well if I am being dragged out of my bed."
His servant bowed and hurried off to do as he was ordered.

An ill feeling of doom pervaded the palace as the new guest was led through the courtyards. As he reached the gardens the plants all died under the sheets that protected them from the worst of the snow. Courtiers and servants peered through the shutters of the covered corridors, who would arrive so late at night and why did he put fear in their hearts so much that it felt like an invisible hand squeezing all the blood out of them?

Spotting the visitor Guang-fu knew who it was. This was his new lord, the man, the demon, who would make him the most powerful man in the country and maybe the known world. He headed up to the Audience Pavilion meeting the Crown Prince heading that way as well. The Crown Prince was still rubbing sleep out of his eyes, "who's visiting this late in the season? Has someone come from Keytel seeking a new wife?"

"Don't be silly, but it is someone who is going to shake things up." Guang-fu smirked.

"What are you talking about?" The Prince frowned at his friend and cousin. Something had changed in him.

"You'll find out soon enough."

They slipped into the side of the Audience Pavilion. The lights had dimmed in the presence of their guest. The King and his two advisors were fighting the urge to shrink away. They ruled supreme here, safe in the knowledge that no one would ever attack. Their mountain home had nothing to tempt anyone with. It was easier to trade with the kingdom then try and take it.

The guest sneered at them, sensing their inflated egos. He turned slightly, barely noticeable by most but Guang-fu knew his presence had been acknowledged.

The king puffed up his chest and demanded, "who are you?"

"I am your worst nightmare. I am Strife."
The wind rose up and blew through the palace whipping up the snow and rattling the doors in their frames. The men in the room felt the cold fingers of decay and shrank into themselves.

"And war and death follow me wherever I go. I have been imprisoned for far too long by my kin and now I am free, courtesy of a sacrifice. This is now my kingdom. You have lived far too long with peace but no longer."

"No it's not." The king found his voice, "guards, kill him!"
The guards at the doors remained still. Strife laughed, "you feeble, pompous, ignorant man. You should have listened more to those tales of warning told to you by the hag you suckled at. None of your weapons can destroy me and I have control of your men. If I chose to I can make them kill themselves."
The five men pulled their swords out and turned them so

they pointed at their own chests. Their eyes were wide with fear as they tried to fight the urge to push them into their hearts, hands and arms shaking with the effort. Strife had left them with enough conscience to know what was happening and he was enjoying the waves of fear rippling out from them.

"No one threatens my father and this kingdom!" The Crown Prince shouted and charged at the visitor with his knife. He never reached Strife who thrust out his hand, palm out. The Crown Prince was flung against the wall, stunned and the knife was now pointing at his heart. He didn't dare move.

Strife looked around, "anyone else want to challenge me?" The two advisors dropped to the floor and cowered there, faces in the wooden floor. Strife raised an eyebrow at the king who was still trying to be defiant, though the willpower was beginning to fail.

Guang-fu didn't like the disobedience of the king and he wouldn't be able to rule until the old man was gone. He heard Strife's voice in his head encouraging the spark of an idea he had. He marched across the pavilion, pulling out his knife. He took the king by surprise as he stabbed him in the neck. Strife laughed as Guang-fu pulled his knife out and blood sprayed out. Guang-fu grinned maniacally at his new overlord, grabbed the king's hair and yanked it back to cut the older man's throat, right to the bone. After trying a few times he realised he wouldn't be able to take the head off as an offering. Changing tact he heaved the heavy body up enough to throw it at Strife's feet.

Splattered with blood Guang-fu looked at Strife, "accept this sacrifice as my dedication to you."

"You are certainly worthy of my attentions." Strife smirked, savouring the scene of blood, "what are you going to do with the rest of them?" He couldn't stop himself from licking his lips.

"Why don't I step out for a moment." Guang-fu suggested with a bow of his head.

The Crown Prince whimpered, silencing it with a hand across his mouth as the God and his cousin turned and glared at him. Guang-fu remarked casually, "you can eat him too."

Guang-fu strolled out as if he didn't have a care in the world and didn't know what was about to happen. Inside the Audience Pavilion Strife let out a satisfied sigh as he changed into his dragon form, growing to fit the large room. A couple of minutes later there was no evidence of the nine men in the room apart from the weapons and blood splatter on the wide bench that was the throne. He roared his pleasure.

Returning to human form Strife slid open the door to the Pavilion and with a mock bow said, "come in and take your new position in life."

Feeling smug Guang-fu took his seat on the throne. From being about ninth in line he had jumped all the way to first. He looked to Strife, "what is next Great Lord?"

"We sort the wheat from the chaff." He picked at his sharp teeth with the Crown Prince's knife.

"Certainly. Let me arrange that for you." Guang-fu pulled the brocade pull rope that was beside him. A bell rang in a discreet room behind the throne and a terrified servant appeared. He kowtowed to his new king and 'advisor' and with a shaking voice said, "may I be the first to congratulate you on your new position my Lord."

"Of course you may. Now, if you want to remain alive send for everyone."

The servant glanced at Strife and saw the man's eyes flash red. Remembering what he had just seen he definitely didn't want to be eaten. He ran from the Pavilion to do as he had been ordered.

Soon the first group were knelt before their new king, afraid and bewildered.

Guang-fu's own father did not look happy that his son had suddenly taken the throne without even a hint of mutiny. From the throne Guang-fu looked down at all of his extended family. Around the walls of the Pavilion stood the palace guards, faces glazed over. With the tension in the room spilling over that women in only their bed robes were beginning to weep Guang-fu stood and announced, "I am now King. This is a new era that is about to begin. War is coming and you are either with me or you aren't."

Three

Hidden in a bush outside a white-haired nursemaid wrapped up against the cold in a padded cast-off coat from one of her charges' mothers, peered through the shutters before they were slammed shut. She had been brought up on the old tales and guessed that an ancient evil had been released. She knew that she had to protect her charges and hurried back to their shared room via the storeroom for clothes and shoved money and two small sharp knives in the pockets.

She had left them hidden under their bedding. Use to obeying her orders they waited till they heard her voice to come out. They peered out from under the bedding into the dark room. She got down on creaky knees, "come, I must get you away from here."
The two young half-sisters glanced at each other and then back at their nursemaid. The elder of the two asked, "what's happening?"
  "Nothing good."
The other asked, "Where do we go?"
  "You need to go to Keytel. Remember the stories I told you of the people that live there? Now, quickly, get changed and wrap up warm. There's going to be a blizzard out there soon. Don't stop till you are below the snowline."
Their nurse answered.
  "That's a long way. How far is Keytel?" The second

protested, "can we take ponies?"

"Enough." The nurse said sternly. She got to her feet and began throwing riding clothes at them. They pulled on the trousers and two shirts over the pajamas they wore and tied them shut with a sash. Over that they pulled on fur lined trousers and coats with large hoods. They thrust the mittens into pockets.

"What about food?" The first asked.

"You can survive a couple of days without till you are safely away from here. Now, quick." She pushed them towards the door, "quiet. Go warn your distant cousins of this. They will be able to help. Don't take the ponies." She quickly embraced them both.

The younger protested, "what about you?"

"I'm too old for this. If I stay quiet no one will notice me. Now go."

As quietly as they could they ran through the covered corridors and courtyards to the main entrance. They didn't encounter anyone, not even a guard. Once away from the palace they were surprised to see the stars and moon shining bright, giving them enough light to see by. They passed through the small village of tightly shut houses that served the palace.

Dawn started to come, turning the snow red and the girls sought out somewhere to hide for an hour or so to rest and discuss a plan. Spotting a cave formed out of a pile of rocks not covered in snow they crawled in and huddled together.

"Aerrana what do we do?" The younger asked, "why did Nuna tell us to go to Keytel?"

Aerrana pulled her half sister closer. There was a year difference in age but had both been brought up together under Nuna's care. They shared the same father but their mothers were two different wives. They were often mistaken as twins as they were similar in height and looks and were always found together. If looked at closer they had different shaped faces, the elder had a rounder face and the younger had more almond shaped eyes. Both had their father's brown eyes but their hair reflected their mothers with Aerrana having black hair and Lhateso having dark brown, both of which were tied in a long plait down their backs.

In such a large household of courtiers and extended family they only had each other. They had a governess who preferred flirting to teaching so were left to fend for themselves most of the time with Nuna ensuring they were fed and clean and tidy. There would have been marriage being muted as they turned fifteen and then they would have married some lowly courtier and left the palace never to see each other again.

As for now they were in unknown territory. They had rarely left the palace apart from the occasional picnic in the summer with other women from the court. They were going to have to survive on their wits. They would have to find a town, buy provisions and get directions. Aerrana had no idea where Keytel was.

All she knew was that it was a country where dragons lived and were ridden by men and women and that one of her distant relatives had married its ruler, long before she was born. She knew he had been described as a magician as shortly after the marriage ceremony they had both vanished. Their Nuna had told them tales of the dragon Gods that were once worshipped in Gloabtona but they were all but forgotten now. They were still worshipped in Keytel so maybe that was why Nuna had told them to go there. She didn't know how she would explain their presence if they made it.

Finally she said, "remember the stories Nuna told us about dragons and Gods?"
Lhateso nodded.

"I think that is why she has told us to go to Keytel. The people there will know what to do and we have family there, distant family, but still family."

"Where is it? I don't think I've ever seen it on a map."

"How often did we ever look at a map Aerrana?" Lhateso laughed referring to their limited education. Girls like them didn't need to be taught anything but how to run a household and entertain themselves and their husbands.

"Well, we'll have to find a map with it on."

"And food?"

"And food." Aerrana laughed. Sobering she asked, "think you can keep going? We should take advantage of the daylight and see how far we can get."

Crawling out of their little cave they looked back from where they had come but could only see black clouds and a snowstorm centred around the palace and the village outside it.

Those who had decided to approve of Guang-fu and submit to the new rule huddled in their rooms in family groups counting the cost of their cowardly decisions. Two thirds of the extended family were gone along with Guang-fu's parents. No one was sure what was going to happen next. No one knew what had happened to those who had gone. They had simply vanished and the visitor had grown bigger in stature.

Now Strife was sated, bloated with blood, he could turn his mind to other things. He needed to seek out some weak-willed dragons to build up a terrifying reptilian army and he needed more men to do his bidding. The world had changed a lot since he had been imprisoned and he had already realised that it was now a world dominated by man with the Gods barely remembered, in this country at least.

He retreated to the warm dark room which was

where the women usually hid to view audiences with their king. Now that he had the strength he could begin to seek out the beasts and men he needed. He blocked out all the minds of everyone left in the palace. Mentally he spread his wings, flying across Gloabtona and was disappointed to not sense the beating hearts of any dragons.

Once out of the mountains he had more success and found a few useful men and dragons to call to him. He realised that this new world of man was even better than the one he had belonged to. Emotions were amazing things for generating the anger and rage he fed off. Envy, jealousy, a lover's tiff, unrequited love, desire, drunken fights; all of it so delicious to detect. He could sense the blood absorbed by the soil where past battles had been fought and was pleased War and Death were still around. He would soon call them to his side.

Something piqued his interest then, another trapped soul wanting revenge, an angry soul carrying immortal blood and he laughed. Here was his general, a Godling. He would have to send Guang-fu to seek him out. He was not ready to reveal himself to the self titled upstart Dragon Lord yet.

As he travelled on in his mind something else took his interest. He found the dragon knights in their Valley in Keytel. Here was a readymade elite army for his general and with experience as well. All the rogues who would heed his call would be his disposable infantry. But he also felt loyalty and realised it would be hard work to convert them to his side, but who were they loyal to? There was a haziness to the person as if something was hiding him or her. There was begrudging loyalty to another, a sibling to the first? Could he use this jealous one to reach the other? That would need to be thought about. Perhaps he would send
Guang-fu there as well to investigate.

Time was of the essence but for now it was time to sleep, let all of the bodies digest and let the human enjoy his new power for a bit. He changed into a smaller version of his dragon form, his stomach bloated with food, and curled up on the floor to sleep.

A new day though no one could tell from the dark clouds that hung low over the palace and the blizzard that raged, keeping them all huddled inside. Strife strolled into Guang-fu's room, the previous king's study, "I have a mission for you."

"What do you mean? A mission?"
Strife spotted a pot of rolled up maps while ignoring Guang-fu's confused expression. Finding the one he needed he unfurled it on the desk, "I need you to go to this country."

"But I am the king now. You gave that position to me. I can send men for you."

"And as quickly as I gave it to you I can take it away." Strife snarled, his face contorting into its natural dragon form.
Guang-fu pressed himself into the cushions he was lounging on in fear.

Strife felt disappointed. Once this man had done what was needed he wouldn't be staying around. There were stronger men out there, including the mystery one. Guang-fu exclaimed, trying not to shake, "yes master, sorry master. What do you need me to do?"

Guang-fu scurried over from the pile of cushions on a low heated dais. Until Strife had entered he had been trying to decide what he would do first, fuck a girl or make one of his old but now sniveling bullies do something demeaning.

"Here." Strife stabbed a claw at the map.

"Moronland? That country. It's more enlightened than it

was five years ago but it's not a place to consider an easy target. The woman who leads it has a tribe of female warriors and her brother supporting her back and he leads Keytel's dragon riders." He looked hopefully at his new master and hoped he had shown himself worthy with his knowledge.

Strife was revealing nothing so Guang-fu quickly carried on, "she has a brother blessed by the Gods. It is said they all have some sort of power bestowed on them from their father, the last true High Priest."

Was this the shadowy man Strife could detect but not determine? Ignoring the boy's look that asked if he had done good, Strife said, "you must go and find a mountain that has been broken in half. There you must dig through the rock and find a body and a breastplate."

"I can send someone to do that."

"No, you." Strife glared at the man, "and now. Time is of the essence." The longer he took to get everyone he needed together the more chance there was of him being spotted by his immortal enemies.

"Yes sir." Guang-fu hurried from the room starting to wonder what he had foolishly got mixed up in.

Strife took a moment to calm his frustration. Though men had claimed the world from their dragon overlords it seemed they were still imbecilic. He would be glad when their only thoughts were survival again and he could leave this cold temporary home. A nice desert home would be good or even that Valley he had seen.

With a lot of muttering to himself Guang-fu loaded saddlebags with supplies, wrapped himself up warm and mounted the mountain pony. He was about to become the diplomat he had wanted to be though via a rather violent route. There was a sense of insanity prevailing the palace now and he hoped that once he was away from it his mind would become clear. A snarling spitting voice appeared in his mind, "don't even think about betraying me."

Shaken Guang-fu led his jittery pony through the broken main gates, the guards mindlessly bowing their heads to him. The clouds and snow parted enough to give him easy passage.

Several hours later he didn't even notice the two walkers entering the town of Pokont at the same time as him.

Four

Aerrana and Lhateso shied away from the pony as it walked past. They recognised that the rider was from the palace but didn't know whether he was seeking them out. Once he had passed they glanced at each other. Lhateso asked, "do you think they have realised we are missing yet?"

"We are two of many, they probably haven't noticed." Aerrana reassured her sister, "come on, we need to find food and a map. I have no idea how far away Keytel is."

They entered a tavern and cautiously sat at a table, removing their coats as it was warm in the large room. At one end in a stone fire place a large fire was burning. A server wandered over, "what can I get you?"

"Some hot food and whatever you have to drink please?" She looked them up and down, "have you the means to pay?"
Aerrana discreetly placed a silver coin on the table. The server nodded and departed with her full tray of dirty dishes and tankards.

Neither of them noticed other customers glancing their way and whispering. To the locals they were recognisable as two people who had never been in a tavern in their life.

As in any town there are those who would take advantage of innocents and one such person stood to do just that but was stopped by the tavern door being flung open by an out of breath man who exclaimed, "have you heard?" Everyone turned to stare at him, recognising the livery of the palace village. While still panting he added, "demons have taken over the palace, no one can get in or out."

"Don't be silly, there's no such things as demons. You've got to be drunk." Someone scoffed.

"It's true. A giant snowstorm has covered the palace and village." He protested

Aerrana and Lhateso glanced at each other. Lhateso whispered, "is that what Nuna was scared of?"

"Must be. Sssh, let's see if he says anything else." The liveried servant sank on to a bench, "it was like all the light was sucked out as he came through the village. He broke down the palace gates like they weren't even wood." He took the offered tankard and drank half of it, "I hid before running down here."

"Will they come here?" Asked a nervous woman. The servant shrugged, "no idea."

Food was brought to the young women and Aerrana asked quietly, "do you have a room we could use? And where could we find someone who makes maps?"

"You aren't from around here are you? Your voice is far too good. Where you run from?" The server demanded suspiciously.

Lhateso grabbed Aerrana's arm with fear.

"We haven't run from anywhere if that's what you are thinking." Aerrana answered stiffly, "we can find somewhere else for a bed."

The servant turned to look and eyed them, "where are two girls like you going without a chaperone?"

"She's out getting supplies." Aerrana replied too quickly. She could sense everyone's eyes on them now. The servant stood up and approached, recognising the quality of the clothes they wore. He asked, "where are you from?"

Aerrana grabbed Lhateso and the coats and exclaimed, "run!"

Lhateso snatched the bread off the table as she was dragged away by her big sister. The liveried servant ran out of the tavern followed by several customers, shouting, "thieves, stop them!"

At the end of the cobbled street the watchman was strolling up towards them. Seeing the two running he did what he was best known for and stuck out his foot tripping Aerrana up. She went flying, sprawling across the cobbles, the coats falling in front of her. Lhateso stumbled but recovered. Aerrana shouted, "keep going! Get to Keytel!" Lhateso wanted to look back but she knew it would be foolish to stay. Tears ran down her face, making her cheeks numb, as she ran.

After a few minutes of running she took a risk and looked back but no one was following her. She slowed to a walk and realised that apart from the bread she didn't have anything. Aerrana had had both their coats and it was not warm enough to survive without them. She started to look for anywhere that might have coats for sale. She had no money so she would have to steal one if she could, or a blanket.

She spotted a narrow street of traders and headed down it. She glanced round to see if anyone was either following or watching her. She seemed to have been forgotten. With another quick glance around she snatched a blanket from its table display and ran.

Several streets later she hunkered down on a step, wrapped the blanket around herself and finally ate the bread she had claimed from the tavern table. As she chewed on the hard bread she worked out a new plan. Priority was to get out of the mountains then hope she found someone willing to point her in the right direction of Keytel. For food she would have to see what she could scavenge.

With the bread gone she tied the blanket round her neck like a cloak and with a determined expression on her face headed out of the town and followed others heading down the mountains. No one looked at her.

Guang-fu was tired of travelling. He'd been doing so for the last week and a half. He was saddle sore and Strife was in his mind nagging him to hurry. Finally he had reached what was hopefully his destination and stared at the job ahead of him.

Before him was a huge rockfall of boulders that split the mountain in half. Water trickled out, forming a stream in an old river bed. Around him the ground still showed signs of charring under the new growth. He remembered hearing of a battle between the tribe of female warriors and the previous ruler of Moronland. He, along with his cousins, had wished they had been able to see the awesome sight of all the dragon riders, the Suwars, of Keytel. One thing for certain he wasn't going to move all the stone by himself. He was going to have to find some labourers.

Two days later he had found himself some labourers and they had set up camp by the trickling stream. Some told Guang-fu of what had happened after the battle, of a huge cavern caving in on itself. There were going to find skeletons.

They soon found he wasn't the first to have gone digging as they found a small tunnel which had collapsed and they wondered whether they would find the owner. Even with reusing the tunnel it was still going to be hard work breaking up the stone and moving it. When asked what they were looking for he didn't and couldn't tell them as he didn't know himself.

And this is how Lhateso, with her now cut hair, found herself earning money for food. No one cared where she came from or where she was going as half of the labourers were in the same position. Most of the locals fled within the first week as eerie ghostly sounds started to be heard. She lived in a tent with the three other women on site and kept herself to herself, wary of the men. Some did stare at her and her almond shaped eyes.

Her main duty was to carry the baskets of broken stone away to the rubble heap. As remains of the Daughters of Scyths' life on the mountain top emerged she was called for to crawl through the narrow space to pull it out. All of the metal was dumped in a pile but she claimed a knife with a dragon on the handle to protect herself, the blade speckled with rust.

As they reached the middle of the mountain they found more bodies from where the cavern had collapsed, just skeletons now with skulls leering into view as they were discovered. The sight of the first one had scared her until another camp member told her of the battle that had happened. The ghostly sounds became louder and more frequent. It sounded like a baby crying and whimpering.

As the crying started up again that evening the three women, with Lhateso by their fire, shivered. One remarked, "how many poor little souls do you think have died up there?"

"I heard they used to kill any male babies as they were not needed." Another whispered.

"Don't be foolish Martha. They are women, why would they kill their own babies?"

"How do you think they fed the dragons then?" Martha challenged back.

"You're scaring Lhateso." The eldest there protested though it was more to hide her own fear. She pulled her shawl closer around herself as she remembered the two babes she had lost.

"It won't just be babies. Once they knew they were pregnant they would kill the fathers." Martha continued, warming to her theme.

"Not true. My brother's friend's cousin ended up living up there for a year. They lived in their own enclosure and were well looked after." The third remarked as she poked at the fire.

"Sounds like they were male whores to me." The eldest remarked with a frown.

"Suppose some of them were but the cousin said some of them had been there for years."

"Come on, let's get some sleep." The eldest stood to make it clear she was to be obeyed.

As they headed to their shelter Guang-fu walked over, "Lhateso?"

Lhateso turned, still amazed he hadn't recognised her as one of his cousins from the palace. He hadn't even recognised her name.

"I need you now."

"Now? It's bedtime."

"We are too close to waste time sleeping."

"Hey!" Martha turned, hands on hips, "she's worked hard all day. We all need to sleep and rest."

"You want to be paid?" Guang-fu snarled.

"Of course."

"Well shut your mouth. If you want to be paid Lhateso you come now." He thrust the lamp at Lhateso. She carefully took it off him and checked her knife was at her side, just in case. She said to Martha, "I'll be alright. You go to bed."

"Are you sure?"

Lhateso nodded her head.

"Fine. Make sure he pays you extra." Martha glared at

Guang-fu but accepted Lhateso's nod.

Guang-fu led her to the tunnel. The entrance had been cleared to allow full grown men inside to work the stone. As they reached the entrance she asked, "what are you looking for? Everything I've found hasn't interested you yet. Are you looking for a lost relative?"

"You could say that." He answered stiffly, "we will know when it has been found."

"I need some clue so I know when I have found it for you." She pointed out.
He sighed, "fine. I am looking for a body, not a skeleton."

"Right." Lhateso replied, feeling a little confused at what he meant by a body. There was no way a body would survive considering all that had been found so far were skeletons with scraps of flesh on them, "I'll see what I can find."

She steeled herself for whatever she might find before she picked up a short handled pickaxe and spade and headed into the tunnel. She crawled on her hands and knees, moving the lamp ahead of her. She wondered what she was going to find when she found it. As she reached the end of the tunnel where it opened out to give the diggers space she froze for she heard whimpering. What was she letting herself into here? She rubbed tired dry eyes and began hitting the rock in front of her with the pickaxe. The whimpering baby sounds continued as she attacked the rock. Tears began to roll down her face from the dust, from fear and from maternal instincts she didn't know she had.

She paused when the whimpering suddenly stopped and a voice in her head ordered, "stop! What you seek must not be found."
She glanced round, thinking someone had joined her before returning to the rock she was hitting with her pickaxe. It was almost ready to crumble and shovel into baskets.

"STOP!"

The voice made her head ring. She put her hands to her
head feeling a sharp pain in her brain. She decided to listen
to the command this time and retreated.

At the entrance Guang-fu got briefly excited at
seeing her, "have you found anything?"
She shook her head, black dots dancing in front of her eyes.
She wasn't going back in there.

"Why are you here then?" He demanded.

"I'm not going back in." She retorted, "there's more than
ghosts in there."
Guang-fu rolled his eyes, "fine, give me the tools." He held
out a hand and muttered, "clearly I'm going to have to do
this myself."

He left Lhateso shaking with cold and fear. He
grumbled to himself as he crawled through. This was not
what he thought he would be doing when he took up
Strife's offer. He heard a voice call out, "turn back."

"Push on, you are so close." Strife's harsh voice called
out.

Trying to ignore the voices in his head he attacked
the rock Lhateso had been working on with the pickaxe. It
finished cracking and then broke apart revealing something
metallic reflecting red in his lamplight. He scrabbled at the
loose stone with his bare hands until he revealed a
burnished copper breastplate that had a patch of green
where water had got to it and the metal had begun to
oxidise. He grinned. This was nothing like anything else
that had been found so this had to be part of what he had
been sent to seek. Now he had to find the body.

He pulled out the breastplate and wondered if it
would fit him. He could tell there was true craftmanship
behind it, each metal scale individually soldered together. It
had to have fallen off a body for no one would have thrown
away such a stunning breastplate.

He felt sure that the body Strife wanted must be

nearby. With the shorthanded shovel he began moving more of the soil and loose stone and then a small limb appeared, and it was a limb, not bones. He stopped and stared. He heard Strife chuckle and he kept going. Soon he exposed the body of a grotesque enfant with the snout of a dragon and claws instead of fingers. Its scale imprinted skin was stretched taut across its ribcage.

He gulped. What insanity was this? He reached in and drew the body out and was surprised to find a dragon handled knife just beside it. He reached for that as he cradled the hideous baby in his arm. He heard two roars, one clearly displeased, the other elated. There was a rumble within the rocks and he realised if he didn't leave soon he would be buried alive.

He quickly crawled out backwards, dragging the baby on the breastplate with him. What had been carved out began to collapse in on itself once again. He hurried over to the women's fire, dust from the collapsed tunnel following him.

Lhateso was trying to still her shaking body and calm her nerves with a herbal tea. She looked up as her cousin sat down beside her and then her eyes caught the object in his lap. She couldn't stop herself staring at the ugly creature Guang-fu had placed in his lap to see it better by the light of the fire. She had never seen anything like it and never wanted to see the same again. She tried to turn away but then the still body jerked and sucked in a breath of air.

The baby turned its head and looked around with eyes that were bright and more alert than a normal newborn. It spotted Lhateso and she felt like it was staring into her soul.

It cocked its head then and looked up at Guang-fu's frozen expression of fear. It had heard a voice calling out, *"sup on his blood, my child, sup on all of their blood. Grow strong*

and then come and find me. "
It grinned manically up at its first meal in five years and leapt up to sink its sharp teeth into Guang-fu's throat and allowed the man's pulse to feed his blood into its mouth. Its skin began to lose its deathly pallor.

With the lifeblood of its first meal drained it slipped off Guang-fu's lap. The man's body slumped backwards, barely alive. By morning he would be dead.

Before Lhateso's eyes the baby stretched and seemed to shed its skin like a snake. It shook off the wafer-thin skin and in a slow blink of an eye became the size of a toddler. Some of the more pronounced features had shrunken. Its nose twitched as it sensed more pulsing bodies. It turned away from Lhateso and waddled unsteadily to one of the men's shelters.

Lhateso fled to the women's shelter and pulled the blanket over her head as the first shrill scream rang out. Martha sat up, "what was that?"

"Don't go out there if you want to survive." Lhateso exclaimed from under her blanket.

"Why?" Martha frowned.
Lhateso carefully lowered the blanket and stared at Martha, "we will be safe as long as we stay in here. It will go for the men first and hopefully that will be enough."

"What are you talking about?" The eldest slowly sat up, rubbing sleep from her eyes. Her head whipped round as she heard a shout of fear and a snarl of anger. She turned to look at Lhateso, "what's happening out there?"
Though she had never heard the word spoken by her Nuna she knew what was out there, "it's the first of its kind, a godling, conceived by a god with a woman."

"A what?" Martha asked with a frown.

"It's half man, half dragon god."

"There's no such thing." The older woman protested.

"It is now." Lhateso whispered and pulled the blanket

over her head to muffle the shouts and screams, "and it's not happy."

The other two women huddled closer together, holding their knives at the ready to defend themselves if needed.

Quiet descended on the camp and the three awake women peered out from their shelter. In the light of the dying fire stood a naked man, peeling another wafer-thin layer of skin off himself like a snake. It still had a copper tinge to it and the faint evidence of scales almost like it had been tattooed on with ash. His hair was auburn and ran down his back. He cocked his head as if he was listening to something.

Inside his mind he heard the voice that had told him to drain the living of their blood earlier. It asked, *"satisfied?"*

"Who are you?"

"You are pain, bloodlust and rage. All the human emotions in an immortal body." Strife laughed, *"you have not been named yet."*

"Where are my parents?"

"They are not important. They abandoned you, tried to kill you. I am now the most important thing to you. Now, put on the breastplate and then change into the dragon God you are and come find me."

"I must have revenge." The godling scowled, picking up the breastplate and knife abandoned by the fire. He sensed the scent on them were important to him. He buckled on the breastplate and kept hold of the knife as he concentrated on becoming his serpentine dragon form with scales of bright copper, as if fresh from the furnace. He pushed up into the air with his back legs. He let out a roar before heading towards the snowcapped mountains of Gloabtona.

Five

Further into Moronland, on the border with Keytel Miryama and Ozanus were for the moment playing happy families with their son Shaprour, eating dinner. For anyone looking in from the outside they appeared to be a happy family. Ozanus with his golden brown hair was bent close to his son's own brown hair as they both whispered and glanced at Miryama on the other side of the table. She looked over, not sure whether to be offended or to smile at the way father and son were being. She brushed a strand of auburn hair off her face. It still had the beads and ribbons that identified her as a Daughter of Scyth.

He looked up, sensing her watching them and smiled at her, a soft genuine smile that said he was attracted to her even with their tempestuous, at times, relationship. Her freckle scattered face hadn't changed from 5years ago and her hazel eyes were looking warm. He almost wanted to describe her as a contented cat.

Then the smile disappeared, fell away as his brown eyes screwed up with pain and he went to clutch his head but he fainted before they got there and he fell backwards off the bench.

Shaprour stared at his father before fainting himself. Miryama's bench tipped over and crashed to the floor as she leapt up and ran round to father and son. She gathered up her son as she called for Arno. She had no idea what had just happened and feared a God's claw was involved.

Shaprour came round first crying, "my head hurts mama, my head hurts."

"I'll get you something for it." She answered softly.

"I feel sick." And promptly threw up over himself and his mother.

Ozanus stirred as Arno placed a damp cloth on his master's forehead. He wondered how he had ended up on the floor. He stared around feeling disorientated and nauseous. He winced from pain as he moved his head. Miryama looked across with concern, "what just happened?"

"I heard a roar in my mind, so loud, so angry…." He let Arno help him back on to the padded bench he had been sat on. He looked at her and realised his wife and son wore vomit-stained clothes and Shaprour was crying, "what happened to Shaprour?"

"He fainted as well. Was it the Gods?" She asked tentatively.

He frowned, "I'm not sure. It felt closer than that."

It had felt like his heart had suddenly emptied of blood. The roar he had heard wasn't War or the Dragon Lord, it felt closer to him. He thought then of the deformed body he had stabbed through the heart and he went cold. Miryama saw the shiver and asked, "what?"

"Nothing." All she knew was that the twin had died at birth. He sometimes wondered whether the guilt of what he had done affected his and Miryama's relationship. Looking over at her he wondered why she wasn't affected at all considering she had carried it for nine months.

*

The godling dragon circled the storm shrouded palace before coming into land. Around him dawn was starting to turn the sky the snowy landscape red. He shrank down into his human form and stalked through the blizzard.

43

He headed straight through the palace courtyards up to the Audience Pavilion. He slid the door open harder than necessary and it slammed against the wall making a servant wince. From the throne Strife grinned, *"welcome."* To the nervous servant he ordered, "fetch him clothes, suitable for his position as my general."
The servant bobbed his head and hurried out.

The godling dropped to one knee and bowed his head, *"master, you sought me out. I will do as you command. Give me a name."*

"You are Bloodlust and you are to be the General of my armies. You will lead the men that will heed my call to arms." Strife declared, "stand and come closer. We must equip you."
Bloodlust rose up and approached Strife on his throne.

"You are one of three I must call to me and then we can reclaim this world both on the ground and in the heavens."

"It will be my honour and the revenge I seek?"

"You will get a chance, don't you worry about that." Strife promised, *"aah, clothes. It is cold up here. Dress and then find the armoury and chose whatever you wish to use when fighting as a man. Now,"* Strife stood, *"I must call the other two to me."*
Bloodlust bowed his head again.

"Rest, you have flown a long way, and you are still a newborn. I need you strong and focused."

"Yes sir."

Strife strolled out of the main room to the room in the back. He sat down in the warm dark room and concentrated on his mind. He needed War and Death at his side to take on the gods. Neither of them had responded to his first call which concerned him. They were his dragons, not that upstart golden dragon who called himself the Dragon Lord.

He scanned the world searching for Death. When he had called out there had been a faint glimmer of contact. He zoned in and found himself in a blackened landscape with the smell of sulphur and steaming mud pools. He felt at home here and was glad one dragon god was keeping their true self alive. Ahead of him was the dark mouth of an old lava tube, rocks fallen from its ceiling. He ventured in, determined to find his next general.

Deep in the hot dark tunnel a black dragon stirred, *"who dares venture into my domain?"*

"Your domain is nothing." Strife pointed out and then demanded, *"why are you not out there terrorising man and dragon a like? I sense no fear of death out there."* Death snarled, *"you were imprisoned"*

"I'm back now." Strife snarled, briefly revealing his true form.

"This is a world of men now as you have probably guessed since you come to me in the form of man. I'm happy down here." Death shifted, scales scrapping against stone.

"When did you become a coward?" Death charged at Strife, teeth gnashing. Strife morphed into his dragon form and within the confines they began to fight, twisting their bodies around each other. Jaws snapped and claws scrapped against scales. Death's frill expanded with a long warning hiss as Strife opened his hood. Rock broke in the confined space to make room for the frill and hood.

Minute by minute Strife slowly pulled his fellow basilisk out of the lava tube until with a snarl Death ran out shouting, *"enough! You have me if you have my brother."* Strife slithered out after him, *"that's where I need your help."*

Death frowned, *"you have not sought him out already? You know you won't get anywhere without him. The deaths won't add up and feed us all without him."*

"I know but I can't sense him. He has not responded to my call." Strife growled.

Death closed his eyes so he could concentrate on seeking out his brother. Maybe he was too weak from lack of sacrifices but he couldn't make contact with his brother either but he could sense a hint of him in two places which confused him. Returning to the present he remarked with concern, *"I could not find him but I had a sense of him in two places. He has hidden himself well. He is perhaps weak. Has there been any wars recently?"*

"Are you really that out of touch?" Strife asked in shock.

"I'm not you. I may have been created by you but you are the all powerful being." Death retorted. It had been nearly six years since the last mass dying event which had made him fat and bloated for a while and then it had returned to the few deaths a day again.

"He's out there. These humans are ruled by emotions which easily spill into anger, rage which leads to fights and war...." A thought came to Strife then as he remembered what Guang-fu had said before going to Moronland. A smile crept up on him as he suspected where he might be and that Bloodlust was part of his other creation. Strife laughed then as he remarked to himself, *"clever, very clever."*

It was going to take more power to draw him out of his host.

"Where's home for the moment?" Death interrupted his thoughts.

"The mountains where I have already been joined by a young one, a unique young man with, I now believe, to have your brother's blood within him. He has his bloodthirsty nature. You can meet him when you arrive." Strife disappeared.

Six

Ozanus was at his desk when he felt a presence in his mind and it wasn't the blasted War God either. This felt older, more powerful, more evil and it was probing, seeking something. It blinded him and he fell from his chair gripping his head as he felt a roar of frustration fill his mind.

Arno ran in and found his master's body jerking with some internal battle. He ran from the room shouting, "Miryama, Miryama, come quick!"

Miryama ran in from the garden, "What is it Arno?!"

"Something is happening to Ozanus." He led her into Ozanus' study where blood was now dripping from his mouth where he had bitten his tongue. Miryama knelt down and turned her husband on to his side as he continued to buck and twist.

They could only watch as it continued for what felt like an eternity but was not longer than a minute. Finally he lay still and Miryama and Arno released their breaths. They looked at each other across Ozanus' body wondering what to do now. She asked, "has this ever happened before?"

"Never. Why could this have happened? The headaches and fainting only started recently." Arno replied

"Has he mentioned the Gods recently?"

Arno shook his head and Ozanus groaned and put a hand to his mouth. He squinted and moaned, *"turn down the light,*

he must not find me."
Miryama and Arno glanced at each other and Miryama nodded.

Arno turned down the lamp and closed the shutters, "that better?"
Ozanus nodded and peered at the blood on his hand. He blinked a few times before realising Arno and Miryama were staring at him with concern, "what happened?"

"You don't know?" Miryama asked in astonishment.

"I felt something in my mind, searching…" He screwed up his eyes as a sharp needle of pain pierced his brain, "War…."
There was a growl in his mind and he realised that the god didn't want either of them to be found. He added, as Arno helped him sit up, "something is happening somewhere and it's not good." And he could only hope he wasn't going to be drawn into it. He had a feeling he was going to have to prepare for the worst but he needed to talk to damn War about using his body as a hiding place.

He tried to stand but almost collapsed back on the floor if Arno hadn't grabbed him and Miryama hadn't moved his fallen over chair.
Miryama said, "I think you need to rest before you think of anything else and I'll go check Shaprour hasn't injured himself. I had to leave him in the garden."

"Yes, go, go." Ozanus waved her away. He wanted to be on his own, "Arno, stop fussing and get me a drink."

"Sir?" Arno looked concerned.

"Just go. I don't need you hanging round me." He growled and made to stand again but promptly changed his mind and held tight to the arm of his chair as he sat back down. With Arno gone he muttered, *"what have you got me mixed up in now? Whatever it is, keep me out of it."*
There was no reply from War.

*

Miryama could tell Ozanus was distracted that night, his mind clearly on other things. As she kissed him she ran a hand through his golden brown hair but he didn't respond. She had a feeling it would be a while before she would see him next.

She remembered how they tried to be the couple the gods had made them be after the birth of their son but after a few months of flying around together they had had a huge argument and she decided she would take their son to Duntorn and the fort the Daughters of Scyth had built.

Much like their relationship the sex was just as tempestuous. Sometimes it was long, slow and tender until one of them couldn't stand it any longer and forced it to a climatic end. Other times there was a frantic aggression to it. No new children had come and Miryama felt sure that the stillborn had somehow torn up her womb. Anyway, Shaprour was enough for both her and Ozanus. Though they both loved him they knew that if it wasn't for War he would never have been born.

She sat straddling Ozanus' lap and kissed him again while he lay propped up on pillows. His hands held her hips but there was no pressure from them as if he was going by instinct. She paused and lifted his face so she could see it in the low lamplight. His brown eyes weren't revealing anything. He frowned and she asked, "want to talk about it?"

"I need you to go back to Duntorn tomorrow, I've got to go to the Valley."

"I could come with you."

"No." He answered sharply and she saw a flash of red eyes.

"What happened earlier?"

He shrugged as he didn't know himself. He lifted her off

him, "sorry, I'm not in the mood. I still have a bit of a headache."

She felt frustrated but didn't say anything. She knew he kept a lot inside him. He was still affected all these years later from the trauma of losing his parents at 6 years old. She knew he feared history repeating itself. She knew she had to be the stronger person in the relationship and was, for the most part. She had to protect both her son and her partner.

He waited till she was asleep, buried under the blankets, before getting up. He pulled on a robe, gave her a kiss on her forehead before wandering through the house. He paused to look in on Shaprour who was sharing Arno's bedroom.

He liked it when Miryama visited with Shaprour. The cottage always felt alive especially once Shaprour was toddling and then running around though he could sense Ozanus keeping his distance. Having lost Kittal at a similar age Ozanus didn't want his son to have the same emotions he had had when he lost his father. He couldn't have his son hero worshipping him then have his heart ripped out if he died. At some point he would have to get closer to his son and begin teaching him as currently he was heir to the title until Ioan had a son and whether the father wanted it or not Shaprour was destined to be a Suwar. Miryama always stayed for as long as possible until the arguing got too much and she left again.

Everyone was asleep apart from himself. He felt restless. The sense of War he had always had since the battle with Timijin was currently very faint but he didn't know why.

He stepped out into the cold air and looked up, but a blanket of snow heavy clouds hid the moon and stars making him briefly feel like the only person in the world. He wondered, as he occasionally did, whether he had been too rash in handing over the title of Nejus to his brother Ioan. He hoped he wasn't going to have to bring all of the Suwars together again.   Even though he had handed Ioan the title it didn't stop him keeping an eye on Moronland and Keytel from his new home. Though he had relinquished his title of Nejus he was still the Defender of all dragons. Lylya was still new to ruling and occasionally sought out his advice while Ioan didn't need him at all.

After he and Miryama had parted ways the first time and he had realised he needed to learn to control himself especially after he attacked a group of defenceless soldiers. He had ambushed them, eyes flashing red. With a shout of rage he killed the group of five within ten minutes. They hadn't seen it coming and never got the chance to defend themselves.

His rage had dissipated as he had looked down at the bodies fanned around him. It had been too easy, no challenge, and he actually felt disappointed. The War God inside him muttered, *"is that all you got?"*

"Shut up! This happened because of you." He had snarled out loud.

"Ha! This wasn't me; this was all you." War had chuckled.

"Enough!" Ozanus stamped a foot in frustration. He knew he needed to stay calm and away from people. He couldn't let the War God influence him every time he and Miryama argued which he felt would happen again.

He had searched the mountains between Keytel and Moronland till he had found a hot spring so that Nimib would be warm and then he organised for a house to be built which he then had furnished in a simple style.

The walls were white washed and the oiled floorboards hid the underfloor heating from the hot water.

51

He had a kitchen, a main room for eating and sitting with a small study off it. Down the corridor were two bedrooms and a bathroom. His own bed was a large one made of oak. However much he had wanted to keep his dragon links out of the house the carpenter had found his hand guided by the gods and they were carved discreetly on his bed foot and headboards and on the seating.

It began to gently snow and he retreated back inside. There was a grumble of protest from Miryama as he wrapped his cold body round her warm one but as his fingers began to probe her she softened. He kissed her mouth as she turned her head and she whispered sleepily, "what changed your mind?"
He didn't answer as his cold fingers went between her thighs and she gasped at the cold touch on her sex. She could feel his erection pressed against her buttocks and started to roll her body over but he stopped her. He was wanting to release frustrations, not make love and didn't want to look into her face. She remained still as he adjusted her position and thrust into her. She gripped the edge of the bed as he thrust in again and again, his hands holding tight to her hips until he came.
He rolled away from her without saying a word. She slowly turned over to lie on her back. She glanced at Ozanus' back with the copper coloured dragon tattoo in the low lamplight, and recalled the time when they were forced together to eliminate their joint enemy. They were strangers then and at times she felt they were strangers still. He didn't always reveal what was on his mind as if he didn't think she needed to know.
She reached out with a hand to touch his back to reassure him she was there but he shrugged off the hand.

The following morning all three of them were

dressed for flying. They all wore knee length boots and padded coats, Ozanus and Miryama matching their dragon's colourings. Loosely wrapped round their necks were the headscarves that would, once flying, covered all but their eyes.

As Ozanus handed Shaprour up to his mother he contemplated what the world might turn out like for his son. By now he had started to learn how to ride his own dragon and was at the very beginning of the journey of becoming a Suwar. He had known he was next in line to the title and then his family was ripped apart by the Gods; the Gods who then demanded his own sacrifices to their cause.

Currently Shaprour was next in line for the title of Nejus and he was already asking why he didn't have his own dragon. Ozanus knew it was a discussion he and Miryama were going to need to have sooner or later but was putting it off. He didn't want Shaprour to go through what he had though he had good people teaching and training him. If he made a decision now would he find himself dying like his father?

Miryama looked down at Ozanus. She knew she didn't need to say anything but she could already see his shoulders were heavy with an unknown responsibility. He wouldn't want her help though she would gladly give it to him. She gave him a tight smile as Shaprour wiggled in the saddle in front of her. With one arm round her son she held the other up as Ozanus stepped back to give dark ochre scaled Spilla with his front claws on the joints of his wings, space to rise into the air.

With them gone Ozanus packed his sword into his saddle bags. He hadn't wanted Miryama questioning him on what he was going to be doing. He hadn't quite formulated the whole plan yet himself. At his waist was a new dragon handled knife that Lylya had given him when she realised he had 'lost' his. Even though at the time he had considered himself no longer a Suwar she still did and he had politely accepted it. Now he understood why she had given it to him. He would always be a Suwar, it was in his blood and nature.

He glanced back at the house where Arno was hiding inside, out of the cold and then back at his sandy yellow scaled dragon Nimib. He took a deep breath as Nimib asked, *"where are we going this time?"*

"The Valley."

"It must be serious."

"I'm not sure to be honest but I need to use the library. Have you heard or sensed anything amiss on the wind?" Ozanus asked as he climbed into his saddle.

"Not personally but the Valley dragons are usually quite good at sensing such things. I'll ask around once we've reached there."

"Thanks."

Seven

They circled round the Valley before descending into it. It lay like a scar in the grasslands and farmlands that surrounded it. Linyee was the closest town sat on its many layered tell, with its once again abandoned fortress. The Valley itself was surrounded by cliffs and was the crater of a long extinct volcano. The cliffs were where the dragons of the Valley lived while the floor of the Valley was where the Nejus' house was situated along with an encampment of Suwars. Outside the Valley, sheltered by the cliffs, the buildings pressed up against, was the village that supplied the people that lived within the Valley.

With some reluctance Ozanus told Nimib to head down into the Valley. He hadn't been back for four years but it looked like the house hadn't changed at all. Nimib landed at the far side of the lawn, closer to the Suwars' encampment than the house. He wasn't ready to see Ioan just yet.

As he got down off Nimib he expected white haired Arno to come running to help but no one did. It was then that he was glad Arno had come and found him.

Originally only Miryama and Lylya had known where his new home was, safely away from any well-trodden paths. It hadn't stopped Arno from making his way to him, to the place via Duntorn for directions. He had arrived tired and a little sunburnt but still managed to grin at the sight of the man he thought of as his Nejus still even though Ioan had the title. He had found his liege attacking a thick post of wood he had set upright in the ground. On the top it turned as he hit the sandbag.

Ozanus ducked as he attacked it with a staff and then realised he was being watched, "Arno, what are you doing here?"

"Sir, I wish to serve you."

"You serve the Nejus." Ozanus sighed, leaning the staff against the post and grabbing the swinging sandbag.

"And that is you. I know you think I am just a simple servant, but I knew your father well and even he would still see you as Nejus." Arno stood straight, "you know I am good." He spotted a towel and picked it up and handed it to Ozanus. Ozanus wiped the sweat off his face as he said sternly, "you know that isn't so anymore. What's the real reason? How did you even find me?"
Arno shifted his feet, feeling uncomfortable under Ozanus' gaze, "I went to Lady Lylya and she gave me directions."

"And what story did you tell her?"

"Your brother doesn't need me sir, he has plenty of other servants." He didn't say that Ioan ignored him most of the time now as if the sight of him reminded him of Ozanus, "I am better off serving you."

"Fine." Ozanus grunted, "but I don't need much."

"I am happy with that."

"Any good at cooking?" Ozanus cracked a smile.

"I'm guessing better than you." Arno grinned, "show me the kitchen."

"This way." Ozanus led the way inside, "it will just be me and you apart from when Miryama visits. We'll have to sort out some warm clothes for you. Did you bring anything with you?" He softened towards his father's manservant. It would be good to have some company and

Arno had helped bring him up.

"No." Arno admitted, "I wasn't sure if you would let me stay."

"Shall we see how it goes."

Arno had ended up staying and even managed to learn enough to cling to Nimib to fly to Duntorn for supplies from Lylya. He found Lylya always wanted news of her brother and the obedient servant passed on what little they got up to. Occasionally Ozanus and Nimib would fly off together and then return a few weeks later and his master was always moody then.

Ozanus smiled to himself. He probably wouldn't have survived the last four years without the servant. The man had good instincts and could always sense Ozanus' mood and what he did or didn't need at that time. He was good at coping with Ozanus' fickle moods.

A servant appeared but hung back as Ozanus took off Nimib's saddle. He clearly knew him by reputation than in person as the servant hesitantly offered to inform Ioan of his arrival. Ozanus turned and said sharply, "don't you dare."
The young man turned and fled as Ozanus heaved the saddle on to his shoulder and picked up his saddlebags and headed towards the encampment.

From above he hadn't noticed but now on the ground he realised there were now structures in the encampment. Inspired by the Daughters of Scyth the Suwars' campsite was turning into a village. Some small houses held families that now lived permanently in the village while two long buildings acted as dormitories for the single men and women. Ozanus was disorientated for a moment and had to ask where he could find Gaerwn, the Suwar's Chieftain.

Entering the yurt that Gaerwn preferred as the bachelor he still was the older man by a few years was surprised to see his High Chieftain. They had developed a mutual respect for each other since their second encounter with Timijin that had destroyed him and his army. Gaerwn stood from behind the table he was sat at, "Ozanus, what are you doing here?"

"Crazy as it seems, I need your help." He dropped his saddlebags just inside the entrance and then placed the saddle on a spare saddlehorse.

"You were crazy when you handed your brother the Nejus title." The broad shouldered Gaerwn retorted, a slight bitter note to his voice. He now had a small paunch to his stomach causing him to pull at his belt, "you were born to be Nejus and together you were good."
He knew that on his own Ioan struggled. He didn't have the full respect of the Suwars and not even the whole of Keytel either.

He had had to send Suwars out to quell rebellions who were in favour of trying to persuade Ozanus to take back the Nejus title. Some feared retribution from their dragon Gods because their leader had had a foolish impulsive weak moment. Even some of the dragons in the Valley grumbled and a couple had left having decided it wasn't safe with just Ioan to look after them.

Ozanus had proven himself to be a man not to be messed with after killing Timijin and Keytel had been considered strong again until he had handed over the title and now it was back to being considered weak as Ioan was known for his love of administration, not his strength and fighting skill.

"Enough." Ozanus growled, not in the mood to have the argument again. He didn't want the title back and the Dragon Lord had left him alone which matter more to him. He just had to work out how to get rid of War.

"It's a chilly day out there, have a hot drink." Gaerwn quickly changed tact, "and then tell me what you need. It's got to be something important since you are here for a rare visit."
Ozanus accepted the drink but didn't sit as he had been in the saddle most of the day.

Gaerwn ran his hand through his white speckled brown hair while waiting patiently for his lord to speak. He could sense Ozanus was trying to work out the best way to explain himself which was unusual. He watched as Ozanus took a sip of warmed ale. Ozanus finally said, "there is something amiss in the world of the Gods."
Gaerwn hadn't expected that but thinking about it he was right. The weather in the Valley had grown chilly and normally it was a fairly consistent temperate temperature. He asked, "has He spoken to you?"
Ozanus shook his head, "it's just a feeling."

"Are you going to do an offering to see if He will speak to you?"

"No. It's not him I need to speak to. I'm going to need as many of the Suwars who are up for a fight as possible."
Gaerwn looked bemused.

"I can't explain."

"The Gods don't make life easy do they?"

"No."

"When do you want them?"

"As soon as possible. It might last all day and they need their weapons. It's going to be violent and there will be injuries."
Gaerwn raised an eyebrow.

"I'll explain once everyone is together."

"Where do you want them to go?"

"The dragon's arena." Ozanus answered after a brief think.

"And do I tell your brother?" Gaerwn asked cautiously.

"Definitely not."

Word quickly spread through the encampment that Ozanus was back in the Valley and was spoiling for a fight. The camp emptied as they all headed to the arena with their swords and knives. They found Ozanus standing in the middle of the dirt arena with Gaerwn helping him put on a plain leather breastplate over his shirt and belting on his sword. Ozanus glanced up as everyone arrived, surprised by the turnout.

Those planning to watch sat on the edge of the compacted soil banks while those eager to prove their prowess entered the arena. They gathered in a large circle looking at him expectantly.

He turned slowly in a circle, looking at each fighter briefly before moving on to the next. To a couple, the younger ones, he said, "please step out."
Reluctantly they joined the audience.

With his turn complete and with his hand on his dragon handled knife he spoke, "I asked you here as I need your help. There is something happening in our world but no God has spoken to me bar one. By the fact I can barely sense him means there is something coming but I need to draw Him out so I can speak with Him. I need to grab His attention with anger and fighting. All of you here, are you prepared to be vicious? To draw blood? To lose blood?" There was a roar of acceptance and Ozanus couldn't help a small smile forming. For a moment he realised he had missed this. He added, "are your weapons sharp?"
There was another shout.

"Then who dares be the first?" He shouted, drawing his sword and stepping into a stance suitable for an attack or defence.

There were glances amongst friends and then at others to see who would be the first to dare. Never had they had such an open invitation to attack their High Chieftain. Some had participated in practice fights with him and knew his aggressive skill and steadfast style but wanted to give others an opportunity to discover it for themselves.

Ozanus was keeping an eye on the large group, watching twitching hands and shifting feet, as he tried to work out who was going to take him on first. He heard light footsteps from behind and spun round, bringing up his sword as he did to defend himself from what was nearly a surprise attack.

While distracted by the first attack three older, more experienced fighters teamed up and ran in. The first of the three was taken by surprise as Ozanus pulled out his knife and slashed upwards with it, causing the man to suck in his belly and turn his head so he didn't get cut. He stumbled, re-found his composure and re-joined the fight.

Over the course of the afternoon the fighting continued, insults were thrown and injuries caused. At times some even found themselves fighting each other, Ozanus somehow throwing them off his scent while he continued to fight with others. Blood was soon staining the arena's dirt floor red. Those worn out or too injured to keep going retreated to the banks while others kept it going.

Ozanus had never felt so energised. Practicing on his own was not the same as honing his skills against real people. And the Suwars seemed to be enjoying it as much as him, testing new attack sequences without fear of looking foolish or receiving retribution. They cheered if someone managed to land a blow on their High Chieftain and he would acknowledge their skill with a nod of his head.

By the evening he was feverish and his senses were heightened and he could sense the War God inside him again. The fighting and blood was too much for Him to resist and he could sense War. He was savouring it all. He declared the fighting over though he had to fight off a few last attacks from those blinded by the fighting.

With it over he let a Suwar bandage up his wounds on his arm, leg and a deep cut on his shoulder at the edge of his breastplate, a lucky slice, which had to be stitched up. Offered the chance to eat with Gaerwn he declined. He didn't need his senses dulled with food and drink.

No one would be up at the ruined temple on its cliff top, as he headed up, following the worn path and steps that hugged the cliffside. Once it was a building open to the sky, the pillars connected with walls but now all that remained of it was crumbling pillars and arches. Ragged banners hung under the arches, moving in the cool breeze.

Stepping on to the exposed platform he lit a torch with his flint and iron kit. Ahead of him was the altar on a low dais with a stone carved bowl on the top always ready to accept an offering. Once at the altar he unwrapped the bloodstained bandages and put them in the bowl. He touched the flickering torch to them and watched as they began to smoulder and then burn. He knelt down before the altar and closed his eyes to concentrate on calling the God of War to him as his empty stomach grumbled. He felt War's presence fill his mind as He shouted, *"you fool!"*

"You chose to live within me." Ozanus answered scathingly, *"but now you are hurting me. What is happening?"* His tone demanded answers.

"This is nothing to do with you."

"I think the fact you are hiding within me means it is now my problem as well."

"He has been seeking me out, that is why you have been fainting. He has a lot of power, more power than the Dragon Lord. The Dragon Lord is pathetic compared to him. He could kill you if he wanted to."

"You knew this was coming?!" Ozanus accused.

"Perhaps."

"I would have thought you would be pleased for another war?" Ozanus sneered.

"Not like this. This will be worse if He is allowed to grow strong. He knows who He needs to ensure it happens. If He gets hold of you we are doomed."

"And I'm guessing you are one of them…?"
They both paused as they felt another presence. War fled.

There was a flash of gold in the darkness of a physical presence that was the Dragon Lord. He remarked, *"he is right."*

"What is going on?" Ozanus demanded, frustrated he was being dragged into immortal issues just like his father and realising his own son might end up growing up fatherless; history repeating itself for the third generation in a row.

"I want to say it does not concern you but you are going to get dragged into this whether you like it or not. A Basilisk has been released from its prison and now it is seeking its revenge and taking the known world back to another time."
Ozanus frowned and huffed, another cryptic message.

"And you have aided it by not doing as you were ordered." The Dragon Lord snarled and flicked his tail angrily, breaking a column, *"you should have burnt the body, destroyed it, but you didn't and now it lives to help Him in reclaiming this world."*

"I want nothing to do with this!" Ozanus shouted angrily.

"You may have foolishly given up the title of Nejus but you are still the defender of all dragons and High Chieftain of your Suwars. You cannot hide a future of your creating."
The Dragon Lord snarled, *"prepare for it!"*
With a flick of his tail again that barely missed Ozanus' head, forcing him to bow down, the God disappeared as the last of the sun also disappeared on the horizon.

War skulked in the back of Ozanus' mind and whispered, *"do not even think about me. The dark is his friend and he will try to seek me out. If he finds me he will discover what's inside you and will want you too."* Ozanus remained where he was until the stars came out so that he could make his way back down to the Valley floor. He needed more information and fast. He had never heard of a Basilisk and was going to have to use the library, which would also mean having to see Ioan. He wondered also why War was hiding within him. If the end of the world was coming, wasn't that ideal for him? Or had residing in a man's body toned down his blood greed?

The stars disappeared behind clouds and he felt the presence again of something cold and evil. This time he refused to let it affect him. He closed his eyes and concentrated on emptying his mind even as he dropped to his knees, hands pressed to his head as if he could hold it together and stop it from shattering at the intense pressure pushing at his mind. He sensed the Basilisk knew that War was close and felt the frustration that it wasn't making contact.

The stars came out and the presence faded and Ozanus realised how tired and hungry he was. His body ached from all of the earlier fighting. The library could wait till the morning. He staggered to his feet and slowly headed back down to the Valley floor, a hand resting on the cliff face, and to Gaerwn's tent.

At the sight of a pale faced Ozanus Gaerwn grabbed the man and pushing him on to a stool and exclaimed, "what have you been doing now? Where are your bandages?"

Ozanus sighed heavily, "the Gods."

"Damn them, you are only human. Here, drink this." He passed Ozanus a goblet of warmed ale.

"We can't say no though."

"What did they want?" Gaerwn asked as he put together a piece of cold beef and bread, "did today do what you wanted?"

"Yes it did and I don't really know what they want." Ozanus replied carefully as he stared into the cup of ale. He wasn't ready to share everything yet but he was ready for bed.

As if Gaerwn had read his mind the Suwar Chieftain remarked, "I've made you up a bed in here if you want to go to bed."

"Thanks." Ozanus gave him a tight smile, "have you got any more bandages? I burnt mine."

"Wrong time for the Blood Moon festival." Gaerwn chuckled and it raised a more relaxed smile from Ozanus.

"It's what I had to do." Ozanus replied as he stood and dropped heavily on to the bed and pulled off his bloodstained shirt.

Gaerwn rebandaged the shoulder wound as he remarked, "he did a good job on that didn't he?"

"He was vicious, ferocious, almost as if he wanted to actually kill me. It went in deep, slipped off the edge of my breastplate. That girl was good as well."

"Which one?"

"Blonde hair in a plait with beads like the Daughters of Scyth. She kept dancing. She was really light on her feet."

"Yes, I know who you mean. She lost her mother in the battle. She was a year and a bit off from being made a Suwar at the time, not quite ready like the other apprentices who we took with us."

"She's someone to watch and develop."

"Already on my radar. There. What are your plans for the morning? I can get Nimib saddled for you if you are heading off."

"I'm going to be here at least one more day, but I want nothing special."

"Fine by me. Others will think differently."

"Shuang can think all she wants but I'm here on business, not pleasure." Ozanus retorted.   He knew his younger sister had married a Suwar. It had surprised him and his siblings, but she had it the easiest with no high expectations put on her. By all accounts she was happy and someone in the family needed to be happy with their lot. He knew Lylya still struggled at times with her role as ruler of Moronland even with Kenene and Sigwear supporting and advising her. Only once had he stepped in after giving up the Nejus title and that was when he had set up Kenene and his old group to support her.

Eight

He slept in later than planned and frustrated with himself he stomped through the house and into the study with its shelves of books collected by generations of Nejuses. He announced himself with, "I need to use the library."

Ioan stared up from his desk in shock at the sight of his gaunt faced older brother and protested, "you can't come barging in here. You aren't Nejus anymore remember."

"Produced that heir yet?" Ozanus sneered back. His brother didn't look any better than he felt, the strains of ruling a country getting to him as well. His brown hair had started to go white and there were pimple scars from greasy skin caused by stress.

Ioan scowled as no children had happened so far with his wife who had previously been his mistress. He felt sure the Gods were snubbing him unlike his brother. He retorted, "you'll have to send Shaprour here sooner or later you know, especially as you can't seem to take care of yourself. And what was yesterday about?! Are you going mad like our great great grandfather?"

"You wouldn't understand." Ozanus snapped as he headed for the shelves. He didn't even acknowledge Rafferty's replacement who was staring at the brothers with wide eyes of shock on how they were talking to each other.

Ozanus found the book he wanted and retreated

outside for privacy though he was soon joined by a cat who rubbed against his ankles while he sat in a chair. He carefully opened the cortina'ed book. He opened it to what he considered the first page with the painted image of the Dragon Lord. He felt sure he was missing something. He worked through the rest of the folds but didn't find what he was looking for. He frowned and felt sure he was missing something.

He returned to the front of the folded book and realised the cover was thick and he could feel a little bump like a button. He slid a finger carefully through the pressed folds and felt a piece of string wrapped round a wooden button. He pulled out his knife and very carefully with its point broke the old brittle string. The folds popped open to reveal a painted landscape.

Painted high in the sky was a large serpentine black scaled Basilisk, it's mouth of sharp teeth open revealing a forked tongue flicking out. A hood framed its head with the outline of a crown detailed within it. To either side of it was another black dragon and a dark burnished copper coloured dragon, blood dripping from wounds. He recognised the two smaller ones as Death and War, bodies in their mouths with arms and legs handing limply down.

Below them was a desolate landscape where the dragon gods he knew hid in caves and forests. Men and women struggled in the dark empty spaces which should have been fields but were either muddy quagmires or dustbowls. They were either bowed down or knelt praying for release from life, faces turned up to the skies and the three ancient gods.

Man and beast fought each other below War, feeding his bloodlust and addiction to anger and rage. Below Death there was a huge burning pyre of bodies with more being added to it. There were bodies missing limbs or covered with disease. Others cowered as dragons flew low in the sky, reaching down with mouths and claws to grab at them. Another group of dragons fought amongst themselves around War.

The Basilisk had no name but it came to him, Strife. This was the new god he had to deal with if he chose to. This was the god War currently hid from. He wondered where Strife was hiding himself.

He carefully closed the book and stared out into the Valley with all of its greenery. He couldn't imagine it destroyed and black and desolate with its dragons hunting the Suwars, the household and the villagers. He wondered whether he would find out more information about that time and returned to the study which was now empty much to his relief.

He went for the book of knowledge first but there was nothing in there. He was going to have to search out the oldest books.

He soon had several books open around him and a pencil and paper in his lap as he made notes. There didn't seem any straight written account of that early time. There was mentions of the Dragon Lord rising up and with the weather gods taking on Strife, War and Death, but not how it was done. With Strife locked away deep in a mountain Death retreated to darkness willingly and War was subdued but not imprisoned. The Dragon Lord knew death was needed to keep life under control.

Then the Dragon Lord and his gods were worshipped with their own bloody and violent ceremonies led by men who ordained themselves as priests and the holders of the knowledge, his own ancestors amongst them.

With this knowledge he decided this was something the gods alone could deal with. No army of Suwars would be able to take down a Basilisk like Strife.

He carefully closed the books and returned them to

the shelves.

      His research done it was time to go home. Gaerwn saw him off as Nimib rose into the air. He called out, "don't take so long to visit next time."
Ozanus laughed and waved a hand.
      In the air, high above Keytel his silence was broken when Nimib asked, *"do you know more now?"*
    "Yes and it's ominous but it's the Gods problem, not ours. Did you get a sense of anything?"
    "Just that the air has become chiller than it has ever been in the Valley. There was mention of a sense of something happening far from here, the other side of Moronland, in your mother's homeland."
    "Gloabtona? That's interesting."
    "They aren't worried though as you are around to protect them."
    "Hmpfh."

Nine

The women had waited till daylight to emerge out of their tent and give the nightmares enough time to slither into dark holes, out of the sun. Lhateso peered out first before crawling out followed by the others. They stared round at the silent campsite taking in the human shaped snake skin and the blood splattered tents of the men.

Lhateso crossed to where her cousin was slumped by the cold fire, pale and hollow cheeked from where the blood had been drained from him. She wanted to feel sad but couldn't. She kicked the body, "you idiot! What did you release?! You idiot!"
She began to cry then for herself and her sister. What would happen to them now? One of the women crossed over, "hush child. There's no need to mourn these men."
She gulped, "I'm not."
  "That's good then. It's shock, isn't it?" Martha said knowingly.
Lhateso just nodded.
  "What are you going to do Martha?"
Martha shrugged, "there is always work to be found. Lhateso, want to join us?"
Lhateso brushed the tears from her face with the back of her hand and shook her head, "I have somewhere I should be going."
  "Good luck then. Come on ladies, let's see what we can

71

scrouge from this lot. Lhateso, you should too, for eating, for selling."

It had taken Lhateso two weeks, walking on her own and then joining a traders' caravan travelling into Keytel. They had pointed her in the direction of the Valley as they were headed in the opposite direction. She now stared up at the entrance to the Valley and its two giant stone statues marking the entry. One had a dragon guarding an egg, standing high above it with one claw on the egg, snarling. The other had lost most of its body, but the large egg remained. The snarling dragon scared her but she reminded herself of what she had seen back at the camp in Moronland and with a set face of determination she walked into the Valley.

She made her way slowly through the Valley, astonished by the amount of vegetation and flowers. She had never seen the like up in the mountains. There were the short-lived summer meadows but she rarely got to see those hidden away in the palace. It felt hot and humid compared to her mountain home making her want to pull layers of dirty clothes off and there was a faint whiff of rotten egg that caused her nose to wrinkle. It was with relief she saw the path opening up ahead of her but it was then her presence came to someone's attention.

Out of a bush stepped a tall woman, her hair braided all over and a scowl on her face, "you don't belong here. I think you should turn around now." Her hand was on her knife, thinking that would be enough to scare the slight girl in front of her.

"I… I was told to come here."

"Who by?" The Suwar demanded.

"I must speak to the Nejus. There is an evil coming. It's already taken the court of Gloabtona. I have family here." Lhateso hurriedly explained.

The Suwar looked her up and down with suspicion considering the clothes she wore needed a wash and were looking travel worn. Her black hair was unbrushed and dust covered her skin. She ordered, "come with me, the Chieftain can decide if you can see the Nejus."

Lhateso was led straight across the lawn past the house. She looked over her shoulder at it and wondered how a ruler of the country could live in a house. It did look impressive with its dragons carved into the eaves of the two storied house and its veranda but it wasn't a palace. Where were its defences? Where were the servants and guards? Where was the women's quarters?

She was led down a well worn path to another site which had a mixture of tents and buildings. They stopped outside a large yurt and the Suwar looked in and then grumbled to herself as she pulled Lhateso in and forced her on to a stool and ordered, "stay here, don't move." The armed woman stepped out and called to someone passing by, "can you fetch the Chieftain?"

"Sure."

While they waited Lhateso looked round and couldn't believe how messy it was. The bed was unmade, a chest to hold clothes was actually covered with them. Behind her was what looked like a giant saddle beside a T bar that held a breastplate and a bow. The only tidy bit was a table where an ink stand was placed on one side and a neat pile of paperwork with a large book on top of it was on the other.

Ten minutes later Gaerwn showed up, sweating still from practice, with his deputy trying to keep up behind him. He scowled as he entered the tent and demanded of the Suwar, "why have I been called away?"

"Sir. An intruder. Claims they've been sent here." She stood tall, not afraid of her leader.

Gaerwn looked at the fidgeting girl on the stool and demanded, "who are you?"

"Lhateso. Are you the Nejus?" She stopped fidgeting and sat straighter as she asked hopefully.

Gaerwn laughed then and began to relax.

The Suwar who had found her said, "she had this on her." And held out the dragon headed knife.

His eyes briefly widened as he recognised the blade and took it before he carefully asked, "where did you get this?"

Cautiously Lhateso answered, "I found it."

"Where?"

"Why?" She warily asked, "are you the Nejus?"

"Why do you want to see him?"

"I was told to come here. Something evil that eats people has taken over the palace and the Nejus can help." She answered, "can I have my knife back?"

"Not yet." He sat down opposite her, "you two, go…. Go on."

The two Suwars glanced at each other before saluting, fist on chest, and then leaving

Lhateso watched them both leave and then back at Gaerwn. He softened, "you aren't in trouble but we don't need to bother the Nejus just yet."

She looked at him and she saw something in his face and posture that suggested he understood and potentially knew something but didn't know how much.

"Where is your palace?"

"In Gloabtona. A demon has taken it over and eaten half of the court. It's hidden in cloud and a blizzard. My Nuna told me and my sister to get here but she was caught. I found work helping look for something in a mountain that had broken in half and another monster was freed." Her eyes had grown wide from remembering it consuming all the men, draining the blood from their bodies. She found herself whispering, "it drank their blood."

She held out her hand, "can I have my knife back please?"
Gaerwn had become very still, forgetting that he even held
the knife. He glanced down at it and then handed it over,
"this is a special knife. Do you know why?"
She shook her head as he let her take it.

"Not everyone is allowed one. The dragon headed handle
marks the owner out as a Suwar, a dragon rider. This one
belonged to a Nejus." Gaerwn wasn't aware that Ozanus
had even lost it.

"He can have it back." She offered.

"He has another one now so don't worry about it."

"Can I see him now? I got told I had to tell him."

"Not at the moment. I need to find out more
information."

He knew Ioan was the wrong man to be informed.
He didn't know whether Ozanus would be interested in the
information. However, for himself, he needed more
information other than some strange girl claiming man
eating monsters were walking the world. She could be
delusional for all he knew and would probably have
ignored her if Ozanus hadn't been in the Valley a week
earlier acting mysteriously.

He looked over at the girl who was shifting
nervously on her stool. She challenged, "you don't believe
me do you?! You aren't going to let me see the Nejus?"
She jumped up, ready to run to the house but Gaerwn
grabbed her arm and hissed, "you are not going anywhere."
He pushed her back on to the stool. More gently he said,
"you can stay with the single women while I find out more
information. I don't disbelieve you but I haven't heard from
anyone else about this. Now, stay here and I'll find
someone who can get you cleaned, fed and some new
clothes."
He left her in the tent while he sought out a couple of
people.

Ten

Three days later Gaerwn was meeting Kenene in Drakgong. The dragons were left on the edge of the trading town and Kenene and Gaerwn walked to a nearby tavern where they were familiar visitors. They often met up to discuss what was going on in Moronland and Keytel.

Kenene was one of those men who reached a certain age and then didn't seem to age any further. His dark brown hair was greying but had been for the last five years. His beard had greyed completely and hid a scar on his cheek. His weather beaten face showed a long life in the sky.

They embraced as the comrades they were and although Gaerwn was the more senior in leadership they considered themselves equals. Kenene looked after the men and women stationed in Duntorn.

Once in the tavern Gaerwn said, "thanks for meeting up with me."

"I sent some men out to check what your girl said." Kenene remarked and waited till the server had brought them a jug of ale before going on, "I sent someone over to the mountain the Daughters used to live on. There has definitely been some activity there though couldn't tell you what they had been looking for. There was a camp but looked like it had been attacked. What Terran said was strange. From what he could tell from the decomposing bodies was their necks were torn open but no scavengers had had a go at them."

"What could have been there to find?"

"Weapons, metal, pots, clothes." Kenene shrugged, "who knows what they were after. There wasn't anything to suggest what. There was a caved in tunnel in the rockfall. What did this girl say she saw?"

"A monster transformed from a baby into a child and then into a man. It ate all the men. It took some armour, turned into a dragon and flew away."

Kenene frowned, "do you think it's a new god? Did one get unleashed in that temple?"

"I think we need to talk to Ozanus. Can you get in contact with him?"

Kenene shook his head, "only Lylya and Miryama know where he is. They won't tell me. That other bit. Davida headed over to Moronland's border with Gloabtona and he said there were rumours of things happening up at the palace. They were afraid as there was a growing black cloud and rumours of a never ending blizzard spreading across the mountains. They didn't know why."

"Ozanus needs to be told. You need to find him, though be careful. There's something amiss with him." Gaerwn said carefully. He took a deep drink from his cup of ale.

"Something I should be worried about? He's been different ever since those battles with Timijin and that blessing in the temple." Kenene replied with concern.

"I'm not sure. Do you ever see him?"

"Not since he set me up here."

"He came to the Valley recently and had everyone fighting him and then took himself off to the temple. Do you know where he lives?"

"No, but Lylya does. I'll talk to her. Does Ioan know about this?"

Gaerwn shook his head, "he'll just get frustrated that he

would have to ask Ozanus."

"He really shouldn't have given up the title."

"His choice. Anything else I need to know or let Ioan know about?"

"Nah. I'll send a message with what is decided." Kenene finished his cup of ale and threw some coins on the table.

Walking back to the dragons Kenene asked, "what you going to do with the girl?"

"She's in with the other women at the moment. I've just got to keep her away from Ioan. She has Ozanus' old knife so she could have been marked by the gods though I hope not. Right, see you soon."
They had reached their dragons and climbed into their saddles.

Lylya loved and hated the role that had been foisted on her by her older brother. She was glad to have Sigwear to advise her and Kenene with his group of Suwars as well as the Daughters of Scyth. Over the last five years she had removed all evidence of Rudolf from the Tower and with Sigwear's guidance she had made Moronland a stronger and more civilised country. It would never be Keytel but it was better than what it was.

She entered the room she had turned into a council room and with a smile demanded, "what trouble are you getting us into Kenene?"

"Not planning anything but there are things happening that will affect us." Kenene remarked from his chair as Lylya in an embroidered high collared blue coat over a shirt and trousers, sat down. Her golden brown hair was swept away from her face, held off it with ribbon wrapped twice round her head. He glanced at Sigwear, Miryama and Harrietta, the leader of the Daughters of Scyth. They were all curious about the reason why Kenene had called the meeting.

"Gaerwn came to me with an odd story and there is some truth behind it." Kenene said solemnly once all eyes were on him, "a girl from Gloabtona turned up in the Valley demanding to see the Nejus. She came claiming a demon has taken the palace. Then on her way through Moronland she stopped at the Daughters' old home." He looked to Miryama and Harrietta. "There she was involved in some digging where another monster was apparently found."

The two women glanced at each other and then back to the table. Harrietta spoke, "there's nothing left in the mountain. There was only the one temple as far as we are aware unless it was…."

"No." Miryama interrupted, "there was nothing else. Ozanus would have known. The Gods would have told him."

"Perhaps he chose not to tell." Sigwear remarked.

"No." It was Lylya's turn, "Miryama is right. The Gods would have spoken. And if it was that power in the temple keeping it locked up, wouldn't it have emerged when the power was drained? Kenene, you say there is truth to what this girl said?"

"There was an abandoned camp at the base of the mountain with decaying bodies, their necks all torn. The scavengers hadn't touched them. As for Gloabtona, there is a huge storm over the mountain tops, growing bigger. I've sent someone to monitor that situation."

"And does my brother know?" Lylya asked with concern.

"Which one?"

"Ioan."

Kenene shook his head, "Gaerwn hasn't told him yet."

"And Ozanus?"

"Not yet. What do you want us to do?"

Lylya was quiet as she thought about it all. She knew they all needed more information for the issue to be dealt with and the best person by far was her older brother. She could feel their eyes on her and looked down at the table so she didn't have to look at anyone.

Finally she lifted her eyes and looked at everyone, "this isn't what he wanted but he is the best option we've got. We have to protect Moronland and Keytel from whatever is coming. The Gods have to be involved in this somehow."

"And Ioan?" Sigwear quietly asked.

"For the moment he doesn't need to know. Whatever it is has to get through Moronland first. Kenene, can you send a message to Gaerwn and tell him to be prepared."

"Sure."

"Now, I need to speak to Miryama and Kenene in private."

Miryama and Kenene glanced at each other while the other two left.

Though she trusted them she still checked the other two hadn't lingered outside the door. She closed the door and leant her back against it. She sighed, "of everyone here we three know Ozanus best. Is he up for this?"

Kenene frowned briefly as he remembered what Gaerwn had said and Miryama looked away. Lylya's eyes narrowed suspiciously, "what are you both not telling me?"

"I think he already knows something is amiss." Kenene admitted, "he was in the Valley the other week."

"Doing what?" Lylya frowned.

"Apparently getting all of the Suwars fighting him."

"What for?"

Kenene shrugged, "he didn't tell Gaerwn the reason behind it. Miryama, you know anything?"

Miryama looked like she was fighting with her conscious. She knew they needed Ozanus to step up again to ensure their countries were safe but she wasn't sure he was in a good place mentally and physically.

"Miryama?" Lylya prompted.

Miryama shifted uncomfortably, "he knows something is up, but he thinks the gods should be dealing with it."

"Kenene, I think you'd best talk to Ozanus." Lylya said after studying Miryama's posture. She could see the woman was holding something back but wasn't sure what.

"Are you going to tell me where he has set up home then?" Kenene enquired.

"No." Lylya answered firmly, "I promised him."
He turned to Miryama, "Miryama?"
Miryama shook her head, "I promised as well. He stepped away for a reason and didn't want to be dragged into everything."

"Well, if you won't tell me where he lives, where does he go when he's here?" The tone of his voice revealed the frustration he felt. He still couldn't understand why Ozanus hadn't trusted him with the whereabouts of his home.

"He sits in the taverns listening and watching." Lylya admitted.

"Why did you never tell me?!" Kenene exclaimed as he stood and leant on the table in frustration.

"I didn't know for a long time. It was one of Sigwear's informants who made us aware. You know now though." Kenene grumbled as he left the room to start a search of where Ozanus hung out and have people watch them. He felt sure his old Nejus would be in town soon.

Eleven

A few days later the word was that Ozanus was in the city. Kenene threw on a coat and hurried out into the streets.

Ozanus sensed someone sitting down at his table and was about to tell them it was a waste of their time when he glanced up and saw it was Kenene. He scowled, "what do you want?"

"Glad to see your temper hasn't improved." Kenene remarked with a sneer, "you are a hard man to find."

"And that's the point." Ozanus replied as he folded his map up and then softened, "it is good to see you. How's life been treating you?"

"Did you not trust me to keep your new home secret?" Ozanus frowned, "I didn't and don't want everyone coming, seeking me out for trivial matters. Would you?" Kenene shrugged his shoulders, but he felt disappointed in his leader and friend, that he hadn't trusted him enough even after everything they had gone through when they had been behaving as mercenaries.

"You've found me now so what do you want?" Ozanus asked stiffly.

"We need your help."

"No you don't. Ioan is in charge now remember and there is Gaerwn."

"Not in regards to this matter. We've all talked."

"We?"

"Gaerwn, me, Lylya and Miryama. Look, you are the best person for this."

"Does Ioan know you are talking to me behind his back?" Kenene shook his head.

"Well, go talk to him then." Ozanus stood as if to go.

"The Daughters' mountain was dug over." Kenene said, taking a chance. He saw Ozanus' eyes briefly widen and a hand clench and knew that Ozanus knew something. He quickly added, "go to Gloabtona."
Ozanus felt a pulsing inside him that was warning him against the idea now that it had been spoken.

"You are the best to interpret what is going on there. You don't have to do anything if you don't want to. You can report back to us if you want and we'll take the next steps from there." He turned in his chair as Ozanus slipped round the table, hand gripping the handle of his knife. He added, "come on, the Suwar in you must be tempted."
Ozanus waved a hand and left leaving Kenene unsure if he had agreed or not. He hadn't managed to see what was on the map to work out what Ozanus was planning.

Ozanus returned to the fort that the Daughters of Scyth had constructed next to the ruins of the arena. He noted the dragons roosting in the high walls The map he had bought was tucked into his coat. He was annoyed that Kenene had found him as he had been internally debating with himself. He knew War was against him going.
He could feel it but it didn't mean he would listen. The fainting and headaches were becoming frustrating. If he went to Gloabtona perhaps War would leave and then he could get some peace.

He headed to Miryama's home and was relieved to find her out with Shaprour. He sat down on a bench by the low fire and threw a log on to it. He pulled out the map to continue studying it. If he went he wasn't going to be able to fly. He wouldn't want anyone to know he was in the country.

Miryama appeared as he was folding the map up, "oh? What are you doing here?"
He looked up with a small smile, "only passing through. Where's Shaprour?"

"Playing. Are you alright?" She asked with concern. She could tell from his posture that something was wrong.
He gave her a tight smile, she didn't miss much these days, "I have to go away."

"To the Valley again?" She sat down beside him.
He shook his head, "no, further than that. I am going to Gloabtona."

"Are you sure?"
He nodded, "there are strange goings on and it's the one place War does not want to go. If I go perhaps he will leave me and I will be well again."

"How long do you think you will be gone? We really should talk of Shaprour's education."

"A week? If you don't hear from me in two tell Lylya, tell Gaerwn, tell my brother. Warn them that danger will be coming and fast."

"What are you not telling me?"
He pulled her to him and kissed her hard. She wrapped her arms round him and felt his urgency as he undid the ties holding her blouse closed. He pulled her blouse out of the culottes it was tucked into and his hands found her skin. She shivered at his cold hands on her warm skin. They moved up and found her plump breasts and gave them a squeeze.

She wanted to stop and get Ozanus to tell her the full truth but before she could he had swept her into his arms and carried her to her large bed. The urgency dissipated and he slowed down, wanting to savour her body. Slowly he explored her naked body until she felt she couldn't take anymore.

Finally he penetrated her, slowly at first, until he was deep inside her. She wrapped her legs round him as he leant down to kiss her again and moved in and out. She hugged him close, not wanting to let him go. He groaned as he came and then collapsed at Miryama's side. He pulled the blankets up over their naked bodies and Miryama snuggled against him. She wanted to savour the moment but she needed answers as well. She asked into his shoulder, "do you really think you won't come back?"
He was playing with a curl of her hair, half asleep, "hmm?"
She sat up and looked at him, "Ozanus? I'm serious now. What is happening? I have heard there are monsters. Is this related to what has been happening to you and Shaprour."
He was no longer half asleep, "yes and I don't know."
She threw the blankets off, "you'd best get dressed before Shaprour comes back and play with him for a bit." Already she was getting dressed herself.

He spent the afternoon playing with Shaprour though his attention ebbed and flowed. He was preparing himself mentally for what was to come.

The little boy threw his arms round his father at bedtime. Ozanus smiled. He was glad his son was having a carefree childhood. Sat on the edge of his son's bed he said, "when I get back we'll start your education?"

"Will I get to ride my own dragon?"

"We'll see. It should be my dragon's daughter but Nimib doesn't have a mate. Maybe there is a dragon mama-to-be who doesn't have a Suwar. I'm sure they would be honoured to have their child as your dragon." He smiled down, "there's going to be lots to learn. We'll get you some weapons and your mother and I will decide where you'll go to learn."

"How long are you going away for papa?"
"Two weeks at most." He hugged his son again.

Twelve

He slipped out in the morning. He paused at his son's bed and rested his hand lightly on his son's small forehead and sent up a silent blessing. He couldn't help smiling at his son sprawled on his back with only one foot covered. Miryama hadn't stirred either as he had given her a kiss. He didn't know if he would see either of them again.

He landed close to the border town of Kacper. It was quiet at this time of year as Gloabtona was snowed in. In the summer the one street town tripled in size with tents as traders from both countries made their deals. He looked up to the sky and saw the black clouds hiding the mountain tops. He heard War moaning in his mind, as if he was dying, and muttered, *"you can leave whenever you want. I have to do this to protect Keytel."*

"You'll regret this." War growled.

Ozanus ignored the god and proceeded to empty his saddle bags into a backpack of supplies. He buckled his sword to his waist. Nimib looked on, *"do you want me to wait here?"*

"No, there's no point. Head home but come back in a week and a half. If I don't arrive a few days later seek out Miryama."

"What are you going to be doing? Why can't I come with you?"

"I don't want whatever is coming to know I'm coming. I'm sorry Nimib." He would have loved to have flown up on Nimib and show that he was not a man to be messed with, *"I need to know what I am up against before I can make a plan, and that means going in discreetly. I have no contacts in Gloabtona that can feed me information."*

"Please be careful sir." Nimib replied with feeling, *"I have a bad feeling about all of this."*

"Me too, me too." Ozanus remarked soberly as he slung the bag over his shoulder. He headed through the quiet street and out the other side. He glanced back as he heard Nimib lift into the air.

It took him a few days getting up the mountains. He had never been so high before and there were times he felt lightheaded or sick from the altitude. He slipped quietly through the towns, hoping not to draw any attention to himself. There was a sense of being more suspicious of strangers than normal and any transactions he made were hurried to completion.

The higher he went the darker it got and he could barely see through the snow swirling around in the winds. He wore his head scarf tight round his face and neck as it was even colder than when he flew on Nimib. As well as his flying gloves he had wrapped cloths round his hands inside them as an extra layer of warmth.

He had no idea whether it was night or day as he staggered through a wall of snow and into silence and stillness. It was still dark but there was no snow or wind as if he was now in the eye of the biggest storm he had ever been in. Ahead of him was a village and beyond that the front walls of the palace. His mother had once told him about it but he couldn't remember any of the details.

Though no one was about there had been a little activity as there was a path dug into the foot deep snow that led up to the palace. There were a few lit lamps hanging outside gated buildings but not many. A few gates hung open with snow drifting high in the gateways suggesting the buildings had been abandoned. A tiled roof had already collapsed on one of them from the amount of snow on it.

Whether it was the altitude, the cold, the continuous darkness or War trying to get him to turn around he felt weary and exhausted. He had the overwhelming urge to fall asleep. His mind told him to rest so he was alert for whatever he found in the palace. He waded through the snow towards an open gate and then pulled himself up the snow-covered steps to the veranda that ran the length of the front of the building. With a hand on his knife he carefully pushed the double front doors open.

The air was cold and musty when he stepped in and his breath rose in a cloud of frosty steam that then fell as ice. He stumbled over something in the dark but had no idea what it was. Sat on the mat floor he used his fire starting kit to strike sparks and was relieved to find it was a brazier that had been knocked over.

By feel he lifted it up and checked there was something to light within it before striking some sparks. With a few glowing sparks on the remains of the last fire he stabbed at the reed matting with his knife to feed the ember with fibres. Gently blowing on it the spark grew stronger and then he added some bigger pieces of matting.

Soon he had a small fire going. It wasn't going to heat the room but it was enough to warm him and give him some light. By its light he worked out that he was in some entrance hall or waiting room. Benches were against one wall and in an alcove there were several dead plants in pots. If it wasn't for the situation he was facing into he would have gone exploring but currently all he wanted to do was wrap himself up in his blanket and go to sleep. In a few hours time he would venture up to the palace and find out what terrified War and what his country was up against.

On careful inspection Strife had found the ancient altar hidden in the top garden of the palace under a large bush. It seemed no one had dared move it though they no longer worshipped the dragon gods. He had it cleared and then the coarse grass lawn removed revealing the rock the altar sat on. The altar itself was carved with channels which ran down the long sides of the altar which in turn led to channels in the rock which ended in a stone bowl situated below the edge of the rock so it would fill with the blood of the sacrifices made on the altar. With disgust Strife had ripped out the dead plant that had been potted in it.

Already the locals were reverting to the primitive old ways in their desperation to survive. Children and young women were being sent to the palace in the hope of placating the demons now living in it. All the blood was making them stronger and Strife was now eyeing up Moronland and the potential there.

Strife had been resting when he sat up, alert. He sensed a strong presence that up until now had been distant. He smiled and called out, "find me Bloodlust, now!"

Bloodlust was quickly found and he was soon in Strife's presence, wiping blood from the corner of his mouth. Strife sneered, *"enjoyed another sacrifice?"* Bloodlust grinned.

"There will soon be more to enjoy. The last piece needed for us to start expanding our reach has arrived. He's down in that silly village, find him and bring him back alive." Bloodlust frowned.

Strife chuckled, *"you are still a child. War is in a man's body. He may put up a fight. He seems to be reluctant to come to me."* He continued with a sneer, *"he's had it too easy in this world. Go armed, but remember, don't kill*

him."
Bloodlust grinned and left the audience pavilion, he finally
had something to do.

He was so hot blooded that the snow melted at
every footstep before freezing again seconds later. He
walked down through the village throwing open doors and
gates demanding terrified habitants where they were hiding
the stranger. None knew what he was talking about and
even after the threat of death none of them changed their
stories.
He wished he had a clue of who he was looking for.
Even a smell would be better than nothing. Grumbling to
himself he moved on to the empty houses. Sensing just the
hint of heat in one of them he spotted deep footprints
crossing the courtyard. He moved carefully, not sure
whether he would be ambushed or not. The closer he got
the more he could sense there were two heat sources and he
grinned, two he could easily take on. Neither heat source
seemed to be moving which was even better!
He gently opened the door, wanting to catch them
unawares and was surprised to find only one person curled
up close to the dying brazier. He approached and poked the
person with his sword and was surprised when a claw
reached out and grabbed it. A voice snarled, *"no you don't
child of my blood."*
The person uncurled and there was the strong outline of a
burnished copper dragon with streaks of green on its scales.
Bloodlust demanded, *"who are you?"*
War laughed, *"you are just a child. Wait and see, wait and
see."*
In a blink of an eye the outline was gone but a pair of
brown eyes stared at him, daring him.
"Get up!" Bloodlust demanded.
"And who are you?" Ozanus demanded back as he sat up
91

and felt for the grip of his sword at his waist.

Bloodlust glared down at the man. He had thought this would be easy. With a toddler like stamp of his foot he demanded again, "get up!"

"And what if I chose not to?" Ozanus asked quietly as he carefully moved into a crouch. From there he leapt up and went for a slash across the young man's chest only to hit metal.

They froze. Bloodlust grinned, eager for a fight and forgetting Strife's orders. He swung his own sword at Ozanus but as he hadn't been trained it came down at the wrong angle and Ozanus dodged it. Ozanus, his face set in a grim expression, remarked, "I don't want to cause any trouble."

"Why are you here?" Curiosity got the better of Bloodlust.

"Get on with it. I need him here now." Strife snarled in Bloodlust's mind.

Ozanus was wary as he saw Bloodlust's posture harden again. He prepared himself as the youth charge him. He spun round the youth and grabbed the boy's sword arm. He held it tight enough for the youth to drop his sword and then pulled his arm behind his back and put his own sword to Bloodlust's throat. He hissed in the young man's ear, "who are you and what do you want?"

"Unhand me." Bloodlust snarled, wiggling like a snake with its head trapped but he could not escape the hold Ozanus had on him.

Ozanus' grip tightened, cutting off oxygen as he demanded, *"who are you?"*

Their heads were so close that there was a spark of energy that threw them apart, the immortal energies inside them behaving like magnets repelling each other. Images flashed into their minds.

Ozanus was stunned to realise the youth was the

92

deformed enfant he thought he had killed. Considering what the newborn had looked like he couldn't fathom how it now looked like a normal person. He wondered how he had survived, let alone been found. What immortal traits had War bestowed on the… No, he refused to call it a baby.

As for Bloodlust, through a blurry baby's vision he saw his father five years younger stabbing his newborn body with a knife and throw it into the sinkhole. He saw red that the man he had been sent to fetch was his father and he decided he had to kill him. With a roar of pain and anger he leapt up and jumped on the older man throwing him back to the floor.

His hands went round Ozanus' throat. Ozanus grabbed at the hands that were gripping his neck, thumbs pressing into his esophagus. His legs kicked as he fought for breath. He realised he wasn't going to be strong enough to get his son off him. Stars started to flash in his vision and the edges began shrinking.

Ozanus blacked out as there was a roar and the roof crashed in as a large black scaled dragon dove in. Its tail knocked Bloodlust away and its body curled round Ozanus' unconscious body protectively. The wooden walls of the house creaked in protest as the serpentine dragon's body pressed against them.

Bloodlust snarled and stretched into his own dragon form. Nothing was going to stop him from killing the man who had left him for dead! He leapt at Strife with his mouth wide open. He was swatted away by Strife who snarled, *"keep back!"*

Bloodlust shook his head to clear away the floating spots and exclaimed, *"let me at him! He left me for dead!"*

"No! We need him alive." Strife growled. He lifted Ozanus' inert body in a claw and pushed off out of the building.

The roof and walls fell in on Bloodlust as he roared

his frustration. He had used a lot of energy changing into a dragon and now didn't have enough to shake off the remains of the house. He roared again before shrinking back to his human form and crawled out of the rubble. Grumbling to himself he picked up the two swords and the bag before stomping back up to the palace.

Slowly Ozanus stirred, his head pounding. He tried to remember what had happened. His throat and neck felt bruised. He realised he lay on a cold hard surface and when he tried to sit up he found he was tied down. The leather strap on his left arm had been removed, exposing his large scar. He flexed his muscles to try and break whatever was holding him down. He couldn't feel any physical rope or chains but his body was too weak from the cold to free himself.

He heard footsteps and turned his head and saw a tall black skinned man approaching dressed in a pair of black trousers with a sash belt and a heavy sleeveless black coat edged in black fur. His skin was tattooed with scale markings. One hand was a stump while the other had nails that looked like talons, before both hands disappeared from view. His black hair hung down his back in a long que and Ozanus could feel the heat radiating from the heavy set muscular body.

Strife, hand behind his back holding the wrist of the other, smiled as he remarked, "you are a very interesting young man, all that rage inside you and that generous gift from the traitors being wasted." He ran a claw along the scar that had allowed Ozanus to accept the Dragon Lord's gift six years previously in the now destroyed temple under the Daughters of Scyth's mountain home.

"Who are you?" Ozanus challenged.

"Let me show you."

Ozanus' heart missed a beat as he was shown a dark

world where dragons hunted man and lording it above them all was a huge black Basilisk, Strife. Flying around with him were two dragons, War and Death, the bodies of men hanging from their claws. Chained to altars as offerings were small dragons and humans, waiting to be accepted by dragons that had a similar stature to the Valley's dragons.

Hiding his fear well Ozanus, his hands as fists, demanded, "what do you want with me?"
His eyes flashed red and dared Strife.

Strife's smile slipped a little as he looked thoughtful. He walked round the altar, hands back behind his back, "well, I was going to kill you or drain you of your blood and drive my kin out but now I think it will be better to keep you alive. It doesn't mean I will release you from your bonds. You can remain here till one or the other of you see sense."

"My son?" Ozanus asked warily.

"Stop sulking back there Bloodlust and apologise to your father." Strife called to the youth skulking in the background.

Bloodlust stepped out of the shadows and into the light of the torches positioned either end of the altar. Ozanus stared at the auburn haired young man wearing the burnished copper breastplate he thought he had thrown away. There were green stains on it where water had rusted it. On it now was the scar of where his sword had slashed across it. Bloodlust's arms were crossed in front of him and he glared defiantly at his father. With a sneer he muttered, "father."

"But how?! I stabbed you through the heart."
Strife laughed, "what a lovely reunion this is. You may have thought you had killed him but you forgot the immortal blood in him."

Ozanus' eyes widened as now he realised why his Dragon Lord had ordered him to burn the body. What was happening now was all down to him not following orders and now it was too late.

"Now, I will leave you to decide what path you are going to take. *War, I know you are there!*" As Strife walked away he added, "come Bloodlust."

Bloodlust glanced at Ozanus before following his lord. He grumbled, *"why do we need to keep him? I could drain his blood and then be just as powerful as them."* Strife turned on him and snarled, *"don't even think about it! You will never be as powerful as my kin and as for your father I need him too."* He wasn't going to explain himself but if he could get Ozanus on his side then the dragon riders would surely follow him What an army that would be?! He had seen the records in the palace's library of the encounter between Timijin's army and the Suwars. He smiled to himself.

Once back in the Audience Pavilion he called for a servant and when one appeared ordered for some wine to be brought to him. With the carafe bought he poured a glass half full. With sharp teeth he broke the skin on his wrist and allowed the blood to pour into the glass of red wine. Once full he closed the wound between two fingers and let the skin knit back together. He stirred the glass of blood and wine with a blood stained finger and handed it to the terrified servant, "give the man on the altar this to drink. Don't let any drops be spilt."

The servant approached what he thought was a soon to be sacrifice carefully and with a bowed head said, "I am to give you this."
Ozanus wanted to reject the offered drink but his throat was sore and dry. He replied, "I can't sit up. You are going to have to hold it for me."
The servant came closer and held the glass to Ozanus' mouth and held the man's head up. The wine tasted bitter and strongly of iron but he was too thirsty to care. He heard

a sigh of satisfaction in his mind.

Thirteen

Strife fed Ozanus for two days with his blood, pulling the man closer and closer to him. As he stood at the end of the altar, long finger nail tapping on the stone, he studied the man. They, as a species, had certainly come a long way since his reign of terror, though there were still plenty of fools that weren't worth nurturing.

Ozanus appeared to be asleep, conserving energy as it was cold lying on the blood stained altar. As the cold had got to his body and mind War had come to the fore, keeping him alive with the God's own internal heat. Sensing a presence Ozanus slowly opened his eyes and they glowed red. Carefully he sat up and stretched his back and rolled his shoulders. He slowly turned and swung his legs over the side on the altar, noting the fresh blood frozen in the channels of the altar with a frown.

Strife walked round to face the man. He smiled, *"welcome brethren. I have been waiting for you. Why have you not come to me sooner?"* The tone of his voice hardened.

War glared out of Ozanus' face, morphing it into the face of a dragon overlying the human. He refused to answer the question.

"War, come out of that shell of a body." Strife demanded, *"I have fed you my own blood to give you strength."*

"Not yet."

"Have you grown soft?" Strife challenged, *"I need you. I'll drain the body of this man if I have to."*
War chuckled, *"no you won't because I know you need him. I have seen and felt more than you but I will release this man from my thrall so that he can train my son."*
Strife's eyes narrowed, *"what are you not telling me?"*

War chuckled and vanished. He knew that Strife was underestimating men. They had grown stronger since the days he, Strife and Death had ruled. For the moment he will ensure Ozanus was pliable to Strife's needs but at the right moment he would unleash all of Ozanus' rage that was sure to grow in the confines of his locked mind.

In a sudden charitable mood Strife gestured with his hand, "come my friend, let's get you into the warm and see to that wrist."
Ozanus blinked and remarked with a flat tone of voice, "some warmth and food would be good."
He ignored Strife's offered hand and jumped off the altar and grimaced as pain shot up his left wrist as he leant on it. Glad that the man was surprisingly docile Strife remarked, as he led the man to the audience pavilion, "I have work for you."

"What can I do for you my lord?"

"I am told that you are a great warrior. I need you to train your son. As you have seen he has no training. I need him to be formidable, unbeatable." Strife replied as he sat on his throne.

"What do you want me to train him on?"

"Everything." Strife answered as he pulled a rope which rang a bell. A servant appeared and he ordered, "take this guest to a room and ensure he is fed and his wounds looked after."

It was then that Ozanus looked down and realised the scars on his hand and arm were seeping blood. He felt tired and weak and thought he could sleep forever. He bowed his head to Strife and then let the servant led him to a small room with a bed and a hot stove. His bag sat at the foot of the bed looking as if someone had rifled through it. He pulled off his clothes and said to the servant, "burn them and I'll want food and a bath when I wake."

"Yes sir." The servant left hugging the stinking clothes to him.

Nimib waited as she had been told to do so. She had to fight the urge to fly into the mountains and go find her rider. With no sign of Ozanus and the black clouds spreading over Moronland now something had gone wrong and she didn't know what. She lifted into the air and flew as fast as she could to Duntorn.

She called out as she circled the Daughters' village, *"I need Miryama."*
She came into land outside the village and hoped Miryama was being found.

Miryama hurried out of the village, *"Nimib, what's wrong? Where is Ozanus?"*

"I don't know. I waited for him but he didn't return. Those black clouds.... They are coming!" She couldn't hide the panic at the unknown that was coming.

"Calm yourself. Ozanus will want you to be strong. Now, I need to go find Kenene." Miryama ran off into the fort to get Shaprour looked after before she headed into Duntorn.

Kenene, Lylya and Miryama flew to the Valley. There was no point hiding what was coming from Ioan any longer. Their first line of defence was gone as far as they were concerned. With the clouds and wind and rain, at the lower altitude of the high plains, encroaching on Moronland, people were fleeing the borderlands.

They knew Ioan would be alerted to their arrival and should go and see him first but all three wanted to meet the girl and discuss their next steps with Gaerwn as a priority. They walked over to the encampment trying not to hurry and reveal anything was wrong to anyone they passed.

They surprised Gaerwn as he stepped out of his yurt home to go and watch the apprentices. He frowned, "this is ominous. What's brought all of you here?"
They found seats while Gaerwn remained standing, arms crossed, "What's happened?"

"Ozanus went to Gloabtona. He told me if he didn't return in two weeks we needed to prepare ourselves." Miryama carefully said, fiddling at a loose button.

"Prepare ourselves for what though? We still don't know what we are up against. We are going to have to send someone else into the mountains but do we risk it? If we've lost Ozanus than how would someone with less skill survive?" Lylya pointed out, trying to remain calm. She didn't want to think her big brother was gone. She felt sure he was alive, just unable to get back. She looked to Miryama and hoped she was thinking the same.

"Can we speak to this girl?" Kenene interrupted, "and then we should probably let the Nejus know."

"Alright, though I don't know how much more she can tell us." Gaerwn remarked, "I'll go fetch her." With a sigh he headed out.

Back in the yurt the three looked at each other again. Kenene was the one who finally spoke, voicing what they were all thinking, "do you think he is dead?"

"No." Miryama answered firmly, "do you think War would really let him die?"
Lylya shrugged, "who knows what goes on with the Gods. I bet he's never told us half of what has been communicated to him."

"He's always been like that." Kenene remarked, "who goes to find him?" They all looked at each other.

"I'll go." Miryama stood, "I've got nothing to lose, have I?"

"What about Shaprour?" Lylya challenged while trying to keep her tone of voice level. She was having a vision of history repeating again.

"I won't die." Miryama answered firmly. She definitely wasn't going to let that happen. She was determined to get Ozanus back if he was alive so he could be the father he struggled to be.

"Are you sure?" Kenene asked.

"How do we get her up there?"

"That's where I come in."

They all turned at the new voice and was surprised to find Ioan in the entrance of the yurt dressed in a pale red robe over a fine linen shirt embroidered at the collar with vines. His well-manicured appearance made the other three, including Lylya, feel scruffy. His arms were crossed in front of his chest and his face showed his anger as he continued, "what have you been hiding from me? Have you forgotten I am Nejus?"
They shifted uncomfortably under his gaze.

"Oh?! Sir." Gaerwn commented from behind.
Ioan turned, "Chieftain, you should know better. If you want to keep your job then you'd best tell me what is going on. And who is this with you?"
Gaerwn's eyes narrowed and stiffly he remarked, "you don't have the power to remove me from my position. Only the High Chieftain can."

"And it seems he is missing so I think that makes me High Chieftain, don't you?" Ioan challenged. He made enough space for Gaerwn to slip past before continued, "so what has my brother got himself involved in now? And who is this girl?"

"There's a monster in my home." Lhateso exclaimed, "why aren't you doing anything?!"

"And you are?" Lylya enquired.

Tears welled up in Lhateso's eyes in her frustration. She looked at Ioan, "are you the Nejus? I was told to talk to you and that you can help. I am Lhateso of the royal family of Gloabtona." She stood as tall and as proud as she could in clothes she didn't feel comfortable in, "a demon has taken the palace and used one of my cousins to release another one. I saw that one, it drank the blood of all the men in the camp I was at. Please," She turned to look at each one in turn,

"And you thought that it wasn't important to tell me about this threat to Moronland and Keytel." Ioan turned to Gaerwn.

"We had to check whether she spoke the truth." Gaerwn calmly pointed out though a hand tightly gripped his knife handle.

"And did she?" Ioan challenged pointedly.

"I think we have to believe so since Ozanus has gone missing." Lylya fought to keep her voice steady. Kenene rested a hand on her shoulder and squeezed it as he said, "we still don't know what we are up against."

"It's growing more powerful though. I have been getting reports of black clouds spreading over Moronland from the direction of Gloabtona. People are leaving that region out of fear." Lylya pointed out, now with her leader head on.

"We need more information to somehow soften this threat." Ioan remarked.

"Soften?! We need to prepare to defend. We need to protect the Valley, the dragons and the people of Keytel, in that order." Gaerwn retorted.

"What about Moronland?" Lylya protested.

"It's a lost cause now. It will be where we'll probably fight."

"You've been thinking about this haven't you?" Kenene remarked, acknowledging Gaerwn's leadership.

“Of course.” Gaerwn remarked stiffly.

“We must send an embassy and sue for peace.” Ioan decreed.

“What?!” Everyone exclaimed.

“Who’s in charge here?” He retorted, “we can ill afford another war.” What he wasn’t going to admit was that without Ozanus he knew they wouldn’t survive a war, let alone a battle. The Suwars would follow his older brother not him and his brother had the skills needed.

No one would say it out loud but they knew he was right. A third of the Suwars were killed in the last fight with Timijin and a large number of Keytel’s population in the first one. Five years was not enough time to rebuild a population that could sustain another war.

“Sue for peace it is then.” Kenene remarked reluctantly.

“And you won’t be going in heavy. I know you Suwars like to show off but we need to appear open.” Ioan warned.

“I’m going with them.” Miryama added.

Ioan turned and looked at her for the first time, noting her long auburn hair tied with ribbons and her short double breasted jacket with toggles which revealed the sash she wore round her waist and the culottes tucked into her boots. It seemed fashions had changed with the Daughters moving their home next to Duntorn. He enquired dismissively, “who are you?”

“I am Miryama.” She answered stiffly.
His eyes widened as he recognised the name of Ozanus’ independent wife and then he shrugged, “suit yourself.”
He didn’t know enough about her to care. Her son was more important and if she died then Shaprour would come and live in the valley as the heir.

“I’ll plan the embassy and you select the riders, sensible ones. Lylya, I will see you in ten minutes.” Ioan ordered before leaving the tent.
The four of them looked at each other, stunned. Kenene

remarked, "I think Moronland is about to be sacrificed for the cause."

"Gaerwn, you'll have the support of the Daughters in this." Miryama said.

"I know, but thank you for saying." Gaerwn replied while his mind was already trying to work out the best people to go on Ioan's foolish peace trip.

Lylya headed off to be told off by Ioan and soon Kenene and Gaerwn were having their own discussions. Miryama approached Lhateso, "shall we go for a talk? I have some questions for you."

"Does this mean you are going to help?" Lhateso asked hopefully.

"Possibly." Miryama carefully answered. She glanced at the two men planning and then led the way out of the yurt.

Once out in the Valley they found a quiet spot not too far from the Suwars' encampment. Sitting on a large rock Miryama remarked, "I see you have a nice knife. May I look at it?"

"Sure." Lhateso carefully removed the knife from its new leather sheath and handed it to Miryama.
She studied it. It had been cleaned and polished well and the blade sharpened. Miryama softly remarked, "I know the owner of this and he wasn't the first to own it either."

"Someone told me it belonged to a man called Ozanus. We have heard of Ozanus, he defeated the previous ruler of Moronland." Lhateso eagerly replied and then with reluctance, "he can have it back if he wants."

"No, it's alright. He has a new one now and the Gods gave it to you though I couldn't tell you why. I have my own as well." She showed Lhateso hers briefly as she didn't know how innocent she was. The two dragons on her handle were intertwined with each other, "now, this is where I need your help. The man who owned this knife, Ozanus, is my partner and I need to find him."

"Partner? Have you not had a blessing?"
Miryama sighed, she hated having to explain. Although
War had tricked them into marriage they never saw
themselves as husband and wife. They thought themselves
a partnership when they weren't getting angry with each
other. She changed tact, "look, he's very important to me.
He went to Gloabtona to find out what was going on."

"Can he save my country?" Lhateso interrupted.

"I don't know. Now, I need to go and find him. Something
has happened to him. You know the palace, are there any
secret ways in?"

Lhateso fought with herself. She didn't want to go back to
Gloabtona for fear of what was there but she had to find her
sister. Staring at the ground she admitted, "my sister was
taken from me. I need to find her as well. If I came with
you and helped, will you help me find her?" She looked
into Miryama's face, pleading with her.

Wary of making any promises she couldn't keep she said,
"we can try."

The young woman seemed happy with that, "thank you.
There are a couple of ways in and out that only us women
know of. I can't really explain where they are. We are
shown them and then told to memorise their locations and
then sworn never to tell a man. Compared to here my sister
and our other female relations lived a very secluded life."

"Do you want to go back to it?" Miryama asked out of
curiosity.

"You are one of those Daughters of Scyth aren't you?"
Lhateso realised now why Ozanus had been described as
Miryama's partner rather than husband.

"You have heard of us?"

"Oh yes." Lhateso said with excitement, "I can't believe I
am talking to a Daughter of Scyth. We idolised you back in
Gloabtona, even the men…" she trailed off as she
remembered hearing her male cousins crudely describing

what they would do to a Daughter of Scyth if they ever met
one. The women of the court knew differently and envied
the freedom they had.

"Now you have escaped, you don't have to go back."
Miryama said into the silence, trying to reassure her, "we
welcome anyone who has lived a secluded life and give
them a chance to get use to their freedoms and learn that
men can be equals, not just masters of all they survey. Have
a think about it. Now, I need to get back to Gaerwn and
Kenene as I need to see what they are planning. I'm sure
we'll meet again soon so be strong."
A part of the speech was reminding herself to be strong as
well. She didn't need Ozanus but a part of her had learnt to
crave him when he was far away, even when they had
argued. She handed back the knife to Lhateso and gave her
a tight smile, "take care of it for now."
She left Lhateso staring at her in awe while she tried to
keep tears of fear at bay. She was sure Ozanus was alive
but didn't know what state she would find him in.

Fourteen

Ozanus woke after ten hours sleep and had never slept so well since… He couldn't remember. He felt sure he had slept only one other time like this. He had woken a few times, sensing a presence but his eyes had stared blankly out as if he had actually still been asleep. He had slept so deeply that he hadn't realised someone had come in and bandaged up all his seeping scars from when he had been on the altar.

He felt sure he was going to die on that altar, just like his…. He frowned as he sat in the bed. He felt sure he was forgetting something. He wondered whether he was losing his mind as he couldn't remember anything from before getting off the altar. He shouted into his mind, *"War! What have you done to me?"*

"Protecting you." Came the whispered reply.

"I can protect myself!" He found himself shouting out loud and then winced as a shot of pain went through his mind as War roared a warning to behave.

There was a scratch at the sliding door and then it slid open to reveal a servant, "do you want a bath or food first sir?"

Ozanus frowned at the man, "how long have you been out there?"

"It is my role to serve you so I will wait for orders for anything you need." The servant in his padded coat bowed his head.

"What of sleep?"

"I have a bedroll out here sir. Thank you for your concern but we should not be talking like this. A wash or food first sir?" The servant glanced around warily, unsure how far Strife's surveillance stretched.

"A wash."

"This way then, we have a bathhouse." He gestured behind him, "I put a robe out for you to wear earlier." Ozanus looked to the end of the bed where in the tangled blankets there was a robe.

Two hours later, after a hot steaming bath and a decent meal he felt almost normal apart from the fact he still couldn't remember much beyond three days ago. He knew his main job was to train his undead son. He tried to think of something else but his mind went blank. He scouted out an area before sending the servant that was still discreetly following him to find Bloodlust.

He found the armoury and sought out a pair of wooden practice swords. With the servant back he had a circle of torches set up so there was good light to see by. The servant returned to the shadows, curious to what was going to happen.

Bloodlust arrived and strode into the circle with confidence dressed in the burnished copper breastplate. He had a sword and a dragon handled knife at his side. He was quite pleased with the knife that he had claimed off his father. He stood before his father, hands on hips and feet spread shoulder width apart. He sneered, "I don't need training."

"Yes you do. Think back to how I disarmed you." Ozanus calmly pointed out. He studied the young man in front of him trying to see if he could see either himself or Miryama in him. He stared at the breastplate and a flash of a memory came to him. Frustrated that he couldn't remember he snapped, "take off that breastplate, you haven't earnt the right to wear it yet. Before you get the privilege of wearing it as protection you must first feel the pain and learn how to defend yourself from attacks."

"And if I refuse?" Bloodlust sneered, "I don't need to know how to fight as a man when I can do this!"
The youth transformed into his dragon form though he had to concentrate on it and with his tail went to trip Ozanus up.

Ozanus sighed, all young dragons were the same it seemed whether mortal or immortal. He hit the approaching tail with the wooden sword he held. The tail was whipped away and Bloodlust changed back with a snarl of rage. He pulled out his sword and ran at Ozanus.

Ozanus adjusted his feet and then at the last moment stepped to one side and hit Bloodlust in the small of his back with the pommel of the wooden sword. Bloodlust fell forward, sprawling across the dirt yard. He rolled over and glared up at Ozanus. The elder blinked, "and that is why. Not even armour can always protect you. I currently have an injury where a sword slipped on armour."

"So you aren't that good then, are you?" Bloodlust sneered.

"Don't be so sure of yourself." War hissed through Ozanus' mouth. The man's eyes flashed red.

"Why should I believe you who hides in that body?" Bloodlust spat as he got to his feet and pulled his knife out, *"Strife would be pleased if I freed you from that body."*

"You are a newborn who has not yet experienced this world." War snarled, *"I am an ancient being and I know a man of skill when I see one. I watched him kill a man with no hint of rage on the surface, in full control but underneath his blood boiled. He could have exploded like you are doing but that is when mistakes are made and he*

knew that from his training. He practices with sharp blades and not just one on one. He took on all the dragon riders to get my attention."

There was awe in how Bloodlust was looking now. Satisfied War retreated.

Ozanus blinked and looked slightly confused then he spotted Bloodlust holding a knife pointed at him, "have you not given up yet?"

He realised then it was his knife, he recognised the nick on its top edge. He held out his hand, "I'd like my knife back please. You have not earnt it and you are not a Suwar."

"And if I don't."

"Do you really want to risk finding yourself face down on the ground again?" Ozanus raised an eyebrow and continued to hold his hand open, palm up.

Bloodlust fought the urge to rebel and reluctantly handed it over.

"Breastplate off and then we will begin." Ozanus ordered as he removed the long padded coat he had been wearing up until that point. He tucked his knife into his belt before rolling up the sleeves of his shirt.

From a dark corner of the yard Strife smiled with satisfaction. With Ozanus training him Bloodlust would soon be a godling to fear. He slipped away leaving father and son to build a relationship. With both of them together he would be able to dominate and influence this world of man with or without War.

Fifteen

Before she joined up with the envoy she had Spilla fly her to Ozanus' house. She knew he had a statue of the Dragon Lord in his study. She had no idea where he had found it but knew he occasionally gave it offerings. There was a bowl already on the shrine and she wondered if Arno had placed it there.

Any other time she may have offered up some of her blood but she didn't want a hand that had a self-inflicted wound as she didn't know what she would be heading into. She poured wine into a cup and placed it beside the bowl. She stared at the Dragon Lord statue with its cracked gold paint hoping for a sign of acknowledgement. Nothing. Feeling a little self-conscious she said out loud, *"oh Lord, please accept my humble offering to aid you in your protection of Ozanus. Please watch over Shaprour as I seek your reluctant disciple."* A golden glow pulsed in the room but it was weak as if the Dragon Lord's powers were declining as the new danger grew stronger. She bowed her head, *"thank you."*

Arno appeared as she left the study and asked, "what's happening Miryama? Nimib said that Ozanus hasn't returned, and I have heard nothing since. Is anyone going to try and find him?"

"His brother is sending an envoy seeking peace and I am going with them to find him. I suggest you go to the Valley where you'll be safest. I fear Moronland is going to become a giant battlefield. Shaprour is already there. I'm sure Nimib will fly you there if asked."

"Thank you for your honesty. I'll pack a few things and head over. Good luck and I hope you find him."
Thank you Arno. You are a good servant to him." She gave him a tight smile. She began to walk away and then paused and turned back, "Arno?"

"Yes?"

"If, only if…. If something happens to me can you watch over Shaprour like you have Ozanus."

"Of course." He could sense how much effort that had taken her. He would have done it even if she hadn't of asked. He would give his life for the boy to ensure he had some sort of childhood unlike his father. He would ensure he had the right mentor as Diego had been for Ozanus.

They quickly had to give up riding on horses as they didn't like the never-ending snowstorm. They could sense the evil ahead of them and bucked and protested. Reluctantly they organised backpacks and started the long walk up into the mountains. Lhateso stayed close to Miryama.

After a week of walking they stepped out of the snow into the village below the palace, unable to believe that they had reached the eye of the storm. It was still a gloomy light but at least it had stopped snowing. Lhateso tapped Miryama's arm, "this is where we leave them." Miryama nodded and with barely a glance at the group of men followed Lhateso between two walled houses to the lane that ran along the back of them.

It was quiet as they made their way past the houses. They soon came to the wall of the palace and Miryama asked, "how do we get in?"

"We have to go further up. The palace is made of a series

of courtyards. Where do you think Ozanus could be? Depending upon where he is will mean a different secret passage."

"I don't know. He could be a prisoner or he could be a guest."

"We'll see if we can find my Nuna. She'll know where he will be."

"And where will she be?"

"I'm hoping still in the family quarters or a servant there will be able to find her. Come on, this way." Lhateso beckoned her forward, "be careful as the path is narrow." She kept a hand against the crumbling plastered wall to guide herself in the gloom.

As they came to the top of each courtyard it stepped in or out, adjusting to the contours of the mountain slope. The biggest two were at the bottom and then they became a little smaller till the top which was dominated by the Audience Pavilion.

At one of those division points Lhateso stopped. She had felt the briefest of change in texture of the plaster and smiled. The slim gap was always in shadow so no one had guessed that it was there. Due to its narrow opening only the younger women used it. Matrons and those that had had children had a different secret passage they tended to use. Glancing at Miryama Lhateso hoped she would fit though it might be a bit of a squeeze. She said, "it will be a bit of a squeeze but this will take us to the main court compound."
Miryama peered into it, "let's give it a try, you lead the way."

Miryama pulled her chest and stomach in as she followed Lhateso into the narrow passage. She side stepped down it, not daring to breath until she stepped into a room screen leaning against the wall at an abandoned angle.

Lhateso reached for her hand and pulled her under

the leaning room screen into a store room filled with chests and shelves of folded cloth. The air was filled with the scent of old and new lavender. Lhateso said with a grin, "welcome to my home. Now we need to look the part." She began searching through the shelves and chests for the appropriate robes to layer up.

Soon they were both dressed for the court, wearing several layers of robes over their blouses and trousers, holding the quilted and brocade layers in place with a sash. Lhateso released her hair from her plait and brushed it out with her fingers. Looking at Miryama she realised that wasn't going to be anything they could do about the beads in her long plait and could only hope no one would notice since they could already hear the envoy being led through the courtyards. She said, "where do you want to go first?"

"Let's go see what happens with the envoy and our mysterious enemy."

"We need to go to the Audience Pavilion then. We have a screened room that we can look through."

The leader of the envoy had presented himself at the gates of the palace. The rest of the small group stood behind him with the armoured and armed Suwars on either side of the group with hands on the pommels of their swords. They were made to wait while a messenger was sent up to the top of the place and Strife sent someone back to bring the group up.

They were led up through the palace and they paused at the sight of the exposed altar. None of them had seen an altar like it with drips and pools of frozen blood. They already knew what they would be meeting but this put fear into them. The sight of it put them on edge. Lhateso, on the journey up had told them as much as she knew and then imagination had taken over. The blood was proof of some sort of monster. Had it sacrificed Ozanus on the altar to itself?

The servant who had brought them up slid open the double doors that opened from the garden and bowed. Looking at each other the six members of the envoy, two from Moronland and four from Keytel, nervously approached the dark room. The doors were slid shut behind them, slamming together, making the group jump and the Suwars left outside grab hold of their swords.

They looked round, trying to work out what was going on and what the dark stains on the floor were, noting the torn hanging cloths. Fire bowls sprang alight revealing Strife in all his black glory, red eyes glowing. He sat upright with crossed legs on his throne, hand and stump on his knees. He blinked and the group of six found themselves dropping to their knees and bowing forward. A small smile played on Strife's lips.

With them now where he wanted them, shaking with cold and fear on their knees, he snarled, "what do you want?"

The leader of the envoy slowly lifted his head and then sat up when he couldn't feel anything forcing him back down, "Noble Lord, I am Kristoph of Keytel. We come seeking a treaty between yourself and us."

"What sort of treaty?" Strife asked suspiciously.

"On behalf of Keytel and Moronland we seek peace." Kristoph carefully said, aware that they were all in travel worn clothes and not looking presentable. He hadn't expected them to be taken straight to their mysterious enemy.

"Peace?! You come seeking peace?!" Strife stood.

Ioan's envoy shook with fear. Strife seemed to grow before their eyes to dominate the dark space when he stood. He went on, "I do not agree to peace on any terms. I am going to take your countries and nothing will stop me. Soon the world will be mine again."

He continued growing. The six of them leapt to their feet and ran to the doors but found them locked. One shook at them calling out, "let us out! Let us out!"
Another turned to face the monster with the knife he had in his belt. A claw knocked it from his shaking hand, and it wasn't a man's face that came in close but a dragon's with a grinning leer. Strife licked his sharp teeth and then snapped. The man shrieked.

Miryama and Lhateso were in the women's room which they found had been taken over by someone. They peered through the screen. Miryama noted the blood that dripped through the viewing holes but didn't point them out to the girl beside her. They watched, unable to take their eyes off the scene unfolding before them. They held their breaths in hope of not being detected as Strife transformed into his dragon form and ate the six men. Miryama smothered Lhateso's forming scream with a hand clamped tightly to her open mouth. Lhateso closed her eyes to the sound of crunching bone.

They didn't dare move as Strife morphed back into human form. Miryama watched as he wiped blood from his lips and with a sigh settled back on the throne. He chuckled to himself, *"so tasty. Peace? Ha! Did they really think I would agree to that?"*
Miryama squeezed Lhateso's arm and gestured behind them. Slowly they crawled out.

Outside by the altar the Suwars shifted uncomfortably as they watched the servant slam the doors shut and put a bar across them. Hands went to knives and swords, checking they were easy to pull out since it was so cold which could cause the metal to stick to the leather. The servant stood with arms crossed in front of the barricaded door.

They didn't like how quiet the palace was and they could sense how tense the atmosphere was. They had seen about four people since being led up through the palace whereas normally they would have been stared at as strangers from a far off country.

They turned instinctively as a group when they sensed a presence behind them just as there was a scream from the Audience Pavilion. They didn't know which way to turn. The need to survive kicked in and three turned to the hidden presence as the other three faced the pavilion where the doors shook as a body slammed against them. They pulled their swords out. A figure stepped out of the shadows and remarked without emotion, "no point looking that way as they'll all be dead by now."
The leader of the group demanded, "who are you?"
Bloodlust grinned, "your own nightmare."
He pulled out his sword and ran a finger along its edge and sucked the blood off his finger. He was going to take this opportunity to prove his prowess to all three of his fathers.

The three facing Bloodlust gripped their swords tighter and adjusted their feet, preparing themselves for the coming fight, as the other three turned to face their new enemy. It was going to be one of survival.

Bloodlust ran at them and swung his sword. He was ready for a defensive strike but wasn't ready for them to work as a team.

As the first defended himself his comrade next to him swung his sword in, slashing Bloodlust's arm. Bloodlust howled in anger and pain. He lashed out again then remembered what Ozanus had been teaching him. He retreated and calmed his heightened emotions, concentrated on burying them, before heading forward again.

Miryama and Lhateso heard the clashing of swords and froze in their shadowy passage. They peered out through the trellis that allowed a little light into the room within the walls of the gatehouse between the garden quadrant and the one below. Lhateso whispered in horror, "that's the man who was a baby when he was found."

"Those Suwars are having a hard fight. If he was a baby only a month ago…?"

"He shed his skin like a snake." Lhateso whispered but Miryama wasn't listening.
She was looking to see who the puppet master was. There had to be someone training him, no one would have the developing skills that the young man was showing naturally. She spotted him in the darkness of the gate, watching. Ozanus.

She bit her lip to stop herself from calling out to him. There was something odd about him but couldn't work out what. He looked so apathetic, as if he wasn't seeing what was happening. His gaze looked like it wasn't even focused on the fighting. It looked like he was staring into the middle distance as if his mind had shutdown.

She was brought back to where she was when Lhateso nudged her. She turned back to the fight which was coming to a surprise end considering it was six against one and that one was unlikely to have actually fought six people before.

The last knew she was close to defeat and decided that she needed to survive and report back even if it killed her. She had put up a good fight but her energy was waning. She parried another attack with one eye on the gates as she tried to determine the distance. She made a move towards their attacker causing him to step back caught by surprise as he hadn't expected her to lunge at him.

She took a chance and began to run. Bloodlust worked out her plan and stuck his arm out. She ran into it and stumbled backwards gasping for breath as the arm had caught her in the throat. He grabbed her arm and yanked her to him. He zoned in on her pulsing throat as her chest struggled for breath. He bit into her throat and let her heart pump hot blood straight into his mouth till her skin turned grey. He let her body drop to the ground before moving on to the next one.

A mortally injured Suwar tried to crawl away but was pulled upright by the back of his coat. Bloodlust clamped his mouth to the man's neck and began drinking again.

Before Lhateso fainted or screamed Miryama dragged the young woman away. She had gone very pale.

Lhateso's colour recovered as they returned to the compound they had started in. She asked, "what's going to happen to us?"

"I don't know but we need to get back to Keytel and warn everyone, but I still need to get to Ozanus. I've seen him. He is alive but I don't know where he is staying."

"Nuna will be able to tell us. Come on, we'll find an empty bedroom to hide in and I'll go find Nuna."

Sixteen

They kept the shutters shut and Miryama remained in the bedroom while Lhateso slipped back out. Miryama wanted to be the one out there but Lhateso knew the palace and would be able to get around without being out of place. She paced the room. She was angry and scared. She wanted to shake Ozanus back to his senses. How could he be involving himself on the wrong side? She was scared for herself, her son, for the Daughters. She found herself hugging her body as a shiver ran up her spine.

Waiting in the dark it felt like hours when it was no more than half an hour before Lhateso came back with an older lady behind her. They slipped in and knelt on the reed matting and Nuna exclaimed in a hushed tone, "now can you tell me why you foolishly came back? Your sister is back here already."

"First, this is Miryama, a Daughter of Scyth."
Nuna's eyes widened, "who'd have thought. Welcome. How did Lhateso convince you to bring her back here?"

"We came as part of the envoy from Keytel." Miryama answered warily.

Lhateso threw herself at her Nuna, the only one who had ever cared for her, with tears running down her face as she was finally able to speak of what she had seen, "they were all eaten by the two monsters. And Aerrana was taken. I've been on my own."

"One is a God and I know about Aerrana, she is back here and she is well. Did you manage to speak to the Nejus then?" Nuna whispered hopefully as she stroked her charge's hair.

"The man who is best suited to save us is here." Lhateso sat back on her heels trying to contain her excitement.

Nuna looked over at Miryama for guidance and saw a strained expression on the woman's face. She guessed that though there was truth to what Lhateso had said there was also something terribly wrong. Lhateso was oblivious to the look as she went on, "do you know whether there are any visitors staying here?"

"They only get to stay if they are of use to the ancient God." Nuna remarked, her eyes still on Miryama who shifted uncomfortably.

"Ancient God?" Miryama asked.

"Even older than the ones worshipped by everyone in Keytel. Did he tell you that?"
Miryama shook her head.

"He is here, but he is under some sort of spell." Nuna went on, "I'm sorry. It's been a wasted journey."

"No." Miryama exclaimed, "no. Take me to him and I will break it. When he sees me…." She was trying hard to believe that the sight of her would bring him round but the image of him earlier came back to haunt her and she wasn't sure if she would be enough. If she could get him back to the Valley perhaps the hold the black God had on him would weaken and the Dragon Lord would then be able to break it completely.

"Not yet. Give it an hour." Nuna said softly, "I've got to go but I'll be back with some food."

An hour later Nuna reappeared and beckoned Miryama out of the door, "quickly. I've distracted the servant that is always with him but I don't know how long he will be gone."

Miryama followed Nuna who was moving quickly up the corridor to the compound between the Audience Pavilion and its altar and the minor royalty one they were hiding in. Nuna remarked, "there aren't many left in this one so be discreet as otherwise you will be noticed."

She stopped at a door and carefully slid it open. She gestured in. Miryama said, "thank you."

"I'm doing this so the girls can be safe wherever they end up. I hope whatever you have planned works."

"I hope so to." Miryama stepped into the room.

"I don't need anything so bugger off." Came a snarl from the dimly lit room. When he didn't hear the door slid shut he turned to look at who was standing in the doorway.

Miryama saw that Ozanus sat at the far side of the room where there was another door open to a small private enclosed garden. He sat against the wall staring out of the door at the deep snow. He stared at her, not recognising her. He frowned, "who are you?"

She stepped into the light of the lamp, "Ozanus?"

"I asked who are you?" He demanded, his hand going to his knife.

She frowned with concern and wondered what Strife had done to her husband, "Ozanus, I am Miryama, your wife, your partner, your lover, the mother of your son." She took a step towards him and softly said as if he was a child, "I've come to take you home."

"I am home." He replied in confusion.

"War?!" She called out sternly, *"what have you done to him?!"*

Ozanus' eyes flashed red, *"protecting him."*

"I need to take him home." She tried not to sound like she was pleading.

"It's not the right time."

"How can it not be the right time?!" She exclaimed, *"the*

Valley needs him, Keytel and Moronland needs him. I need him. Let me take him home." She was pleading now.

"No." He answered.

"But he will just make the monster stronger and harder to defeat." She protested.

"Return home and tell them of what is to come and prepare for it." War ordered, *"go now, start back before Strife realises you are here. I can't stop him."*

The red eyes disappeared and there was a flash of recognition on Ozanus' face. He started at her in shock, "Miryama? What are you doing here?"

She flung herself at him, crying. He held her tight and kissed the top of her head. He could feel the tension in her body softening but then everything he knew of her began to fade. He reluctantly pushed her away, "go, go now! Tell them all it will be the biggest fight we will ever see."

She stared at him and saw a blankness return to his face. He frowned at her, "who are you?"

She turned and fled.

Miryama came back to find Lhateso gone and briefly panicked but looking round the room nothing was disturbed as if to suggest she had been taken. She would give the girl ten minutes before finding her way out of the palace. There was no time to waste.

She impatiently walked up and down the room but froze as the door slid open and Lhateso slipped in. She exclaimed at the younger woman, "where have you been?!"

"I've found my sister." Lhateso grinned.

"That's great but we need to leave now and get back to Keytel."

"We need to take my sister with us." Lhateso demanded, the smile vanishing.

She had found her sister in a suite of rooms dressed in clothes they had only ever dreamed of. The copper coloured robe was layered with quilted underrobes of various colours that complimented each other. Her hair was up in a complex bun, with a large hairpin that had a head which was a stylised cloud on it, pushed through it, marking her as now being married.

Aerrana had slowly turned to look at the door that slid open and blinked. She didn't react as Lhateso, in a crouch, ran over to where she knelt on a padded cushion, hand resting on her knees. Lhateso exclaimed in a whisper, "Aerrana?! You are alive. You can come with me." Aerrana shook her head and emotionlessly said, "I can't. I am now his and he will seek me out if I disappeared." Lhateso spotted the cut on her sister's face then, "what has he done to you? And who is he?"

"A monster." A tear trickled down Aerrana's cheek, "now go before he comes back."

"No. You must come with me." Lhateso cried and grabbed her sister's hand, "I have a Daughter of Scyth with me. Remember Nuna telling us about them? She can protect us."

"No, he's too strong. Only the Nejus can defeat him."

"The Nejus who is here you mean?" Lhateso exclaimed.

"He's here?" Aerrana grew hopeful.

Lhateso wanted to shake her sister, "he's on the wrong side now so he won't be defeated." She released her sister and reluctantly got to her feet.

At the door she glanced back and saw Aerrana had already turned away to stare blankly at the wall opposite. She whispered, "I'll rescue you soon, somehow."

She slid the door shut and ran down the half-covered passage back to the room she and Miryama had hidden in.

Miryama looked relieved and angry at seeing her return. She ignored Lhateso's demand to take her sister with them. She felt sure there would be another time and place where a better opportunity would be had to rescue her. She hissed, "we must leave, now!"

"Now?" Lhateso asked with fear.

"Yes, now."

"What about my sister?"

"Now is not the time for that. Come on, take us back to that storeroom and let's head back down the mountain. I have to get back and warn them of what is coming." She pulled Lhateso to her feet.

Spilla was relieved to see Miryama. He knew there was something very wrong with the world as the storm Gods had joined whatever was in the mountains. It might be an ongoing snowstorm up there trapping the citizens of Gloabtona in their homes but it was a rain storm on the plains of Moronland. It wasn't always raining but there was a continuous wind that rose and fell, knocking over trees and sweeping through any open doors.

Miryama and Lhateso clambered up on to Spilla's back. He quickly rose into the air, narrowly missing being hit by a fork of lightening which felt aimed at them. Thunder rumbled and seemed to be following them, trying to make them afraid.

They flew over people heading away from the Moronland-Gloabtona border, heading for the safety of Duntorn. Spilla remarked, *"there are dragons leaving Duntorn."*

"Which way are they headed?" Miryama asked with concern.

"The wrong way. I've heard something calling to me as well, promising a return of the dominance of dragons."

"Thank you for your loyalty. Something big and dangerous is coming and he is likely to head to the Valley."

"It is the home of the Dragon Lord. He's out for revenge."

"Do you know who he is?"

"He's an ancient God. He's told us himself when he began calling us to him. We have to stop him Miryama. Where is Ozanus? We need him." Spilla looked back at her.

"That is complicated." Miryama sighed and frowned. To try and deter any more questions she asked, *"who, if anyone is at Duntorn?"*

"Some of the Daughters have gone to the Valley with all of the children. Others have remained to fight. The Suwars have retreated. They are planning to keep the Valley as secure and safe for as long as possible."

"Lylya?"

"Don't know. I haven't heard anything. Why has Ozanus not returned with you? He is alive isn't he?" Spilla asked with fear.

"He is alive." She reassured him and tried to hide the fear tightening her throat. Her gloved hands gripped the saddle tighter.

"Where are we going?"

"To Keytel."

Ioan heard the slow steady sound of dragon wings and ran through the house, surprising the two servants who got in his way. He leapt down the steps and slid to a stop on the grass as Spilla came down to land. He didn't care much for the woman Ozanus had taken as his wife but for the moment she was the only source for information.

As she helped Lhateso down off Spilla's back before slipping down herself Ioan demanded, "well?!"

"Well what?" She retorted.

"Have we peace?"

She stared at him in shock. Her mind went back to what she had witnessed. She shook her head to get rid of the images as she didn't want any nightmares which must surely come, however exhausted she was.

"Well?"

"Just forget it Ioan. You were foolish to even hope." She exclaimed, "have you heard what is happening to Moronland? He's coming and peace is definitely not on his mind." She turned away to remove her saddle from Spilla's back.

"He?"

"He is a monster in sheep's clothing." She replied as she turned to face him with the saddle in her arms.

"What do you mean by that?" He frowned.
Miryama rolled her eyes and headed past him to go to the encampment where she knew she would be welcomed.
Ioan stamped a foot in frustration, "stop!"
She turned and bluntly answered, "we are in big trouble so start preparing." She began walking again.

"And Ozanus?" He asked with reluctance. However much he didn't want his brother he knew the only way to ensure the help of the Gods would be to have Ozanus in the Valley. He wanted to show the country that he was as good as Ozanus but also knew his brother was the right man for the situation they were heading into.
Miryama stopped in her tracks and turned again. She carefully said, "he's alive."

"Is he coming?" Ioan asked hopefully.

"Not in the way you hope." She replied and then hurried away with Lhateso trailing behind her before he could ask any more questions.

Part Two: Seventeen
1 Year Later

Miryama sat in the lookout post, one of many built around the Valley's clifftops. It was a moment of peace in the crazy world. No one could explain it but the Valley was hanging on and just about repelling the attacks from Strife and all who had joined him. Wild dragons that no one had been aware of had come out of hiding at his call. It wasn't just dragons either. Men and women also responded and now lived in a growing lawless camp at the base of Titan's old castle.

She stared out across the grass plains that now looked like a desert with the wind causing sandy dust devils. She wondered if across the country Ozanus was doing the same and was thinking of her like she was doing him.

In the past year there had been expeditions by the Suwars to try and take Strife out but most had failed. The survivors came back with stories of seeing Ozanus which were quickly subdued by those in the know. It had been agreed that no one would know what had happened to Ozanus for fear of mass demoralisation. Instead they had created a rumour of hope that he was out seeking allies and a solution to their predicament. It seemed to be enough to keep everyone going, keeping them hoping there would be an end.

She turned and looked down into the Valley. The lawns around the house had been taken over by refugees from Keytel as well as the Valley's villagers and the survivors of the Daughters of Scyth. When Strife had made his entrance in Moronland those who had stayed put up a brave but short fight, destroyed by Bloodlust and Strife's human followers. The dragons had destroyed Duntorn and the Daughter's home.

The survivors were part of an encampment supporting the fight for survival and ensuring there would be the next generation to help repair the lands. Forges and armourers had set up and were in demand for repairing weapons and armour.

Other parts of the Valley had been turned into land for growing vegetables and sheep and chickens. Children still ran around with a carefree nature but grew nervous when the Suwars went out to fight.

The temple was back in use with new banners. The altar had offerings of food and drink and was stained with blood offerings from the Suwars. It had also witnessed many hasty joining ceremonies.

With a reluctant sigh Miryama climbed down from the lookout post and returned to the Daughters of Scyth's camp. As she headed down the cliff path she passed a volunteer watcher heading up to take their turn. She was asked, "anything happening?"

"No. All quiet for the moment."

"Thanks. It's been quiet for a bit now. Do you think a big one is being planned?"

Miryama shrugged her shoulders, not really in the mood for small talk, "who knows."

They hadn't heard back from the man they had sent into Strife's camp of villains for a while and he might now be dead for all they knew.

"Well, best get going." The volunteer gestured up the

path, taking the hint.

Miryama grunted and continued on her way, her thoughts turning to her son who had started training with other children of his age from the Suwar encampment.

It was that evening that she received several visitors she was not expecting. She had stepped out of the tent she was living in with Shaprour and Lhateso. Somehow the young woman had attached herself to Miryama, probably from their shared experience in the mountains. She frowned at the sight of Gaerwn, Ioan and Lylya approaching. She settled on the stool she had outside the tent and waited for the three of them to reach her. She noted their serious expressions.

Under her gaze Ioan shifted uncomfortably and then glanced at Gaerwn who rolled his eyes and then said, "Miryama, we've decided we need to organise a rescue mission. Whatever War said Ozanus isn't going to come back to the Valley. We are going to have to fetch him back, kidnap him from Strife."

"It's suicidal." Lylya objected, her tone suggesting that a discussion had already happened, and she still disagreed with the decision.

"Quiet Lylya." Ioan snapped.

She crossed her arms and looked sullen, "she has a right to know."

"To know what?" Miryama frowned.

"Lylya is right but it's the only thing we can do. None of us have any idea how long our invisible defences will survive. At some point they must weaken as our Dragon Lord's power weakens." Gaerwn replied and shifted uncomfortably on his feet, "if we can get Ozanus back we'll have War as well and maybe we will be able to stand up against Strife. The longer we leave this the stronger He will get."

"You still haven't told me what has been discussed." Miryama remarked and recrossed her arms. She also wondered why she hadn't been involved in the earlier conversation.

"Look, stop pussy footing around this." Lylya turned on the men, "she is a grown woman and has the right to know and decide for herself." She turned back to Miryama, "we all know you have a reluctant relationship with War and when you went to the palace He let you speak to Ozanus. What the men," she shot them a glare, "are skirting around is that we need you to lead this rescue attempt. War isn't going to let Ozanus go with just anyone. This is a one time only chance or die trying. There, wasn't so hard was it?" She looked at the men again.

Ioan cleared his throat and croaked, "that."

"Thank you Lylya." Miryama replied, "and if this plan of yours fails? What happens to Shaprour?"

Reluctantly Ioan answered, "he is my heir, he is Ozanus' heir so he will always have a home here and he will be well taken care of."

"And Keytel?"

"We can't plan for that." Gaerwn commented, "I'm sure you will have the Dragon Lord by your side. He won't want this mission to fail any more than us."

Miryama sighed, "let me get this straight, you want me to go and rescue Ozanus? Do I get any help?"

"Of course you will."

"And what if I say no?" She challenged.

"I don't think you will." Gaerwn looked directly at her, daring her to say no. He knew she wouldn't as there was too much at stake not to try. Yes, it was going to be an extremely dangerous mission but if it meant the situation they were all trapped in would have an ending then so be it.

"I'll need dragons as well otherwise I won't even be able to approach the castle."

"I'm sure there will be some."

"Let me think about it." Miryama said without emotion as she stood.

"How long?" Ioan asked.

She shrugged her shoulders and entered the tent, leaving the three of them glancing at each other. Lylya remarked, "come on, let's give her some space."

Lylya was the last to leave. She stared at the tent and sent a silent prayer that Miryama would do the right thing though every fibre of her body was also screaming don't. She certainly wouldn't want to be making this decision. She wondered then if her father had felt the same before he offered Ioan to the Gods. With a heavy heart she turned away and headed back to the house.

In the tent Lhateso gave Miryama a few minutes before stepping out of the shadows, "I'm coming with you."

Miryama turned and stared, taking a moment to register Lhateso's presence. She replied, "I don't want to talk about this now. I haven't made a decision yet."

"You have to go and I have to go too. I need to get my sister back as well as your Ozanus. Do you really think he is the key to our survival?"

Miryama sighed, "I don't know, I really don't know. I don't want to talk about it right now Lhateso. I want to go to bed. We'll discuss this properly in the morning."

She turned away from the younger woman and pulled off her outer clothes before getting into bed. Lhateso glared at her with clenched fists before reluctantly going to bed herself.

Miryama tried to sleep but found herself tossing and turning and in the end she gave up. She pulled on Ozanus' bed robe and felt a little calmer at smelling his fading scent. It was times like this that she missed him the most, just

having him there as someone holding her and as someone
to talk to. She turned a lamp up and sought paper and a
pencil to write a list.

Lhateso stirred an hour later but didn't move in her
bed as she watched Miryama intently writing and planning,
a plan of Trajan's castle spread out on the table. She
watched as Miryama stood and stretched and then bent over
Shaprour lying sprawled across his bed.

Miryama had written and planned as much as she
could. She had come to the conclusion that Ioan, Lylya and
Gaerwn were all correct. There weren't any safer options.
On a fresh piece of paper she had written a wish list for
Shaprour for if she didn't survive. Ioan was right that her
son was the heir to a long line of notable Nejuses and he
would have a lot to live up to whatever happened. It would
be terrible if history repeated itself but at least he was
currently in a happier place than Ozanus had been. In fact
he was thriving with being around all the other children and
starting all of his training. Though the situation was
dangerous the adults tried to keep it away from the
children.

Shaprour barely stirred as she placed a kiss on his
cheek and pulled the blanket back over him. She wrapped
Ozanus' robe tighter around herself and stepped out into
the cold night air in the hope of clearing her mind.

For once the stars were out and she stared up at
them wondering whether Ozanus was also looking at them.
She remembered him telling her that each star was a dead
dragon and she couldn't help smiling and then laughed. The
one person she would have spoken to for advice was the
one person she was going to have to rescue.

The cold air had cleared her head and she returned
inside. She glanced over at Lhateso who had sat up.
Lhateso asked, "you are going aren't you?"
Miryama nodded.

"And me?"

"It's suicidal, I wouldn't advise it. I can only have the best come with me."

"Then my sister…?" Lhateso asked hesitantly.

"I'm not going to promise anything."

Lhateso lay back down and Miryama returned to bed herself, throwing the robe over her blankets.

Eighteen

There were eight of them standing around the table in Ioan's study. On the table was a plan of Titan's castle. The eight of them were going to be the core team who would be venturing into the castle and tracking down Ozanus. A larger group of riders and dragons would be outside distracting as many of Strife's men and beasts as possible. They looked up as Kenene entered and announced, "I'm coming too."
The others all looked to Miryama. She looked at him and asked, "what about your wife and child?"

"She understands. I don't know about anyone else here, but that energy we were all gifted, I think this is it's time or it is coming soon."
There were a few nods around the table.

"Thank you Kenene. Your experience will be welcomed." She gave him a tight smile.

"Where do you think the Nejus will be? We'll all surely die if we had to scour the whole castle." One of the Suwars remarked bringing everyone's attention back to the task at hand. Miryama was glad Ioan wasn't in the room to protest at that slip of the tongue. What was notable was no one corrected the young man. She knew a lot of riders who still considered Ozanus their ruler and that Ioan was only temporary until their true leader saw sense.

Kenene leant over the table and studied the plans

before pointing at a pair of rooms on the second floor, "if we go off what Miryama told us of the palace in Gloabtona last year Strife will take the best rooms and I bet Bloodlust will have the next best."

"So we'll start on the second floor then. We need to land on the battlements, according to these plans there is a bridge linking the walls to the main building." Miryama replied, "we'll all need to be prepared to swing down from our dragons' claws." She glanced round at the group and knew she had never done it herself though she had seen Ozanus do it a few times. She could only hope every Suwar learnt how to, "now, we must prepare ourselves. You've got the rest of the day to do as you please but we must leave before dawn tomorrow."

Everyone left apart from Kenene. He walked round the table and put a hand on Miryama's shoulder and felt the tension in it. He remarked, "if he was here he would be impressed."

"Once I wanted to lead the Daughters, wanted this sort of excitement but now…" She looked to him for reassurance.

"You still have it in you." Kenene replied, "you were the one to go and find that Ozanus was still alive and now you are preparing to go drag him out of the hellhole he has to be in, potentially sacrificing your life for all of us and potentially leaving your son parentless. Everyone will ensure Shaprour is proud of you for trying but you are more than capable of achieving this. Come on, we need to make our peace and ensure we have the blessing of the Dragon Lord."

"Thank you Kenene." She gave him a tight smile, "I appreciate it."

"Do you think they would have come to you if they didn't think you capable?"

"Who knows what they were thinking?" Miryama replied with a slight sneer. She knew that she was in some ways dispensable. The only two people who needed her were Shaprour and Ozanus and for one to survive she needed to fetch the other back. She would protect them both no matter what and hoped the Dragon Lord would understand when she gave Him her offering of blood.

"We are all just trying to survive." Kenene commented as they both walked from the room and the house. He added, "see you tomorrow then and be wary of the Gods."
She frowned as he walked away and called out, "what do you mean?"
He waved a hand in reply.

She returned to her tent and searched through her few possessions for the Nejusana robe with its high collar that Ozanus had given her. She pulled the knife in its sheath from her pile of armour and weapons she had made ready the previous day. She thought it mad that she would be incapacitating a hand just before a major fight but everyone seemed to have adapted, including herself.

As she left the tent to head to the clifftop temple she spotted Arno hurrying towards her, "Arno? What's wrong? Is Shaprour alright?"

"He's fine. I was hoping to catch you." He replied while trying to catch his breath.

"Me?"

"I know you are about to go give the Dragon Lord an offering but I suggest you come with me. For what you are about to do for Ozanus, for this Valley and Keytel I think you deserve a more special place. I don't think Kittal or Ozanus would object."

"You have lost me Arno." She frowned.

"It's a private shrine that only a few are aware of."

"I don't know." She was hesitant, "I think I'll stick with the temple on the cliff."

"No, no, please. Come on." He beckoned her to follow him.

With a sigh she began to follow him. She concluded
that she didn't have to go in once they reached wherever
she was being taken. She followed him down a path that
she was surprised looked barely used considering every
other path was showing the evidence of the many footprints
treading them. The bushes and grasses made the path look
abandoned

They soon came to the cliffs where Arno turned left
and walked along the base of them. He wasn't going to tell
Miryama how he knew where it was but he had once
followed Kittal out of curiosity of where his master was
going. He had returned a few times in his own time to study
the cave shrine for himself and thankfully nothing bad had
come of it.

He reached the spot where an ancient rockfall half
hid the shrine a few metres up the cliff face. He pointed up
to it, "up there."

"Up there?" She looked up and then back at Arno, "what
is up there?"

"A shrine to the Dragon Lord used by the Nejus."

"But I am not the Nejus." She protested.

"You are his wife and Ioan doesn't know of this place.
Ozanus will always be the Nejus in the eyes of the Gods."
Miryama studied the servant, surprised how knowledgeable
he was. He had always been so quiet but like any good
servant he had learnt a lot over the years. He bowed his
head and departed with a quiet, "good luck."

With him gone she found herself alone unsure
whether to venture into the small cave or whether to return
to the familiar. She looked up at the cave and saw then the
hint of hand and footholds that had formed over the years
and realised how privileged she was. Whatever was inside
the cave had been sacred to generations of Nejuses and
their heirs.

She took a deep breath and then began climbing up

the few metres to the entrance. She peered in but couldn't decern anything in the interior apart from a shaft of light. She had to bend slightly to get in.

"Welcome Nejusana."

Miryama looked round with wariness and curiosity, trying to work out where the voice had come from. In front of her was a dragon carved out of stone with flames of faded red paint. In front of it was an empty bowl also carved from the stone.

"I was wondering how long it would take for you to find your way here."

"Arno...."

There was a chuckle, *"yes, I used him."*

"I am not Nejusana. Ozanus relinquished the title." She pointed out, staring directly at the statue now.

"He will always be Nejus, with or without the title and you are a worthy mate for him."

"Mmm." She didn't particularly want to recall how she became Ozanus' 'mate'.

"You are. I have not seen someone venture into the depths of the demon's home to seek their mate and then repeat it to bring him out."

"Why did you let War do this?" She demanded, trying to keep frustration out of the tone of her voice for fear of angering the God.

"Conflict is what He lives for. He has no side though Strife might think so. How do you think He was defeated the last time?"

"No stories are told."

"They are ancient. I'm sure if Ozanus looked he would find them."

"I need War out of Ozanus if we are to survive."

"That will come." The Dragon Lord remarked cryptically.

Miryama glared at the statue, not in the mood for vague

promises. She instinctively reached for her knife as if she would try and stab the God if she could.

"I need no blood from you today." The soothing voice remarked, *"see this place, today, as a sanctuary. Let yourself find peace and seek out that power and strength within you that will serve you well tomorrow."*

The small cave began to glow golden as if the sun was shining directly into it. She settled herself on the floor, her robe pooling around her. Briefly she wondered if Ozanus ever did this then that thought was whisked away.

She found her senses becoming heightened. She could suddenly hear individual cicadas rather than a mass of them. She could taste the cool air of the cave. She could see individual flakes of dust in the sunbeam coming through the hole in the cave's roof and each one looked like a fleck of gold. She could feel the rock shifting under her like a faint heart beat. She wanted to open her mouth and speak but found she couldn't. She knew she was receiving the blessing of a powerful God and hoped He had some spare for Ozanus.

She woke several hours later and blinked at the sight of Arno's concerned face peering down at hers. She blinked a few more times to check it was Arno and not someone else. She licked her dry lips before saying, "are you some sort of seer?"

He laughed, "no, just someone who has been round this family a long time. As you hadn't reappeared I thought I'd best come and find you and make sure you hadn't done anything foolish like bleed out."

"Bleed out?"

"Kittal lost a lot of blood when the Dragon Lord gifted him the powers of a High Priest." Arno remarked soberly, "would you like a hand up?"

"Please, I think my legs have gone to sleep."

She froze briefly as she heard a growl in her mind and glanced round.

"What?"

She shook her head, "nothing."

"Ready for tomorrow?"

"I think so."

They returned to the centre of the Valley in silence, Miryama contemplating what had happened. She felt almost serene, with all the worries of the next day gone though she didn't know how long it would last. She smiled at the sight of a group of children playing and realised everything she was about to do was for them, so the next generation could grow old safely.

The smile grew bigger and warmer as she saw Shaprour split from the group and fling himself at her, "mama! Where have you been?"

Hugging him back she replied, "I've just been a little busy."

He stepped back and looked serious as he asked, "when is papa coming back?"

She was taken by surprise for he hadn't asked much of his father during the last year. Had he sensed a change that only a child could detect or were the Gods involved in the prompting of the question? She tried to see if she could feel it too but all she felt was the prevailing tension and fear that lingered over them all. He repeated sternly, "is papa coming back soon?"

"Maybe."

He seemed satisfied with the answer as he gave her a brief grin and then ran back to the others who were calling him back. She looked to Arno but he just shrugged his shoulders as he hadn't mentioned anything. Softly he remarked, as he could see she was distracted by her son, "I will come and wake you later and help you dress."

"Thank you Arno. You are too good for me."

"Only doing my duty to you and the Nejus." He smiled.

144

Nineteen

The dawn was a thin strip of red as everyone heading out across Keytel gathered together just outside the Valley. Only a few friends and family had come out to see them off, holding torches for the Suwars to see by. Many didn't want to jeopardise the mission by appearing to celebrate.

Gaerwn approached Kenene and Miryama dressed in their armour, curved swords at their sides and dragon headed knives tucked into their belts. The last year had caused the Suwars to wear armour they had never felt the need to do previously. They wore leather breastplates and shoulder plates linked together.

Miryama wore her dragonscale breastplate to give herself the confidence of Scyth. She felt eyes on her but ignored them as she crossed to Spilla. She didn't really want to talk to Gaerwn and pretended to tighten Spilla's saddle and make sure her quiver of arrows wouldn't fall off. She was surprised that she still felt calm and ready for what was coming though there were others who were a bundle of nerves. No one knew what was going to happen to any of them or if they would return.

Gaerwn coughed for Miryama's attention and Kenene touched her arm. Reluctantly she turned and frowned at Gaerwn. He shifted uncomfortably, aware of what they had pretty much forced her to do. He could sense a new aura around her even if she didn't know it. He wondered where she had been the previous day. He felt drawn to the strength that seemed to emit from her. He cleared his throat, "I came to see if there is anything else you need?" He wanted to wish them luck but didn't want to jinx the mission.

"I think we are all as prepared as we can be. Are you ready for whoever gets back?"

"As much as we can be."
She acknowledged his reply with a nod.
He gave her a tight smile and then stepped back as a Daughter of Scyth ran up exclaiming, "I thought I might have missed you."

"What's wrong? Is Shaprour alright?" Miryama asked with sudden fear.

"No, no. He's fine. I was thinking about what you said about what happened up in that palace and I made you this." The woman handed over a dart with the tip wrapped in a scrap of cloth.

"What is this?" Miryama asked as she felt Kenene come closer out of curiosity.

"Be careful with the tip. It's a sedative. It's for just in case you can't persuade him to come willingly. You just need to jab him with it. I think it will last long enough to get him back here."

"Thank you." Miryama gave the medicine woman a tense smile.

"Come on Miryama." Kenene remarked.

"Yes of course." Miryama came back to the present. She was wondering how they would get War out of Ozanus when he was the only one who would be able to initiate that.

Soon they were all in the air, Suwars on their dragons and solo dragons. Only eyes could be seen through

146

their headscarves revealing every emotion they were feeling- fear, determination and excitement. They were all armed with any weapon they thought useful. As well as bows some also carried several short throwing spears. They had also tied themselves into their saddles as they knew their dragons would be doing most of the fighting and they didn't want to be falling out of their saddles. The team heading into the castle all had their swords at their waists.

As Titan's castle came into sight the large group split away and pushed forward. Miryama, Kenene and her team of seven hung back watching as several dragons rose into the air to meet the challenge.

With a roar the wild dragons flew in hard and were soon fighting Strife's dragons with claws and teeth. More dragons rose into the sky to engage the Suwars.

Fifteen of the Suwars slipped past, rising above the fighting though some had to dive sideways as two fighting dragons rose upwards. They circled round the castle bringing men and women on to the battlements armed with bows. Below in the courtyard a large arrow was being pulled back and angled upwards to take out a dragon with its scale piercing head.

Arrows were soon flying through the air. Spears were thrown down and hit their mark. The huge arrow was released and flew high into the air, ramming into a dragon without thought whether it was friend or foe. Dragon and rider fell to the ground into the middle of the encampment and both were quickly engulfed by its inhabitants. The rider didn't have any chance to escape and was dragged to his death as he tried to crawl away with his broken leg.

Miryama put a hand in the air and then pointed forward. They circled around the fighting that was concentrated in the sky above the encampment. The paved road led up to the large gatehouse. There was a large, cobbled courtyard which was filled by the arrow firing catapult which they had all hoped would have disappeared with Timijin's death. Wide steps led up to the double doors of the Keep which towered above the courtyard in a series of steps. One corner of the top most tier had crumbled from being hit by a dragon in an earlier attack. Two bridges connected the walls with the keep.

She looked around her handpicked team, calmed her mind that was leaping ahead to what may or may not happen. Spilla asked, *"ready?"*

"Yes. You know what to do?"

"We'll keep an eye out for wherever you come out."

"And Ozanus is the most important, if you have him and you can't get to me just go." She said sternly.

He turned his head and eyed her and knew by her eyes she meant it. He nodded his head and remarked, *"down we go then."*

The eight of them unwrapped their headscarves for better visibility as they prepared to slide down their dragons' bodies to their front clawed feet. They rested there briefly as the dragons flew down lower to the battlements. A well-placed arrow took out one of them and their dragon rose into the air to make room for the others.

The other seven hung from the dragons' forearms as one by one the dragons flew low enough for them to drop down on to the stone wall safely. Each one leapt to their feet, drawing out swords or arming bows ready for any attacks.

Apart from one moaning man there was no one alive enough to attack them. They all staggered back as a dragon fell past the castle to land in the river below. Water began to spread out and around the sudden new dam, flooding nearby tents.

Miryama maneuvered herself to the front of the group and ordered, "work in pairs. If you find Ozanus find

me. DO NOT challenge him as he could do anything."
There were nods as there were shouts from the courtyard
and opposite battlements as they were spotted.

They ran towards the open wooden door. Miryama
shouted, "keep it open, we need escape route options. Now
go, before they really come for us."
The group split up as the passage went both left and right.

Kenene followed after her and she was relieved he
had when they met their first opposition in the narrow
space. They found themselves fighting opposite the enemy,
backs against the wall. There was no room to swing a
sword. The other two Suwars with them were fighting dirty
with fists, knees, elbows and feet until their opponents
slumped against the wall. They ran as soon as they were
free leaving Miryama and Kenene fighting two against
three.

Miryama's attacker got right up in her face,
sneering at her. She winced at the bad breath before
kneeing him in the groin. He staggered backwards but
didn't get far as he reached the wall. She pulled out her
knife and went in through his belly where his leather jerkin
didn't quite close, thrusting upwards. The injured man let
out a scream and grabbed at his stomach.

She went in again and slashed at his neck. Blood
poured out and he gurgled up blood as he slumped to the
floor. She turned to help Kenene who was fighting two of
them with fists and knife. She leapt on the back of one and
pulled his head back by wrapping her arm round his
forehead. She slit his throat and jumped back as he
scrabbled at his wound while gurgling.

Kenene gave his opponent a final punch, breaking
an eye socket and knocking the man out. He grinned at
Miryama while breathing heavily and she couldn't help
returning it. She wiped blood from her eyes, smearing it
across her face. She let out a laugh, high on adrenalin and

exhilaration.

"Come on." Kenene said beckoning her on, "it will only get harder."
She grabbed her sword from the stone floor and followed Kenene down the passage without a backwards glance.

They came out of the passage into a wider corridor with several doors opening off it. Those doors were already open and scuffling could be heard in one. Miryama said, "upstairs?"
Kenene nodded.

They made for the staircase at the other end of the corridor, swords in hand. It came out into a small ante-chamber lined with tapestries, dust hiding the bright colours. They looked like they had been used for target practice with broken arrows on the floor and holes in the bodies of man and beast. One wall had a long bench against it. The door ahead of them was closed.

They crept up to it and Kenene put an ear to it to see if he could hear anything. He shrugged and adjusted his grip on his sword before slowly turning the handle. Miryama stood in front of the door ready to defend or attack.

The door swung open with a push of Kenene's booted foot. They released their breaths when nothing leapt out at them. They glanced at each other before venturing into the darkened room. The only light came from around the edge of the shutters on the window. The room was still, as if it wasn't used. Kenene asked with a frown, "where do we go from here? There has to be a door in here somewhere. Can you remember what was on the plan?"

"I'm not sure. Maybe there is a secret door." She crossed the room and opened the shutter to let some light in to reveal a room lined with wood paneling scratched with deep claw marks. The furniture in the room was all upturned and a chair lay with a broken leg. A smashed plate lay against the wall, food splattered on the walls and floor. Blood pooled near the fireplace.

Kenene stared around, "who is living here? This feels fresh."

She nodded in agreement.

"Something or one who is very angry."

"There's been a fight." She fought back the hope Ozanus had been fighting to escape then the opposite thought came to here; was he now dead?

"Let's get this done quickly then." Kenene remarked as he crossed to the wall opposite the window. Miryama went for the wall opposite the door where the fireplace was.

After a few minutes Kenene grumbled, "there's nothing here, I'm going to head down and see if there is something we missed? Coming?"

"He's got to be here somewhere. Could he be outside? I bet he is outside." Kenene walked over to the window and looked out of it. There was fighting happening around the ballista, the huge machine that could fire scale piercing arrows. Some of the other Suwars had dropped down to try and destroy it.

"No, something tells me he is in the castle."

Kenene looked round at her, "what has the Dragon Lord said to you?"

"Whatever Strife might think War is his own entity." She answered as with a smile she heard a click and a small door opened to reveal another room in semi darkness.

Kenene hurried over and peered in, "maybe there are two ways to get up to this floor."

"He's on this floor, I know he is." She said firmly enough that Kenene didn't dare challenge it. He knew they had an unusual relationship with the Gods heavily involved at all sort of levels, even more so than his father's relationship with the Gods.

"Shall we go on then?"

"After you." She said, something warning her not to go first.

"No problem." He responded a little too cockily.

He stepped through and found himself being dragged in and flung across the room by a claw. He didn't even have a chance to try and defend himself.

Miryama hesitated at the growl and shout of surprise. Someone had been waiting in there for their arrival. She definitely didn't want to enter and find herself fighting in the unknown. She stepped away from the door and checked her knife was loose in its sheath before calling out, "show yourself!"

"Why don't you come in?" The voice growled.

"War?"

There was a laugh and a young man stepped into view dressed in a burnished copper breastplate and auburn hair in a high ponytail. She recognised the breastplate and had thought it lost. She demanded, "who are you?"

"Don't you recognise me…. Mother?" The young man sneered.

She frowned, "mother?"

"You let my father leave me for dead but I have found a new one."

"I… I did not know." She was struggling to think straight.

"He's a better one. He lets me have as much blood as I want and my blood father is nothing. And now I will kill you and maybe then I will kill him and War will be freed and my new father will be happy. My foolish real father has been training me." He smiled.

Miryama's eyes widened and then she remembered that even if Ozanus had been teaching him how to fight he wouldn't be as good as her or Ozanus. He hadn't had the years of training and practice. She smiled herself and she saw a look of hesitation cross his face. She realised he may

look like a young man but there was a six year old in there as well, one that craved attention and rewards. She couldn't believe she was doing it but she taunted him, "you think you are better than me? Skill comes with practice and years."
He scowled, "I'll show you. You are a woman."
"Ha. Have you not been told of the Daughters of Scyth?" She adjusted her feet ready for his attack.

Bloodlust glared at her. He fought the urge to charge at her. He remembered what Ozanus had taught him about being out of control. He steadied his childish desire to act impulsively and adjusted his own stance. She could come to him.

She calmly waited for him to come. For now he was a mere distraction, but he must be Ozanus' guard, why else would he be here and not outside joining in the fighting? A new taunt came to her and she wondered if War was nearby influencing her, "why don't you go out and play and leave this to the adults?"

A growl rose in his throat and he began to change but he suppressed it. His anger was up and he couldn't control himself. He went for Miryama, rising his sword up to his shoulder to take a swipe at her.

She dodged past it as she saw it coming. He spun round and came to attack again and she brought up her own sword to deflect it. She remarked as she pushed him back, "you won't win against me. I know all of his tricks. I bet he hasn't shown you any of them."
As he staggered she leapt towards him. She wasn't going to let him have it easy. She exclaimed, "I will make you bleed, how you made me bleed."
Her own anger and frustrations were coming out now, going all the way back to her son's violent conception.

She backed him into a corner, holding his free hand to a deep sword slice on his sword arm. Tears were running down his face from the pain and humiliation. He whined, "I was meant to win."

"Not today." Miryama sneered, "and hopefully never." The point of her sword was at his throat.

A growl came from him and he changed into his dragon form. His change sent Miryama backwards and into the broken furniture. With a roar he flew through the window, creating a large hole in the wall.

With a groan she sat up and reached for her sword. There was going to be a stern conversation with Ozanus and War once she found them, but first she needed to find Kenene. She staggered to her feet and called out, "Kenene?"

There was a groan from the next room and, "if I get my hands on that sonofabitch…. Hey, there is another door in here."

"I'm coming. They've gone for the moment." She stared at the large hole in the wall.

They both looked at the door after Kenene had opened the shutters. Kenene asked, "do you think he'll be in here?"

"I hope so."

"You go first this time. I'm going to ache later."

"Me too." She opened the door and was relieved to find the window open this time. Compared to the last two it was tidy and had no broken furniture. There was a table and chair and a bed. Opposite the window was another door.

The chair was close to the window and they could see a hand resting on the arm of it. Kenene went to step in but Miryama put a hand out and stopped him.

He asked, "you sure?"

She nodded.

Sword in hand she stepped into the room and approached the chair. Quietly she called out, "Ozanus?" The hand gripped the chair arm tighter and then relaxed, *"you have finally come."*

"War? Are you going to let me take Ozanus?"

"Yes."

"Will you let me speak with him?" She stepped round and stared in shock. Sat before her was Ozanus but he had lost weight and his left hand trembled. There was a hollow look to his cheeks. He was dressed in a sleeveless tunic and trousers. His feet were bare. She knelt before him and took the hand. She demanded, *"what have you done to him?!"*

"Not my doing?"

"You could have stopped it." She protested, *"let me speak to Ozanus."*

"Not now."

"Are you going to come willingly?"

A look of contemplation crossed Ozanus' face and then a sneer, *"no."*

"No?! Do you know how many dragons and Suwars have willingly joined this suicidal mission for you?"

"Oh yes." Ozanus smiled, *"I am enjoying the taste of blood."*

"And Strife will be too! Whose side do you want to be on?"

One of Ozanus' eyebrows rose, *"ah, an interesting choice of question there. Who has been speaking with you?"*

"Does it really matter?"

They both turned as Kenene shouted, "what's taking so long?! We need to hurry before we are found. I can hear someone on the stairs."

Miryama remembered the dart and pulled it from a small bag on her belt. She stabbed it into Ozanus' bare arm and War growled, *"what have you done?!"*

"I'm sorry. I'll deal with you properly later. There is much to talk about." She exclaimed and hoped the sedation would work.

She sighed with relief as Ozanus' eyelids closed and

his head slumped forward. She called out to Kenene, "I need your help!"

Kenene ran into the room with two riders close behind, "what's the matter?"

"Just you two?" She asked of the Suwars.

The woman in the pair nodded and asked, "have you found him?"

"Yes. I'm guessing the best way will be up."

"I think there is one more room and then there is a roof of some sort between this tower and the next." The other remarked. He was a large strong man and Miryama asked, "do you think you can carry him?"

"What's the matter with him?" The Suwar asked and stepped round, "oh."

"Do not tell anyone." She ordered sternly, "no one needs to know."

"Yes madam."

"And you?" Miryama turned to the female Suwar who nodded as she stared wide eyed at Ozanus' seated form trying to think if her imagination had remembered him all wrong.

"Let's get moving." Kenene remarked as he glanced nervously at the door.

"Close it, barricade it, and then let's get going." Miryama ordered and then to the strong young Suwar, "be gentle with him."

The female Suwar and Kenene dragged the table over to the door and pushed it up against it once it was closed. The other carefully picked Ozanus up and put him over his shoulder so he could still swing his sword if needed.

Miryama led the group through the door and outside on to a flat roof made of planks. The stonewalls had deadened the sound of fighting and once outside it was an explosion of sound, mainly snarling from the dragons still fighting in the air.

Miryama put fingers to her mouth and let out a piercing whistle as Ozanus was put on the roof surface. Kenene and the other Suwar warily watched the door that they had shut while also glancing skywards for their rides.

Being as discreet as possible the dragons flew down, folding their wings in between the two turrets. The large Suwar made a run and leapt to grab his dragon's clawed foot which was missing a claw. Kenene pushed the female Suwar forward while shouting, "you next!"
Up at his dragon he shouted, *"Eciplso, take him!"* He pointed to Ozanus' prone body.
His dragon flew down and reached for Ozanus with a front claw and picked the limp body up as Kenene ran and leapt for the other.

Spilla came down last and with a running leap Miryama grabbed a claw and swung up on to his wing. He held it still long enough for her to turn in her saddle. As he flapped both wings to gain height he said, *"we need to move now. There is a God about."*
He glanced behind as he flapped his wings. Miryama looked behind as there was an angry roar.

Heading towards them was a large serpentine dragon copper scales glistening in the sunlight and red tail feathers streaming out behind him. He shot between the two towers and pushed upwards as Spilla swerved to the right in an attempt to dodge the attack.
"That is the son I thought was dead! War has a lot to answer for." Miryama shouted as she lay low in her saddle and held tight as Spilla turned tightly to the left to dodge their attacker, *"keep him busy until the others are far enough away!"*
"Think that's pretty easy." Spilla grinned as he turned again to face his opponent taking Bloodlust by surprise.

Bloodlust didn't have time to dodge the large

dragon. He roared in anger and pain as Spilla's claws
racked his back as he turned. He felt one set of back claws
clamp briefly on to his back. He shook himself free and
tried to reach round and bite the dark ochre dragon but
Spilla had already risen higher into the air, out of reach.

With a flick of his tail he flew up to meet with
Spilla, jaws snapping, claws stretched out. He was blinded
by his rage and didn't see the tail coming his way,
knocking him sideways. He couldn't recover from that and
found himself falling. He recovered before he hit the castle.

Miryama looked down and shouted at Spilla,
"leave, now!"
Spilla willingly turned away from the castle and let out a
roar to call the remaining Valley dragons away. There were
ten answering calls, six still carried Suwars though
Miryama couldn't tell how many were alive.

Twenty

The dragons staggered to the ground outside the Valley where a few people were there to meet them. Only Kenene and his dragon had gone into the Valley, taking Ozanus with them. The greeters gathered round each dragon with a rider and helped them down.

Miryama was thankful for the help as she was helped down. She ached all over and couldn't even recall how she had been injured as she looked at her arm. She was also exhausted but needed to find Ozanus before eating or sleeping. Before she left she put a hand to Spilla's nose, *"thank you for today."*

"When you said son…?" He asked with concern. She glanced around and decided there were too many people who could overhear their conversation, *"another day, in private."* She murmured and then added, *"go let Nimib know we have him."*

He grinned then, *"I can do that."* He added with a frown, *"Ozanus did not look well."*

"There is a lot to find out. See you later." She patted his nose again and then headed into the Valley.

She found Kenene, Gaerwn and Arno outside the house talking in hushed tones. She approached them, "what's going on? Where's Ozanus?"

They broke apart to let them join their group. Kenene frowned, "Ioan took him away as soon as we landed, into the house.”

“That’s good, isn’t it?”

“They won’t let me go to him, but I sneaked in and found him. They’ve put him in my old room, but he’s chained up.” Arno answered with concern.

“Has he come round yet?” She asked.

Arno shook his head, “couldn’t tell you. He looks terrible.”

“Did he say anything to you?” Kenene turned to Miryama.

“I had War who was being his obnoxious self.” Miryama replied in frustration. She turned to Arno, “do you think you could get me in?”

“Is that wise?” Gaerwn asked, “you look worn out. Go eat and sleep before you do something foolish. If he is asleep then let him be.”

She closed her eyes and sigh, “you are right.”

“I’ll take you back and help you out of that armour and check that wound for you.” Arno offered.

They were about to split up when Ioan appeared at the top of the steps, “great, you are here.”

“What are you doing with Ozanus?!” Miryama couldn’t help shouting angrily.

He raised an eyebrow and sneered, “the right thing. I can’t trust him. War might still betray us. Strife will come looking for him.”

“Strife is going to come whether you want him to or not!” Miryama exclaimed, “he’ll know where Ozanus is. He could be here in the next hour or tomorrow. We will need to prepare.” She turned to Gaerwn who stood with his arms crossed and she wondered which side he was on. She turned back to Ioan, “and as for War, he is his own entity. He does as he pleases.”

“Then it’s even more important that War is kept locked up with Ozanus.”

“Have you not seen Ozanus’ condition? He won’t be

going anywhere?!" Kenene exclaimed, "we all know we need him but keeping him locked up isn't going to be any use for us." In his exasperation he threw his arms in the air and walked away from the group.

"Gaerwn are we ready for any attack?" Ioan calmly asked as if he hadn't even heard anything that had just been said to him.

"Of course." Gaerwn grunted and walked away before his anger at the situation exploded out of him.
Gauging the situation Arno put a hand on Miryama and suggested, "let's go."
She uncurled her hands when she realised they were fists. To Ioan she sternly said, "you'll let me see him tomorrow." He didn't reply as she turned and walked away.

She sank with relief on to a stool and let Arno take off her breastplate as Lhateso offered her a cup of water. Lhateso asked hopefully, "did you find my sister?"

"Lhateso, this is not the time." Arno said, pausing in his bandaging of Miryama's wound.
Miryama looked up from where she leant forward, arms resting on thighs, cup still in hand, "I'm sorry, I completely forgot."
Lhateso brushed tears from her eyes.

"I'm sure she is fine." Arno offered up, "now let Miryama rest, it's been a long hard day." He stood up and guided Lhateso towards the tent's entrance.

With a heavy sigh Miryama sank on to the bed. She was hungry but sleep called to her. As her eyes closed she smiled, Ozanus was now back where he belonged even if he was being treated as a prisoner. Now she needed him back in her bed.

Ozanus stirred he lifted a hand to his sore head. He had a pounding headache but didn't know why. He realised his arm felt heavy and lifted his head to find a shackle and chain on it. Wincing he sat up and looked around wondering both how he had got to this room and where he was.

Flashes of memory came back to him- Strife and Bloodlust in the palace in the mountains; Miryama in the palace; teaching Bloodlust how to fight. Then he was in his uncle's abandoned castle which he knew he was no longer in. He looked round the wood paneled walls and had a sense he was somewhere familiar. He remembered then through a hazy filter Miryama knelt before him and then it had gone black.

He realised his throat was parched and he felt hungry as if he hadn't eaten for ages. He shook the chain to see how long it was. He was going to be able to stand up but wasn't sure how much further he could go.

He heard roars from outside and swung his legs off the edge of the bed. He paused a moment before cautiously standing up. The chain was three steps too short for him to reach the shutters to see what was going on outside. He growled in frustration and retreated back to the bed. He spoke to himself, *"what have you got me into now War?"*
"Just wait and see." Came the reply.

Outside shouts had gone up from the watchtowers that a mass of dragons were approaching led by a huge serpentine black dragon. A copper one flew close behind and to one side. The black dragon let out a roar so loud everyone had to cover their ears and the dragons following him joined in.

In the Valley, thinking the end was here the human population ran for cover and weapons with no real idea how to defeat the dragons. They could only pray that the invisible barrier would survive. The Valley's dragons answered the challenge and rose on mass to greet their challengers.

As he reached the Valley Strife felt the power emanating around the Valley, protecting it. He roared in frustration as the Valley dragons rose up and the fighting began.

If he couldn't get in himself he would try a different way. He dove down, away from the fighting and began to circle the Valley.

Like a wave that has crashed and travelled across the beach till it is spent a mist began to creep into the Valley and reached out to anyone it touched, before retreating. Those it touched caused them to shiver, nothing more.

It would be a few days before those who had been caught in the mist drifting around their ankles became ill. There was a cough and fevers as the first symptoms, and it was effecting people indiscriminately. What confused them was that no one else became infected.

As people began to die, coughing up chunks of their lungs, a small crowd began to gather on what was left of the lawn demanding to see Ioan. Some were saying they had seen death slipping between the tents and huts, bloated by the number dying. They were fearing the worst and contemplating returning to the ancient ways. Would a human sacrifice be enough to rid them of the pestilence harming their friends and families?

It was in this tense atmosphere that Miryama finally managed to see Ozanus. Arno had informed her he was getting food and drink but he was still chained to the wall.

Ioan didn't stop her pushing past while he stood at the top of the steps trying to come up with the right words to say to the people gathered on the lawn. He didn't know what to say. He realised he needed his brother. The world was falling apart, and he didn't want to believe his brother was the answer. He straightened his back and shoulders, but words failed him as Lylya hissed, "do not say anything about Ozanus." Before following Kenene into the house.

Kenene and Lylya stopped at the end of the short passage to give Miryama and Ozanus space through they desperately wanted to see him too. Miryama was surprised to find the door unlocked as she pushed it open. She cautiously stood in the doorway, "Ozanus? War?" Ozanus looked up from where he sat on the bed, back against the wall. His eyes widened and he pulled himself towards the edge of the bed, "Miryama?"

"Is it really you?"

"I think so. I'm not quite sure how I got here. What happened the other day?"

He was taken by surprise as she ran the few steps across the room and flung herself at him. She held him tight till he grumbled and then held his head more gently to kiss him. His hands reached up and held her face and he felt the tears running down. He gently pushed her back and wiped the tears off her cheeks, "what's the meaning of this?"

"I've been worried for you, for us, for Shaprour, for all of us but now you are back. And we need you stronger than ever."

"What's happened?" He asked with concern, "Why am I chained up here like a prisoner?"

"Strife attacked us a few days ago and there is now sickness. People are getting worried and are suggesting sacrifices."

"No! That cannot happen." Ozanus stood up and tried to head to the door only to be stopped by the chain. He turned and grabbed it with both hands and with a snarl of anger that came from War he pulled it from the wall. Turning back he demanded, "where is my brother?"

"Outside, with the crowd."

He marched out of the room and down the passage, not
noticing his friend and sister who flattened themselves
against the wall to let him past, chain trailing behind him.

He flung open the doors of the house and stepped
out into the sunlight. Everyone looked up and Ioan turned
to see who they were all staring at. He stuttered, "br….
Brother, it's good to see you up."

"Up?! You had me chained in a room. And what is this I
hear about sacrificing someone?!"

"It hasn't been decided…"

"Yet? I know you are thinking it." Ozanus exclaimed, "do
you know what happened the last time we had to sacrifice
someone?"

"Of course I do." Ioan spat.
Ozanus turned to the crowd, "I am here now. Don't even
think of taking anyone to the temple and sacrificing them."

There were whispers amongst the crowd as they
talked amongst each other at the sight of Ozanus. They
waited for more from him, hoping for words of
encouragement. He just stood there, glaring at them.
Slowly they began to disperse to let others know that
Ozanus was back.

Ozanus waited till the last one had gone before
sinking on to the top step. Lylya ran forward and knelt
down beside him, "Ozanus?!"

"Ugh. Get this shackle off me and I need a bath and clean
clothes."

"Of course."

"And something to eat, something better than that
hideous pottage I've been given the last few days."
Lylya grinned, "of course. Ozanus?"

"Yes?" He glanced at her but returned to staring out
across the lawn, astonished to find most of it now a village
of tents.

"I'm glad you are back."

"Me too…. I think."

With a wash and clean clothes and some hot food inside him he started to feel more himself. He was soon dressed in a shirt, sleeveless robe and trousers with bare feet. He got everyone together in the living area. As he had washed he couldn't believe the state of his body. He'd lost his muscle mass. He wasn't starvation thin but hadn't eaten a huge amount since… He couldn't work out when.

He looked around the gathered people, his sisters, his brother, his wife, his friend and the Chieftain of the Suwars. Standing at the edge of the room was Arno and Ioan's secretary. Ioan shifted uncomfortably under his older brother's gaze. There was a clear division amongst them all. Miryama, Lylya and Kenene were one group, Ioan and Shiang were another and Gaerwn drifted between the two groups, arms crossed.

Ozanus took a deep breath before asking, "so what exactly has been happening around here?"

"I could say the same to you?" Snapped Ioan, crossing his arms, "what have you been doing?"

"Ioan!" Lylya exclaimed.

"What?!" Ioan leant forward as he retorted, "he's been gone a year with the enemy and then he berates me in public. He has no right to order me about."

"Well, leave then." Lylya challenged.

"Quiet." Ozanus ordered, a hand on his knife, "he has a point. Yes, I have been with the enemy but not willingly if you can tell by my appearance. War has been using me."

"And now?" Kenene asked with concern.

Ozanus shrugged, "I don't know but I am definitely me. Now, what about here?"

"Strife over ran Moronland and then took up residence at our uncle's castle." Lylya replied, "the Daughters of Scyth retreated to here along with every Suwar to protect this

166

valley and then the refugees came. A lot of Linyee have
ended up here along with the villagers."

"We've lost dragons along the way to Strife's recruiting
and to fights." Gaerwn added.

"Who is currently winning?" Ozanus looked to his
chieftain.

"No one, we are at a stalemate."
Ozanus raised an eyebrow in question.

"There is something stopping Strife from wiping us out.
If there wasn't none of us would be here now."

"What's stopping him?"

"An invisible shield of some sort. I think the Dragon Lord
is involved but it is growing weaker." Miryama remarked.

"And earlier?"

"After we took you Strife attacked with everything he had
but thankfully couldn't get in but there were reports of a
mist and now there are people dead or dying. They are
looking for a way to stop it." Kenene replied.

"Thank you everyone. I'll have a think about this."

"How long do you think the barrier will last?" Shiang
asked with worry.

"He's not going to know." Lylya turned on her sister.

"Ssh Lylya." Ozanus said sternly and turned to his
younger sister, "currently I don't know."

"And War, what about Him?" Ioan challenged.

"He's a God and does as he pleases." Lylya retorted
before Ozanus could say anything.

"He's inside our brother so he should know." Ioan
exclaimed, "he could be spying on us for all we know and
then will return back to Strife and tell him of our weak
spots and how many we have."

"Enough!" Arno shouted from the back of the room.

Everyone turned in surprise to stare at the servant
who had clenched hands. With everyone's attention on him
he added sternly, "your parents would be so disappointed in

you all. You should be uniting against the enemy. This is what War and Strife want. They want you to argue and break apart then it will be easier to either turn us into slaves or wipe us all out. We all know the Gods are playing with us like toys and we are just being used to help them reach their own planned agendas."

He stumbled to a stop and blushed as he realised he had everyone staring at him and he was a servant who had spoken out of turn. He looked to Ozanus for guidance and found his master was smiling in a way that suggested he was trying to hold back a chuckle. Gaerwn turned back to the group and quietly remarked, "you know he is right. We should be celebrating Ozanus' return to us rather than bickering. War is his own entity and is clearly planning something that will be revealed when he is ready. Ozanus is **not** a spy." He looked at Ioan sternly.

"The Dragon Lord said to me that War is in fact likely leading all of this and we can only let him lead it to its conclusion." Miryama added.
Ozanus raised an eyebrow in surprise as she glanced at him.

"I think," Ozanus said thoughtfully, "I think it's now time to stop. There is much to think about. Now, if you will excuse me, I would like to spend some time with my wife." He carefully stood and Miryama quickly tucked his arm into her's, so no one realised how tired he now was. She held the hand tight as she felt it shake. She asked quietly, "where do you want to go?"

"Anywhere but here." He murmured, "we have a lot of catching up to do."

"Shall I fetch Shaprour?" She asked, "he will be so happy to see you."

"No, not yet. I don't want him to see me like this." He turned back to the room and ordered, "Arno, make up a room in the house please."

"Yes sir." Arno called back with a bow of his head.

Miryama led Ozanus to the veranda at the back of the house and guided him into one of the chairs there. He remarked, "it feels like I have been asleep a long time but it has left me drained and tired rather than refreshed."

She stood facing him, "I'm just glad I've got you back. Up at the castle, what was happening?"

"I honestly couldn't tell you. War possessed my body and mind not that Strife liked it. I could hear and see but could do nothing about it."

"Where is He now?"

"Only He knows." Ozanus shrugged. He then turned the conversation to her, "how have you been? And Shaprour?"

She ignored the questions, "Ozanus?"

"Mmm."

"When we were rescuing you. I met a young man who claimed he was my son."

His eyes widened and he growled, "he didn't hurt you?"

"No, no. I think I managed to hurt him more. With a little more experience he would be as good as you. He said you trained him. Ozanus, who is he?"

"A godling." He replied bluntly and stared out unable to face looking at her.

"A what?"

He drew in a deep breath before saying, "he is the son of yourself and War. I thought I had killed him but didn't do everything I was told to do."

"So, everything that has happened is your fault?" She asked in dismay. She sank into the chair beside him.

"I think… I don't know what to think." He stared down at his hands on his knees and went to twist the signet ring he no longer had. He stopped himself and let his hands become fists instead, angry with himself and with War.

She stared at him. She wanted to be so angry with him but for once couldn't find it in her heart to be so.

Instead, she said, "damn the Gods! Damn your family!"
That raised a small smile which then slipped.

They found themselves look at each other, trying to find something to say; the right words. He reached out and took one of her hands. Carefully, as if still thinking over the words, he said, "I've missed you. Seeing you in the palace… Then I wasn't able to even think of you. My mind was clouded. All I could do was go through the motions of living and then even that dwindled and I didn't want to do that. It was like I had outlived my use and it had become a waiting game. For who?" He shrugged as he couldn't answer the question and didn't expect anyone else to either.

"But you trained our son? Why didn't you try to stop that?" She demanded. She pulled her hand away. She suddenly wanted him to suffer, know how alone she had been.

He withdrew his hand with a sigh and swept a hand through his hair. He stood, "I should go…"

She reached for his hand, "don't." It was her turn to stand. She stepped so close they were chest to chest, face to face. She chewed her bottom lip, "Ozanus? I should be mad at you, so mad at you, but I can't be. I'm just relieved I found you alive and could bring you home, well, nearly home. Everyone will be relieved to see you stepping back into the role they see you in."

"And you?" He asked, not moving, but breathing in her scent. He knew their relationship was tempestuous. "Do you want me in that role?"

Her eyes flittered over his face. She didn't know the answer to that. She took his head in her hands and pressed her lips hard on his. She felt some of the barrier between them weaken. When they were both ready to start their relationship again, they would both know it.

He murmured into her lips, "I should go."

"Go where?"

"Just go."
She let go of him and stepped back and watched him walk away.

Twenty-One

Kenene and Ozanus stood on the cliffs beside the head of the complete dragon statue that marked the main entrance to the Valley looking out across the plain. In the near distance was Linyee. The ground between was scorched but vegetation was still trying to survive. Kenene remarked, "it didn't take Him long to destroy the lands, burning them all. Linyee has been half destroyed." Ozanus didn't reply. He turned and crossed the clifftop, past the watchtower and looked down into the Valley. It looked so different filled with people and their homes and fields. Would it stay like that once this was all over?

He looked up and tried to discern if he could detect the barrier. He squinted as he thought he saw a shimmer to it.

"We think it's the Dragon Lord's doing. What you think?" Kenene asked as he stepped up to Ozanus' side and peered up as well.

Ozanus closed his eyes and concentrated in the hope of detecting anything and got nothing. He looked at Kenene then, "I have no idea. Now, I want an honest answer to my question."

"Go on." Kenene replied warily.

"How bad has it really been?"

"We're surviving. We were hit badly at the beginning when a group of dragons left us and we were fighting to protect all of the refugees but since then it hasn't been so bad. We've been over to the castle to get information, any information on our enemy but we have lost good people as well from doing so. They have tried attacking us. They did get in once but then this barrier showed up."

"Numbers?"

"Holding steady. About two hundred in all. We have lost some dragons along the way and have had to crash course some Suwars to ride."

"What about the other side?"

"Fluctuates."

Ozanus stopped and turned, "fluctuates?"

"We haven't managed to get an accurate number. There are dragons and there is the big camp of men below, but they all come and go raiding the surrounding area or further afield. That's how come half of Linyee is now in the Valley."

They fell back into companionable silence. Ozanus didn't even know where to start as he stared out. He rubbed his thumb on the finger that would have had the signet ring on it as he contemplated everything.

"What are you thinking?" Kenene asked.

"Nothing at the moment. I need to have a good think. First though I need to speak with Gaerwn and see if he has anyone who can help me get back into shape." Ozanus subconsciously held his trembling left hand.

"You could join the children." Kenene laughed, "have you seen Shaprour? I think he'll be alright, just needs to improve his attention span."

"He's six, I probably didn't have the attention span at that age either." Ozanus smiled and then it vanished as he remembered why. "Come on, lets head down before someone starts worrying."

"I don't think you need to worry about Ioan. He's one person against the rest of us." Kenene remarked as they headed towards the path that was carved into the side of the cliff.

They walked in silence for a few minutes before Kenene asked, "have you seen him yet?"

"Who?"

"Shaprour?"

Ahead of the older man Ozanus shook his head, "I don't want him to see me like this and anyway I'm probably just a stranger to him now. I can barely recall him myself." Kenene sighed, "come on, come and watch him at the training ground and you are his father, he won't care how you look."

"Not today." Ozanus responded in a tone that said his mind would not be changed.

However curious the adults were they were respecting Ozanus' request for privacy as he started to work on getting back into a fit fighting state. Children, however could not be told and hearing that Ozanus, the man who saved the Daughters of Scyth, was back in the Valley they had to come and see. The group of six, seven and eight year olds crouched giggling behind a large bush while poking each other to see who would fall out into view first.

On the training ground, striped to the waist Ozanus was breathing heavily from the exertion of the training. He was out of shape and out of practice which he wasn't happy about. As he paused to catch a breath and give his muscles a brief rest he tried to recall when he stopped training Bloodlust. Had he shown the youth all of his tricks? The crazy thought that he needed to go up against his son to find out what he had shown him came into his head. He shook his head to remove the thought and then had to wipe sweat from his eyes.

His opponent was also breathing heavily. Normally

he only worked with the children so was a little out of practice himself but he had an eye for picking up the faults that could quickly become bad habits. He was patient as well which is why Gaerwn had recommended him as he knew Ozanus would quickly get frustrated with himself. He knew Ozanus, as a matter of pride, had always trained hard and a year of doing not as much would mean his body would be protesting.

Ozanus' trainer asked, "ready to keep going?" Ozanus adjusted the grip of his wooden sword and nodded. A year ago he would have had no qualms using real ones but after the last few days his body had taken a beating from the wooden sword so was glad they weren't.

"Remember to rest tomorrow. Your body needs a chance to recover especially as you are so out of shape." Ozanus grimaced as he knew the man was right but he was also aware of what was at stake. He nodded again and then he heard a loud peel of laugher and a shout as a child fell through the bush.

Both men turned to look and saw the boy land on his bum on the compacted soil of the training area. The boy staggered to his feet and turned to the men as two more ran out from behind the bush. He blushed and stared at his feet, "sir, sorry sir." He looked up and saw Ozanus staring at him and shifted uneasily on his feet as his two friends ran to his side. The other four still hiding behind the bush fled.

The three of them stared up in awe at Ozanus, unable to believe they were seeing the man they were always being told about in training. They were all repeatedly told that if they practiced they would become as good as their High Chieftain. They had heard how he practiced not just one on one but with multiple Suwars.

The two friends frowned. Their image of who Ozanus was different from what they were looking at and one exclaimed, "you are not Ozanus."

"What are you doing here?!" Their teacher demanded.

"He's meant to be super strong and able to fight forever." The other boy protested.

Ozanus raised an eyebrow and chuckled, "not everyone appears strong. Some are strong in the mind like my brother."

"Where have you been?" The first boy demanded, "if you were here sooner my mother would be alive." The boy brushed tears from his eyes.

That resonated with Ozanus and he handed the sword to the Suwar and beckoned the three boys closer. They nervously approached, fearing they were about to be told off.

Ozanus cleared his throat, "I am sorry that your mother died but she would have died fighting to protect all of this and you from Strife. I'm back now. I'm not going to promise anything but I will try my best to destroy Strife but you must promise me something."

"What?" The boy asked suspiciously.

"We will always need Suwars so remember to keep practicing and then you will become strong."

"And you?"

"I am practicing to become strong again."

"Have you been ill?" The boy who had been pushed out of the bush finally spoke up.

Ozanus looked at his son before suggesting, "why don't your friends go home and you and I have a talk?"

The Suwar picked up the other wooden weapons and then said, "come on you two."

"Is it true he has been ill?" The second boy asked as they were led away.

The Suwar glanced back at his High Chieftain and then said, "yes, but he is recovering now."

Now alone neither son nor father were sure how to

react. Shaprour wasn't sure if the man before him was even his father. He didn't look like how he remembered. Ozanus shifted uncomfortably. He had never quite been sure how to handle his relationship with his son. He had an opportunity now to start a fresh but didn't know where to begin.

Ozanus studied his son with fresh eyes. He had grown in the year he had gone. His brown hair was longer and tied with a leather thong and a bead the same as how the Daughters of Scyth wore it. He wondered how much of War's essence he had absorbed. Was the boy taller than a normal child of his age? Those almond shaped eyes, were they immortal inheritance or from his own mother?

Shaprour said stiffly, as if being polite to a stranger, "mama says you have been away."

"I have."

"What happened to you?"
Ozanus was thoughtful for a moment as he tried to work out the best way to explain it all, "I was a prisoner and your mother rescued me."

"Why did you let yourself get caught."

"Keytel and Moronland were being threatened and I had to check the threat out. If you want to be a good leader you can't act impulsively. Knowledge and the more you know of a situation the greater the chance of winning." Ozanus replied, finding it comfortable talking in such a way, "I was ambushed."

"Will you have to go away again?"

"I'm not planning to."

"Good." Shaprour said with some relief.

Miryama saw the children running back and glanced over them to see if Shaprour was with them as he usually was. She couldn't see him. She shouted, "stop." They turned and looked at her, ready to flee if they were going to be told off.

She frowned at them, "where is Shaprour?"
They shifted uncomfortably; aware they had been doing something they shouldn't have been. They stared at the ground.

"Where have you been?"

"The training ground." One of them quietly admitted.

"Is Shaprour still there?"

"Is that really the Nejus?" One of the others asked.

"Yes he is."

"And will he really save us."

"We hope so."

"He didn't look like he could." Another frowned.

"You should all go home." Miryama suggested sternly as she headed in the direction they had come in.

She wasn't sure what she was going to find considering Ozanus' reluctance to see their son. She hurried to the training ground but paused as she spotted father and son talking. There was an awkwardness about them which she hoped would eventually past now they were back in each other's company.

There seemed to be a lull in their stiff conversation and called out, "there you are."
They both turned to see who it was. Shaprour lit up at the sight of his mother. He ran over to her as he said, "look who's here mama."
Miryama gave Ozanus a tight smile, "not as bad as you feared?"

"Suppose not." He replied gruffly, "he has grown."

"They do that." She laughed. She bent down to Shaprour, "are you happy to see your father?"
Shaprour squirmed and glanced over at his father before replying, "not sure."
She looked over at Ozanus, "will you come and stay with us now?"

"I'll think about it." He replied stiffly. He felt tired from

178

the training and trying to talk to his son. He had found it hard talking to the six year old.

Miryama nodded and asked, "shall I come over tonight?"

"If you want." He shrugged his shoulders. Their relationship was another thing to think about. He pulled on his shirt and left the training ground.

Walking back to the house Ozanus didn't expect to be ambushed by a young woman who looked familiar. His hand went to his knife as he asked, "who are you?"

He looked her over and spotted the knife and demanded, "where did you get that?"

"I need your help."

"Not now." He scowled, "I'm busy."

"You were there, you'll have seen my sister."

His eyes widened briefly. Now he knew why she looked familiar. Bloodlust had been offered the sister as a gift who he half ignored. She had come with them to the castle and continued to be half ignored.

"I have." He answered bluntly.

"Can you rescue her please? Bring her back here?"

"No."

"No? You are a great warrior. We were originally sent to find you to tell you about Strife."

"I didn't need to be told about him. I wouldn't be any good as a leader if I didn't know of things." Ozanus retorted as he began to walk away.

"Wait!" She cried.

He paused and reluctantly turned round, "there is nothing I can do, I'm sorry." He wasn't going to tell her he didn't want to go back. "Don't you dare go asking anyone else either as they would be foolish to even try."

"And if I try?"

"Good luck." He replied dismissively and began walking again.

She stared after him, shocked at his attitude and wondering why everyone spoke so favourably of him. If he wasn't going to help she was going to have to do it herself and to hell with him. The Suwars could idolise him all they wanted but she wasn't going to anymore.

Twenty-Two

Gaerwn was surprised to find Ozanus on the edge of the training ground watching the youths. He came and stood beside his leader and looked out on the group. It was split in two. Some were working in pairs honing a particular skill. The others were working as a group, taking it in turns to be the one in the centre being attacked by the others. He asked, "how are you getting on? Ready for what you are known for?"

"Mmm." Ozanus barely glanced at the Chieftain. He crossed his arms as he added, "they are all doing well. Any really good ones?"

"Some very strong ones are ready to become Suwars."

"And in the younger groups?"

"A few with potential already." He noted how Ozanus' eyes were drawn to the group. Trying not to smile Gaerwn remarked, "you know you want to. You've been working hard the last two weeks. It will be good for all of you if you join them."

Ozanus was quiet for a minute before asking, "have we got knives being made ready?"

"Are you coming up with a plan?"

Ozanus grimaced, "not yet, but I am tempted by your suggestion."

"They can change back to wooden for you."

"No, the real thing is fine."

Gaerwn led him round to the group, who becoming aware of their High Chieftain, paused in what they were doing. They saluted him, fists on chests. Their teacher approached, "can I help? Any issues?"

"No issues." Gaerwn reassured him, "would they be interested in doing a workout with Ozanus?"
A whisper went round the group and their teacher chuckled, "I think that is a yes. We have a couple of spare leather jerkins if you want to wear one for protection."

"I'll take you up on that." Ozanus replied.

A few minutes later Ozanus stood in the centre of the more experienced group. The other half had moved to the edge of the tampered ground to watch. They were all feeling privileged to be either watching or participating.

Standing in the centre of the group a feeling of the familiar came over Ozanus. He adjusted his grip on his sword which he would normally find a little too light. He slowly turned on the spot eyeing all of the youths over, noting any eagerness, nervousness and twitches that he could use to his advantage. With a small smile he paused, facing his first choice and beckoned them in.

The young man was eager to prove how good he was and ran in ready to slash his sword diagonally across Ozanus' chest. Ozanus raised his own sword into the air to meet it and as they closed in he stamped on his opponent's foot. The young man grimaced but didn't let the pain get to him. He retreated enough to change his attack as Ozanus remarked with a smile, "good."

As the two defended and attacked the teacher limped round the outside of the circle and tapped on the shoulders of two of the girls. One ran in eager to show off her skills while the other was more cautious. Holding her spear she stayed wide of the action but circled, watching.

She spotted her opportunity as Ozanus was distracted by both of his opponents. As he stepped back,

being pressured by them, she jabbed her spear behind his knees. Unbalanced by it he found himself falling backwards and landing hard on the ground. He stared at the spear pointed at his throat and the smirking girl above it. He frowned, smiled and then laughed, "bravo. I don't think anyone has ever dared to."
She bowed her head in acknowledgement and pulled the spear away. She held out a hand and helped pull him up.
"Do you want to go on sir?" The teacher enquired.
Adrenalin was pumping through his veins. Ozanus glanced round at those who had yet to have a chance and grinned, "yes."
A cheer rose up from everyone. Gaerwn ruefully smiled, this was what was needed to draw Ozanus out of himself. What he was seeing was the old Ozanus. He turned and walked away, leaving them all to it.

Miryama was surprised to find Ozanus entering her tent with a determined step. She stood up from her stool, "Ozanus?"
He pulled her to him and pressed his mouth hard against hers. She pushed him away, her hands on his chest and stared at him wide eyed. She could smell the sweat and damp leather on him so guessed he had been practicing. His shirt was cut and blood stained. She asked, "what have you been doing?"
"Ssh." He hissed and pulled her close again. His hands ran down her back and found her buttocks. He gave them a good squeeze as he pulled her groin into his. His tongue forced her mouth open.
She found herself wrapping her arms round him and was glad Shaprour was out and she had no idea where Lhateso was and didn't care either. He pulled her loose blouse out of her culottes and she felt his hands move up her bare back making her shiver with growing anticipation.

Still under her blouse one of his hands moved round to her chest and grabbed at a breast.

A giggle escaped her mouth as she fell backwards on to her bed with Ozanus dropping on top of her. He lifted himself up and stared down at her face framed with her auburn hair. He said quietly as he began to undo the leather jerkin he was still wearing, "today… today…"

After an hour of fighting he had abandoned the training ground and had hurried through the Valley. He was all fired up and fighting wasn't going to quell the other things being aroused in him.

"You truly found yourself." She smiled and pulled him down to kiss him herself.

While knelt over her she helped him take off his jerkin and shirt then he pulled her blouse off. They quickly removed their trousers. He pressed her down again and his touch on her skin was steady and careful. She bit her lip to stop herself from moaning too loudly and revealing what was happening to anyone who might be passing outside. His fingers slipped between her thighs and found her wet and eager.

She pulled his hand over her mouth as he slowly entered her, feeling her tight around his penis. She moaned into his hand, as he held himself just inside her. She arched her back, wanting more of him inside her. She had missed sex with him. She lifted his hand and panted, "don't make me wait."

She wrapped her legs round him and arched her back again. He couldn't hold off much longer and thrust deep into her. She held tight to him as she felt him within her, her body stretching and clinging to him.

He came quickly and rolled off her, panting. She found his hand and held tight to it. He glanced at her in the streak of light coming through the opening in the tent and kissed her cheek, "thank you for coming to find me."

"That's alright." She murmured, in a post sex daze. She rolled closer to him and pulled a blanket up over their naked bodies from the tangled mess at the bottom of the bed. He wrapped an arm round her and she, for the moment, felt contented and whole.

Ozanus returned that evening once Shaprour had gone to bed and they made love again by the light of the brazier.

Shaprour threw himself on to his parents' bed when he woke in the morning. He grinned down at his parents' surprised faces. With a smile Miryama remarked, "why don't you spend some time with Shaprour today?"

"What do you think?" Ozanus asked as he looked at his son.

"Yes, yes." He bounced on the bed making his parents laugh.

Ozanus smiled, "what do you want to do?"

Shaprour paused in his bouncing, "umm..."

"Tomorrow then. Let me have a think."

"Woohoo!" Shaprour bounced on the bed again making it dangerously creak.

Twenty-Three

He sensed his son had lots of questions to ask and he decided to give him a lesson in the Gods and being their servant in Keytel. He gathered a few supplies and let Miryama know they were going to the private shrine as he shrugged on his sleeveless robe with its embroidered golden dragon god swirling on the back and checked his knife was secure on his belt.

He led Shaprour through the Valley to the bottom of the cliffs and along them to the shrine. Reaching it he pointed out the cave, "I was about your age when I was first brought here. I witnessed your uncle being named by our father and the Dragon Lord blessing the choice of name."

He paused and remembered the words spoken by the God saying that Ioan would support him and couldn't help sneering at how unhelpful Ioan had been.

Shaprour stared up at it, "what is in there?"

"A private shrine used by generations of Nejuses and High Priests to our Dragon Overlords."

"Dragon Overlords?"

"Come, lets head in and I will give you a lesson on the Gods and our family." He picked his son up to help him up the first boulder and watched him scramble the rest of the way.

They sat together in the entrance of the shrine, the

sun warm on their fronts and the cool air from the cave on their backs. Shaprour had already peered in and seen the Dragon Lord statue as his father had scrambled up using the worn foot and handholds in the rocks. They drank cool water from Ozanus' canteen as Ozanus said, "what do you want to ask me first?"

Shaprour was thoughtful for a moment before saying, "if I am heir, why are you not the Nejus?"

"I was Nejus but I gave the responsibility to my brother, your uncle. He now looks after Keytel but I am still the High Priest and High Chieftain to the Suwars. Currently as the only child out of all of us you are heir to all three titles. I know that is a lot of responsibility but hopefully you'll be an adult before you have to take on those roles.

"But you are both going to die." Shaprour remarked with concern, tears forming at the thought of losing his parents. He couldn't imagine a life without them. The concept was too much for his six year old mind.

"No we aren't yet." Ozanus tried to reassure him, "yes we will be fighting but we fight to live and we have you as a reason, the best reason."

"He said he would kill you both."

With a frown Ozanus asked, "who is he?"

"He says he is my brother."

"You don't have a brother." Ozanus lied, "who is this?"

"I don't know but he comes in my dreams."

Ozanus noticed then the dark stains under his son's eyes. He closed his eyes and sighed. He wished he could go back and do what the Dragon Lord had ordered and burnt the body, not just killed it and dropped it in the sinkhole. He asked, "what else does he say?"

"You aren't going to let him kill you?"

Ozanus stared straight into his son's concerned face, "I promise that with everything within my power I will not be killed. Why do you think I am training as much as I can."

Shaprour nodded solemnly.

"Now, let me show you something." Ozanus reached behind and pulled out of the bag the contina'ed book.

"He said he would kill me too. That you loved him more than me." Shaprour said, fear making his voice tremble. Ozanus froze in shock. Finding his voice he turned to his son, "I will not let anyone kill you, I can promise you that. As for who I love more, you and your mother are the most important things to me. Everything I do is to protect you. Do you understand?"
Shaprour nodded.

"Come here." He put the book down and held open his arms. Shaprour shifted into his father's lap and Ozanus held him tight, "learn everything you can from your teachers and that will mean you can defend yourself. We can do some practice together as well if you want?"
Shaprour nodded into his father's chest.

"Now, let me tell you about the Gods." He unfolded the book, "then you will be better at protecting yourself from them. Knowledge is power remember."
Sniffling Shaprour leant in to look.

"I was first shown this at about your age." He paused as he remembered sitting with his father and sisters looking at it and being most interested in War. He should regret that now, but he couldn't change the past. He asked his son, "which Gods do you know?"

"The Dragon Lord of course." Shaprour smiled and looked up for confirmation.

"Correct." Ozanus replied and began to point out the others.

He decided that he didn't need to show his son the beginning of the book. He didn't need to add to his young son's nightmares. His son carefully took the book from his father's lap and stared at the painted pictures like Ozanus had done. Ozanus gave him a few minutes before asking, "what else do you want to know?"

Shaprour looked behind them, into the shrine, "is that the Dragon Lord?"

Ozanus looked back at the stone statue, "yes that is. Men from our family have been coming here for generations for peace, advice and to give offerings."

Shaprour looked at his small smooth palm and then at the one of Ozanus' that lay on his father's knee, palm up.

"Not today, you are too young." Ozanus reassured his son.

"The scar on your arm?"

Ozanus held his left wrist, recalling the madness of the moment when it had happened and the fact that power seemed to be lying dormant within him. He had no idea when it would emerge. He had a feeling none of the Suwars had used theirs during the battle with Timijin either.

He wondered then if Strife had been destined to happen even if he had properly destroyed Bloodlust or not. He finally replied, "honouring the Gods. You are too young yet but one day when you have earnt the privilege to be known as a Suwar you will do so. Promise me you won't try doing it?" Ozanus ended sternly.

"Yes papa." Shaprour answered solemnly.

In a brighter tone he said, "now, I am actually going to give an offering to our Dragon Lord and you can watch." Ozanus stood and ducked into the shrine. Shaprour followed him in out of curiosity.

Knelt before the altar Ozanus looked up at the statue and wondered whether he should organise for it to be cleaned and repainted. He glanced at his son who was looking at how his father had knelt with his calves tucked under him and was copying. Ozanus couldn't help smiling for a moment before becoming serious again.

He pulled his knife from its sheath and bowed his

head, *"thank you for watching over the Valley, the dragons and the Suwars. Thank you for protecting my wife and son."*

He sliced across the scar on the palm of his hand and winced as he cut a nerve he hadn't destroyed. He let the blood pool in his cupped hand before kneeling up and pouring the blood into the bowl.

Shaprour stared in astonishment as the statue glowed and a voice spoke from no obvious place, *"I am glad to see you back and growing stronger again. War has poorly used you. Your Nejusana did well."*

"Yes she did. This is my son and the heir to Keytel."

"I am aware of him."

"Will I see him grown to be an adult?"

There was an ominous silence.

Ozanus looked at his son who was staring up at him with curiosity. He couldn't think of anything to say. Once again the Dragon Lord had shown His true colours and had justified once again why he had stepped away from being Nejus. He briefly wondered whether he should just let Strife take the Valley out of pettiness but didn't think he had that in him and perhaps the Dragon Lord knew that.

Shaprour tugged at his father's sleeve, "papa, what did you say?"

"I thanked the Dragon Lord for protecting the Valley and you and your mother."

"What about you?"

"What about me?"

"Can I thank him for bringing you back?" Shaprour asked in complete innocence.

"Have you got something to offer him?" Ozanus asked with a soft smile.

"Some water?"

Ozanus nodded, "that will be enough. Go pour some in the bowl and say what you want to say."

Shaprour found the leather canister of water and approached the bowl. He poured all of it in his eagerness, into the stone bowl and shouted, "thank you for looking after papa and helping mama bring him back. Can you make sure he lives?"

The cave glowed golden and he looked to his father, "have I done it?"

Ozanus nodded with a smile, "he has accepted your offering."

Shaprour grinned and shouted at the statue, "thank you!"

Ozanus laughed, "you don't need to shout. Come here." He held his arms open and Shaprour fell into them with a giggle. Becoming serious Shaprour asked, "can I tell mama?"

"Of course."

"When can we come back here?"

"Whenever we need to." Ozanus replied solemnly, "shall we head back, I think you have lessons this afternoon."

"Yes. I'm learning how to shoot arrows. Can you do that?" Shaprour asked with a six year old's enthusiasm as he followed his father from the shrine.

"I used to be able to."

"Oh. Is that because your hand shakes?"

Ozanus was surprised by his son's observation. He paused on climbing down and looked up at where his son waited for help, "when I cut myself on my arm I hurt some nerves in my wrist so I have lost some control in it."

Shaprour nodded sagely, though Ozanus wasn't sure how much his son had understood.

Twenty-Four

He stayed the night again though he didn't sleep as easily as the last time. He lay there with Miryama curled up against him, her head resting on his shoulder. He had his eyes closed but he wasn't sleeping. He was listening for Shaprour to be disturbed in his sleep.

At some point he must have fallen asleep for when he woke it was by Shaprour bouncing on them. Miryama got up with their son leaving Ozanus dozing. She saw him off to his lessons before returning to find Ozanus getting up. As he got dressed he remarked with concern, "Miryama, Shaprour mentioned that recently Bloodlust has been coming to when he sleeps.

Miryama paused in her tidying and turned to look at her husband, "that explains the nightmares. They started after we got you back here but he never told me what they were about. Though he hasn't had any the last two nights while you have been here."

"He's scared that we are going to die and he's going to be killed."

"Is there anything we can do to stop them?" She asked with concern.

"I'm going to try. Do you have anyone as good as Mada now? I wish there was someone alive with her knowledge. I could use her advice right now, otherwise I'm going to have to go through the books." He said with a heavy sigh.

"What are you thinking?"

"I don't know. I'm High Priest, there has to be something I can do but never been taught. I wonder if I can make a barrier in Shaprour's mind like the one protecting the Valley." He frowned in his frustration.

"Have any of them tried contacting you?" He knew who she referred to, "no. I think War is keeping them at bay, not that he is talking either."

"How long do you think it will be before you are ready?" She asked, changing the subject.   She didn't reveal the fact she knew he had tried to hold a bow steady, the key weapon of any Suwar, and had failed. She had secretly watched him as he held his left wrist tight to his chest to try and stop the tremors and silently cry over it. She knew his skills with all weapons were his strengths and his pride was wounded that he couldn't use them all now. He had been able to hide it until Strife had come along. She watched him instinctively go to hold his left wrist still. She wanted to take hold of it and kiss the angry scar away. He said with a hint of anger, "I'm working on it."

"I know you are." She replied, trying to pacify him.

"I need to go to the library, so I'll see you later." He turned and walked away.

"I'll ask around for you." She offered.

"No, it's alright." He waved a hand dismissively.

Reluctantly he went to his brother. Ioan looked up from his desk in surprise at the sight of his brother knocking at the door frame before entering the study. His secretary, who was standing beside him, froze to the spot fearing a fight.

Ozanus, in Ioan's eyes looked haggard and older than his years. A year as Strife's prisoner had taken its toll on his older brother. He knew he should feel pleased but he didn't. He pitied his brother who was struggling to re-find himself and be the man everyone needed him to be.

Ioan put his pen down, "what can I do for you brother?"

Ozanus took a deep breath before saying, "I need some help with finding some books. I know you will have read most of them."

"Of course." Ioan couldn't help being a little smug, "what are you looking for?"

The secretary interrupted as Ioan stood, "sir, we need to finish this."

"Mallon, most of the country is under Strife's rule so I think it can wait." Ioan replied sharply.

"Yes sir, sorry sir. I'm come back later." The man bowed his head and left.

Ioan headed to the shelves, "what are you looking for?"

"Do we have anything that the ancient priests used to refer to? There must be some spell or draft that can block bad dreams."

"For you?" Ioan raised an eyebrow.

"Yes for me." Ozanus carefully lied.

"There are a few scrolls or there's the big book but it needs translating. I haven't managed to yet."

"Get it all out and we'll start looking." Ozanus said as he reached for the referred to big book and took it to the big table.

Soon Ioan was looking through the scrolls while Ozanus was working through the big book with the poor dictionary that had been worked on over the years by other Nejuses. He hoped there were no more pasted shut pages. He came across the pages that were ungummed by his father as he quickly flipped through the pages in the hope of stumbling across the answer he needed. He paused on the page and ran his hand over the tear stains as he glanced over at Ioan.

Annoyed at himself he flicked over the page. Being angry at his brother was not going to help his son right now. He closed the book, took a deep breath and started from the beginning again.

At the end of the table Ioan announced, "I think I've found something."

Ozanus looked over, "what?"

"Come over here." Ioan beckoned his brother across. Annoyed, but curious, Ozanus headed round the table to his brother.

There was an image of a man lying on an altar with a High Priest at the head of it. His hands hovered over the lying down man's head. Ozanus frowned, "that tells me nothing."

"It says about a man struggling with bad dreams, being bothered by the Gods."

"Could have done with this earlier." Ozanus grunted with a hint of bitterness.

"But then you wouldn't have met Miryama, defeated Timijin and become almost equal to our father in reputation and had Shaprour."

"And you wouldn't have become Nejus. I'm sorry you haven't had any children. I probably don't appreciate him as much as I should."

"It must have been tough for you." Ioan said quietly, "can you remember what they were like?"

Ozanus looked down at his younger brother, "a little. They loved each other and all of us." He looked down at the manuscript and contemplated the picture, "my journey with our father had only just begun and then it was taken away. I remember being so angry."

"And War took advantage?"

"I suppose." Ozanus shrugged.

"There is one problem with this possible 'ceremony' is

that you are High Priest and the patient." Ioan remarked, bringing the conversation back to the reason they were actually talking to each other.

"I'll work something out, may I?" Ozanus made to take the rolled manuscript.

"Of course but let's keep looking."

Miryama hurried into the house in the search of Ozanus. Coming to the study she froze in shock at seeing the brothers actually working together. They both looked up when they saw her with Ozanus asking, "everything alright?"

"I'm not sure. No one has seen Lhateso in the last few days. I don't know where she has gone. I'm guessing you haven't seen her?"

"Not since she asked if I would rescue her sister."

"And what did you say then?" She asked with fear.

"I wouldn't do it, but she could though it would be a foolish thing to do."

"Damn!"

"Oh fuck!" Ozanus exclaimed at the same time as he and Miryama realised. In his next breath he said, "I'm not ready, I'm not going."
Both Ioan and Miryama saw Ozanus visibly shiver.
Ozanus looked to his wife and sternly said, "and don't you think about it either."

"We can't abandon her like this." Miryama exclaimed.

"I have to agree with Ozanus." Ioan added, "if Strife finds you there and gets hold of you, he'll know Ozanus will come and rescue you at whatever cost."

"We have to go get her somehow. If it wasn't for her I wouldn't have known you were alive." She protested.

"I'll have a think about it." Ozanus answered sternly with a tone that said he was not to be challenged. He turned his attention back to the table and the books and scrolls on it.

Reluctantly Miryama left but knew she would have some work to do to get Ozanus to go. She knew it had to be him. She knew they couldn't just abandon Lhateso to an unknown but potentially fearful fate.

Twenty-Five

Everyone had been warned away from the clifftop temple for a private ceremony. By the altar stood Ozanus with his son, wife and Lylya, the only other person he felt he could truly trust to this very personal matter. He had spent the previous night and the day in the shrine mentally preparing himself and re-reading his notes. He felt sure it wouldn't work as he had none of the old powers of the High Priests but he had to try. Shaprour was the only heir so he needed to be fit and well to be able to take on such a task and shutting out Bloodlust would be the right thing to do.

Shaprour held tight to his mother's hand as the sun turned the sky red as it descended. He sensed something was going to happen. There was a serious atmosphere as his father appeared and approached the altar. His eyes were wide at seeing his father dressed for the occasion and walking straight backed with a wary confidence. Even his father's hand had lost its shake. He asked, "mama, why are we here?"

"Those bad dreams you are having we are going to try and make them stop."

"That's good." He remarked solemnly.

Miryama looked down at her son and wished she could turn back time somehow to take Shaprour back to a carefree time but she knew she couldn't. He was growing into a boy who would become a man who would have this last year guiding how he would form. She knew he loved his outdoor lessons but struggled with Ioan's teachings.

Ozanus had a feeling his wife had more confidence in him than he did. He had spent the last twenty-four hours preparing and hoping he would be able to carry out the ceremony. The Dragon Lord hadn't come to him but he had felt his father's presence in the shrine and it was that, that gave him the wary brief that he could do this for his son.

Reaching the altar Miryama smiled at him with faith he could do it. He nodded at Lylya to acknowledge her presence, "thank you for coming."

"You know I'll always help you whenever you ask." She responded with a tight smile, "why am I here?"

"I am about to try something that could be foolish and dangerous or something incredible and I didn't want Miryama here alone as I don't know what will happen." She looked down at Shaprour and guessed it involved her nephew, "let's begin then."

"Ready?" He looked to Miryama and Shaprour.

"Do you think you can really get rid of my bad dreams?" Shaprour asked.

"I'm going to try my hardest." He crouched down to his son's height, "now, I need you to drink this so that you sleep and so I can help you without hurting you."
He gave Shaprour a small vessel of liquid. His son cautiously took it and looked to his mother. She gave him a nod. He pulled the cork stopper out and drank it.

A few minutes later his eyes began to droop and Ozanus scooped him up and lay him on the altar. With a sigh the little boy rolled on to his side. Miryama cautiously asked, "what now?"

"We wait." He answered as he moved the bowl so that he could gently stretch his son out on his back. He looked westward to check on the sun and frowned to himself, wondering if it was lingering too long. Lylya moved around lighting a few torches so there was some flickering light to see by.

Miryama placed a blanket over her son and kissed his cheek. The draft had put him in such a deep sleep he didn't even stir like he usually did. She glanced over at Ozanus but he was standing at the edge of the clifftop now, staring out. Though she wanted to go to him she felt sure he needed the alone time more.

An hour later Shaprour twitched and then moaned. Lylya tapped Ozanus on the shoulder, "it's time."
"I know."
"Good luck," She gave his arm a squeeze, "you have it in you. Remember the mountain."
He gave her a tight smile, "thanks."
He took a deep breath to calm his nerves before turning to cross to the altar. He looked up to the moon and hoped it would prove to be a healing one. He dipped his hands in the water in the bowl on the altar that was reflecting the moon.

On the altar Shaprour let out a cry of anguish. Miryama couldn't stop herself saying, "please, hurry."
"This cannot be rushed." Ozanus retorted.
He went to stand at where Shaprour's turning head was. He sent up a silent prayer to the Gods and his father to help him through this, guide his hand when needed. He placed his purified hands on either side of his son's head and closed his eyes.

He felt the dormant power within him stirring and opening like a bud about to bloom. He felt the spirit of his father guiding him into his son's disturbed mind.

He stumbled into a desolate land where his son stood in the middle of it with a body of an indeterminate age but definitely older than his six years. A strand of hair was plaited and beaded in the style of the Daughters.

He stood within a landscape void of vegetation with black scars the only evidence of what had been. Surrounding the flat land was a high ridgeline. Silhouetted against the red sky was the ruins of a temple and the blackened skeleton of a dragon. Bloodlust emerged from the clouds, Miryama hanging from his jaws, dipped down low and then reappeared over the ridge. He circled the young man, taunting him.

Shaprour pulled back the string of his short bow armed with an arrow that looked like it wouldn't harm a fly. He turned on the spot following the copper scaled dragon until he was in a position to release.

It flew true and should have hit Bloodlust if he hadn't swung his head at the last moment and it hit Miryama. Miryama let out a scream. Bloodlust let her fall from his jaws. She landed on the ground with a bone shattering thud as he laughed, *"you failed again. Who should I kill next?"*

As he slowly circled Bloodlust spotted Ozanus and sneered, *"what do we have here?"*

Shaprour turned to see who his brother was looking at. The dreams tended to be one of three scenarios but this seemed to have become a new one. He stared at the sight of his father standing in his robe and cautiously asked, "father?"

Behind him Bloodlust landed and transformed into his human form in his copper breastplate and strolled across the ground to stand beside Shaprour and grinned, "why, hello father. What a pleasant surprise." He glanced sideways at his brother and remarked, "do you think if I kill my brother here he will die in his sleep?" He pulled out his knife as he looked to Ozanus, challenging him.

Ozanus' hand instinctively went for his sword and didn't find it there. He growled his frustration as Bloodlust laughed, "it seems you came unprepared, perhaps I should kill you instead then Strife will be free to rule the whole world and War can rot as I take his place."

"Not if I can help it." Ozanus growled. He stared at his human son and gave him a nod of encouragement.

Shaprour stared at him for a moment and then at his godling brother and realised what was about to happen. He closed his eyes and imagined his father dressed to fight, a dragonscale breastplate, like his mother's, a sword at his side and dragon handled knife tucked in his belt. He opened his eyes and nodded at his father.

Ozanus smiled, back in control. He shrugged off his robe revealing what he now wore underneath. Bloodlust sneered, "come to play the hero have we? You can't stop me. You know you could die here and what then? My mother and brother will still die."

"Then I will have died trying." Ozanus retorted and pulled out his sword. He knew that though Bloodlust had picked up his sword skills quickly he hadn't been taught everything. He added, "Shaprour is no challenge, come and try me."

"Oh, willingly." Bloodlust swept Shaprour out of the way as if he didn't even exist as he pulled out his own sword.

Shaprour landed hard on the ground and couldn't help feeling relieved that Bloodlust's attention was focused away from himself. He watched as his father adjusted his posture, preparing himself for the fight that was coming.

Ozanus knew what was coming and prepared for Bloodlust's first strike. He brought his sword up as Bloodlust's came down. The swords clashed before the two men retreated. Bloodlust went in again and again and each time Ozanus defended himself.

With his father's stamina and skill tested Bloodlust changed tact as he realised his father was returning to full strength. He went to slash at his father's legs. Ozanus leapt backwards out of the way and as Bloodlust approached again his defence pushed Bloodlust's sword out of the way and hooked a leg behind the younger man's. Bloodlust went flying backwards and landed flat on his back.

Ozanus approached and pointed the point of his sword at Bloodlust's throat, "will you die if I kill you here?"

"I am a God and can't be killed." Bloodlust growled and swiped at his father catching his calf. Ozanus staggered back, trying to ignore the pain.

It gave Bloodlust the space to leap back to his feet. In frustration he ran at his father, bringing his sword up to try and slash Ozanus' chest and face. Ozanus easily hit the sword away and in a quick movement hit the other with the pommel of his own sword in his nose.

Bloodlust cried out in pain and tears welled up in his eyes as he grabbed his nose, blood streaming from it. With Bloodlust distracted Ozanus took a moment to line up his next move. He angled his sword to stab Bloodlust in the side and then hoped he would be able to slash his son's throat afterwards.

He stabbed the godling in his side. Bloodlust howled and lashed out with his own sword catching Ozanus off guard. Ozanus dropped his sword and grabbed the deep slice on his arm and retreated.

Bloodlust threw his sword away and ran for the ridgeline, turning into a dragon and flying off. Ozanus sank to the ground breathing heavily.

Shaprour ran over, "father?! Are you alright?"

"I will be. I'm here for you though."

"For me? How did you get into my dream?"

Ozanus smiled, "magic." He searched in a pocket and pulled out a small vial. Becoming serious he went on, "you need to drink this."

Shaprour eyed it warily, "why?"

Ozanus slowly pulled himself to his feet, "to stop these dreams, to stop Bloodlust coming and tormenting you." Shaprour cautiously took the vial and took out the stopper. He downed it in one and threw the vial away. He wondered if he would feel any different. He looked down at his body to see if there were any changes and when he looked up his father had gone.

With a heavy groan Ozanus let go off his son, his hands tried to grip the edge of the altar as he sank to the temple's floor.

Lylya and Miryama had watched in silence as Shaprour had become still and Ozanus' body began to twitch. Lylya whispered, "What do you think is happening?"

"I don't know."

They fell back into silence as they saw blood stain his trousers and shirt until they saw Ozanus fall to the ground. Lylya ran to her brother, crying out his name. He carefully sat up and blinked as he tried to work out where he was. Working out it was Lylya next to him he said, "tell Nimib I need her first thing in the morning and then get me stitched up."

"Ozanus, what happened?"

He looked up at Miryama and without emotion answered, "I have a job to finish."

"Ozanus, what happened?"

"I'll tell you later. Help me up." He held out a hand and Lylya pulled him to his feet. He looked over at Miryama and asked, "how is he?"

"Will he be alright?" Miryama asked.

"He'll sleep it off. Hopefully I've done enough. Can you carry him?"

"Of course." She said as she carefully picked their son up. With concern she asked, "what about you?"

"You know me." He gave her a tight smile, "I'll be alright."

"Let's get you down to the house. You must be exhausted by now." Lylya interrupted, trying not to see the looks passing between the pair. She pulled his uninjured arm over her shoulder and led him limping towards the path down.

Twenty-Six

He ached where Bloodlust's blade had slide deep into his arm and leg but he knew he couldn't rest. As soon as it was light enough to see dark objects he was up, wincing and dosing himself up with a pain killing draft. Lylya watched him from the doorway as Arno helped Ozanus put on a borrowed leather breastplate and then check the bandages on his arm and leg. She asked, "where are you going?"

"I badly injured Bloodlust last night. I can't let him heal. I need to finish him now."

"But you need time as well." She protested.
He turned and looked at her, "Lylya, I don't have the time. I need to get on and do this, take out Bloodlust and then work out a plan to wipe out Strife for good."

"Have you eaten?"

"I'll eat in the air."
Lylya looked to Arno who shrugged at her. She sighed. She knew nothing was going to distract him now, not even sleep, food or drink.

"Is Nimib ready?" Ozanus asked his manservant as he buckled on his sword, "and where is my bow?"

It was Arno's turn to glance over at Lylya. She shook her head, she didn't want Ozanus dying through trying to do something his body was going to let him down on. Ozanus saw the look and turned. He held out his left hand and it was steady, "look, it's fine."

"Are you sure?" Lylya asked with concern.

"Arno, my bow." Ozanus ordered.

"I'll bring it out to you sir."

"Good. And Nimib?"

"I got her ready before coming to you." Arno bowed his head.

"Good." Ozanus answered as he wrapped his head scarf round his head.

Arno stepped back, "done sir." He held out Ozanus' coat for him to slip into.

"Excellent." Ozanus slipped into his coat and took his leather gloves and headed out of the room. Lylya stepped back to let him pass. She asked, "are you going to see Miryama first?"

"No time." He answered stiffly with a dismissive wave of his hand.

She followed him to the veranda and stopped on the steps and watched him stride across the remains of the lawn towards the arena where Nimib waited. Arno slipped past her with Ozanus' bow and a sandwich wrapped in a cloth. She sent up a silent prayer to the Dragon Lord to watch over him.

She waited till she saw Nimib rise up into the sky before heading into the village of tents to find Kenene. She wasn't going to rely on the Gods to look after Ozanus. She burst into Kenene's tent and called out, "Kenene?"

"Tell her to go away." His wife muttered, "we aren't in Moronland."

"Ssh." He murmured and heaved himself out of bed. He stretched and pulled on a shirt before guiding Lylya out of his tent, "what is it Lylya?"

"Ozanus has gone to take on Bloodlust but he can't."

"Why not? Only he knows when he is ready." Kenene shrugged and made to go back to bed.

"No." She grabbed his arm.

He turned and studied what he could see of her face and asked with concern, "what's happened?"

"He fought with Bloodlust in Shaprour's dreams last night. They were both injured, him and Bloodlust, from it and he says he needs to finish the job off. I don't know what happened but he's not ready to do whatever he's planning."

"Where is he now?" Kenene asked, waking up now.

"He's gone already."

"What?! Why didn't you try to stop him?!" He exclaimed.

"I tried but you know what he's like once he has decided on a plan." She protested.

"True, fine. I'll go and try and catch him up." He headed back into his tent to get dressed.

"Thanks." She called out from outside.

"Best let the others know as well, just in case." He called back, waking his daughter who asked, "why are you getting dressed?"

"I've got to go somewhere but I'll be back." He reassured her.

High in the sky, wrapped up in his coat over his breastplate, he said to Nimib, *"it's good to be up here again."*

"Where are we going?" She glanced round at her rider.

"To start the end of all this. Wake me when Titan's castle is in sight."

"Of course." She had more questions but she sensed Ozanus wasn't inclined to discuss his plan.

Several hours later Nimib called out, *"Ozanus?! The castle is in sight."*

"Mmm."

Nimib turned her head with concern and saw him slumped

in the saddle. She remarked to herself, *"what have you been doing to yourself?"* Out loud she shouted, *"Ozanus?!"*

He lifted his head, *"I'm here."*

"We'll be there soon. I hope you will tell me everything later."

He smiled, *"that's a promise."*

"Please be careful. What do you want to do now?"

"Circle the castle. Just to warn you this fight could either end up on the ground or stay in the air."

"Who are we about to go up against?" She asked with worry.

"Bloodlust." He answered grimly, *"we aren't going in quietly either."*

"You sure?"

"I'm back and I want them to know it."

"Are you fit enough?" She asked with concern.

He declined to answer for he knew he wasn't but he couldn't give Bloodlust a chance to heal. He needed to fix where he had messed up.

As Nimib turned to circle the castle he asked, *"ready?"*

"As ready as I can be."

"Let's hear it then." He grinned and rose up in his saddle to get a better view as Nimib let out the loudest roar she could give which echoed around the walls of the castle. As the sound died down he shouted, "get out here Bloodlust! Let's settle this here and now!"

Inside the castle Bloodlust heard the roar and pricked up his ears. He dropped the drained body to the floor where three others also lay. He wiped blood from his mouth. He stood and stretched. He touched his nose and was satisfied that it had healed. He had winced when he had stretched so fingered the area where his father had stabbed him. It was still tender. Another body's worth of blood and it would have healed. For the moment he would have to live with a seeping wound.

He pushed open the windows of his room and without a backwards glance or second thought he responded to Ozanus' call to fight. He leapt from the window. His body morphed into his dragon form in mid-air and answered Nimib's roar.

Nimib turned to see who had responded, *"is that him?"*

"Yesss." Ozanus hissed. He peered over Nimib's head trying to see if Bloodlust's wounds could be used to his advantage. As Bloodlust curled his way towards them he couldn't see any sign of the deep side wound and swore. He had hoped to be able to fire some of his arrows into Bloodlust to bring him down so he could finish him for good, but that wasn't to be. He shouted to Nimib, *"keep him busy."*

"What are you going to do?"

"I don't know yet. Just keep him away from you. Wear him out."

"On it." Nimib shouted with just a little too much glee. She felt sure Ozanus was already coming up with a new plan.

She twisted round and flew straight past Bloodlust, taking him by surprise and flicked her tail into his long body, catching him with her tail. He roared out in anger and twisted round to chase after her as she pushed herself upwards with her wings, creating distance between them. He was more lithe than her and with a flick of his tail quickly closed the distance and snapped at her tail.

She flicked her tail at him again, catching his snout, before diving down to escape. She saw dragons starting to rise up and shouted, *"hurry up Ozanus! More are coming!"*

"Keep going, tire him. He's got to be as tired as me."

In a wide corkscrew around Bloodlust she began to

rise again while wishing there was the heat of the afternoon and the thermals that would have helped her. Bloodlust snapped at her every time she came past, twisting his own body to try and get at her. He felt the pain in his side and the blood seeping out of the not fully healed wound, opening it up.

Bloodlust spotted the dragons flying up, keen to join in the fun, and dived down roaring, *"they're mine! Leave! Now!"*

"No way are we letting you have all the fun." One shouted back and flew past Bloodlust.

With anger Bloodlust turned and pounced on the dragon with his front claws and ripped his neck open. The head hung low and Bloodlust released the now dead dragon and didn't even look down as it fell towards the ground. Another came in to attack him.

High above the squabbling Ozanus looked down in surprise at the turn of events. Nimib remarked between breaths, *"thank the Gods. I wasn't sure how I was going to keep going. Are you alright?"*

His thigh muscles ached from holding on but he wasn't going to say so. He could also feel the presence of War within him that he hadn't felt for the last few weeks. He felt sure the scent of blood was rousing Him out of his temporary slumber. He knew he needed to act now before War or Strife came. He ordered Nimib, *"go down so you are above him and as close as you dare."*

"What?!"

"I'm going to fall on to him."

"Are you crazy?!" She turned her head and stared at him. He gave a chuckle, *"a little."* He hadn't done anything so insane since he was a teenager at the height of feeling invincible, like they all did. They had all learnt acrobatics on dragons and he was about to head into a rather dangerous move that was dangerous even with two willing

dragons.

"Are you sure?" She asked again.

"Just be ready to catch me if I miss." He answered sternly, *"now go, while he's still distracted."*

With some reluctance she descended, keeping an eye on all the dragons but they seemed to be giving up now that three of them had been killed. Bloodlust was still distracted by them and acknowledged the shadow over him too late. He felt something heavy land on his back and turned to look. He hissed, *"you!"*
Ozanus snarled, *"prepare to die."*

"I'll kill you!" Bloodlust roared, beginning to buck in an attempt to get Ozanus off his back. Ozanus stretched out along the godling's back and held tight, digging his hands between scales. With a roar of fury Bloodlust twisted vertically upwards to try and shake Ozanus off.

Ozanus felt wet on his leg and glanced back and spotted the open sore of the side stab he had done to Bloodlust in his son's dream. Carefully he started to shift backwards to stab at it with his knife.

Before he could do it an arrow flew into the open sore. Bloodlust roared in pain as Ozanus tried to work out where it had come from. He looked round and spotted Kenene putting another arrow to his bow string. Neither acknowledged the other. They didn't need too as they had worked together for so long.

The smell of iron rich blood grew stronger as Ozanus reached down to and pulled out the arrow, nearly falling off Bloodlust's back in the process. He held tight. With blood now starting to run from the new wound the scent became intoxicating, but it wasn't his nostrils that was sniffing it. Ozanus found his mind beginning to cloud over and tried to fight it. Now was not the time for War to make His presence known.

From his dragon Kenene watched as Ozanus began

to transform. He shouted to his dragon, *"get further away. Now!"*

"Is what is happening, what I think it is?" His dragon asked as she turned upwards to join Nimib.

"Yes, but I don't think he knows it." Kenene shouted.

Below them Ozanus' body began to stretch and with a groan he submitted to the God's dominating willpower. He shouted inwardly but it wasn't heeded. Ozanus' changing body slipped from Bloodlust's back and with glee Bloodlust flew upwards and then turned to watch Ozanus fall to the ground but that wasn't what he saw.

Twisting in the air was a new dragon. He shouted, *"where is he?"*
The copper and green dragon turned, sun reflecting off his broken and scarred scales and snarled, fresh blood on two limbs where Lylya's stitches had been snapped and reopened on the wounds from the night before. Bloodlust didn't know who this was but his blood ran cold. With a hint of fear to his voice he demanded, *"who are you?"*

"I am your father, I am War." War roared and flicked his tail to push himself up towards Bloodlust, his mouth open wide revealing blood stained teeth and a broken spear trapped between two sharp teeth. One canine had a ragged break to it.

The first thought that came to Bloodlust was to flee. He turned and flew upwards but it didn't take long for the giant immortal dragon to catch up with him. War snapped down on Bloodlust's tail and a high pitched yelp escaped from Bloodlust's mouth as War tugged down and Bloodlust lost all flying momentum. He turned to attack War and felt bone snap. He clawed at War's scarred snout and the God didn't even flinch. Bloodlust snarled in frustration and then the tip of his tail was bitten through and he broke free, blood streaming from it.

War's eyes flashed at the taste of blood. He

swallowed the flesh of his son. He swallowed the flesh and licked his teeth, savouring it like an addictive drug.

Bloodlust didn't care that the dragon was a God, no one was allow to defeat him. He swooped up, all four claws ready to rack War's body. War just laughed, the claws merely tickled him. With one of his own claws he whacked Bloodlust knocking him briefly senseless.

Bloodlust shook his head to clear the fogginess and roared, *"no one kills me!"*
War exclaimed, *"someone can and nearly has, a mere mortal."*

"I would have drunk his blood before I died." Bloodlust retorted.

"You have proven to be no son of mine." War pronounced in disgust.

"I am not your son!" Bloodlust protested, panic in his eyes, *"I am Strife's."*

"You disgust me." War spat, *"you are worthless to me."* He had seen how Bloodlust fought and even with Ozanus' training there was only the barest disguise of control hiding the impulsiveness. To be of use he needed full control of himself and then the course of this time would be different. War was showing his fickleness. He didn't need Bloodlust, he would use Ozanus and all of his followers and then a new world would begin! Strife had chosen poorly.

Bloodlust was not going to die without a fight. The one advantage he had was he was smaller so could twist and turn and nip in and out of attacks on War. But he was weakening from blood loss from his tail, Ozanus' wound and the new racking wounds from War's claws.

Though War looked large and slow moving he was a God fueled on blood and could out pace Bloodlust if he wanted to but he had chosen to torment his son instead. He knew it wouldn't be long before Bloodlust's heart would beat its last. He could smell it in the blood leaving the godling's body.

As Bloodlust came in for one last attempt to save himself, jaws open to attack War's throat and perhaps drink some immortal blood, War snapped his head round and bit down first. His teeth broke through the skull and spine and he swallowed Bloodlust's head whole while the body began its descent to the ground to join those that were already down there.

Twenty-Seven

Strife had kept his senses open to the events outside the castle. With a wiry sneer he acknowledged War's sudden presence and felt a little disappointed in Bloodlust as he felt the youth's lifeblood fading. Another year and he probably would have been undefeatable and might have been more of an equal to War, the War he remembered from when he had ruled the world.

He heard War's roar and responded to it. He burst out of the castle's walls like they were a stack of building blocks not thick several hundred-year-old walls built to protect the inhabitants from dragons. With a deafening roar that was heard in the Valley he rose into the sky. The other dragons who had been beaten back by Bloodlust rose up to respond to his call.

Kenene stared in disbelief and horror at the black dragon emerging from the castle who was even bigger than War. He closed his eyes to hide the hideous image of the Basilisk and sent up prayers. Never had he seen such a colossal monster. Was he about to witness the end? He didn't know whether to flee or stay. Nimib called, *"what do we do?"*

War looked up and saw the two dragons and the rider. He shouted up, *"go now! This is not the right time."*

"What about you?" Kenene cried back, *"and Ozanus?"*

"Just go." War snarled and turned to face Strife. He needed to distract his kin long enough so the others could escape and then he could make his own escape. Ozanus was injured and exhausted from the night and he needed the man at full strength to use him for the battle that was coming.

Kenene shouted over to Nimib, *"let's retreat to a safe distance."*
He felt sure War would have to release Ozanus at some point and if they were all in the sky then he would need to be caught in the air. As the three of them retreated he muttered to himself, "damn the Gods."
He didn't know who had got the worst short straw from their immortal overlords, Ozanus or his father. His dragon asked, *"what do we do?"*
"We just have to wait."
"Is this the end?"
"I don't think so. I think this is a warmup."
"Who's going to win?"
"I honestly don't know. He really is in the hands of the Gods." He sighed and then chuckled, *"well, claws."* Anything to chase away the fear.

Emboldened by Strife's presence those dragons that had answered his call a year previous went on the attack. They could sense War was not up to full strength and it was worth a try especially as they were all still hyped up from their earlier tussle with Bloodlust.

Strife didn't stop them from flocking towards War as it would weed out the weak ones. He smirked, *"War, you have finally decided to reveal yourself then. Are you coming back to me? Why did you have to kill our kin?"*

"He has been a disappointment." War snarled as he swatted a dragon away with his tail as it got too close, *"call off your pets."*

"Pets. I like that." Strife laughed, *"I can't call them off any more than you can. Now, are you going to come peacefully? With you by my side we can rule this world together again."*

War snapped at a dragon who got to close before answering, *"this is a different world now."*

"I am well aware of that." Strife snarled.

War flew upwards and slowly circled the monstrous sized dragon, *"I have things to do."*

"In my favour I hope." Strife snapped as War passed his snout, wary of the god who he once called son. He had always had an independent streak and his presence heralded conflict. That was why he had been created but he had been out of Strife's company too long and he was going to be hard to bring back. Frustration welled up in him and he began to coil around War like a snake with the plan to tighten himself round the god and remind him who he was.

War saw what was happening but the human body he was using was weakening. He couldn't move quickly enough for him not to feel the squeeze. He raked all four claws up Strife's body as he forced his way out.

Strife roared in pain and his coils loosened enough for War to escape but not without returning the favour. As War flew off Strife roared, *"come back you sly snake. This will be my win."*

Returning to the castle to nurse his wounds he knocked the tower off with his tail in rage. He needed War with him to bring the conflict he needed to feed off and truly rule the world again.

Kenene watched War escape Strife's coils and fly upwards into the clouds being chased by the other dragons. Nimib called out in fear, *"What is he doing?"*

"I don't know." Kenene frowned, *"be ready for whatever comes next."*

"I can't stay here doing nothing." Nimib declared and headed into the clouds that were starting to turn black.

"We should leave here." Kenene's dragon remarked with concern and a wary glance at the clouds. Other gods seemed to be getting involved, but they didn't know which side they were on.

Minutes later Nimib came diving out of the clouds, blood seeping from fresh wounds and being chased by a dragon. The dragon pulled up at the sight of Kenene and Eciplso and fled. She cried out, *"look out, here He comes and it's not good."*

She had witnessed War trying to hold on to his form and hoping it was because he didn't want Ozanus to die. She knew that she couldn't let either of them fall into Strife's possession. She attacked the circling dragons who were sensing a weakening dragon, keeping them at protesting bay.

Out from the clouds, attempting to glide towards the ground was War. He wobbled as if he had stumbled over a stone. He spotted Kenene and his dragon and was aware of Nimib near by. He gave up then, retreating back into Ozanus and letting Ozanus be himself again.

Ozanus fell more heavily than War. Nimib flew in and grabbed him with her rear claws. She had to turn hard not to hit the ground. Kenene and his dragon swiftly flew down and called out, *"let's get to the ground where we can check him over."*

"Do you think that is wise?" Eciplso looked upwards expecting dragons to emerge from the clouds.

"Between himself and War he's sustained some serious injuries. I need to check him over first. Nimib, head down." Nimib wasn't going to object, she was tired now from being so long in the air and trying to hover in one spot. She descended, followed by Eciplso.

Kenene crouched over the prone Ozanus as he said,

"keep an eye out for anything. We aren't safe yet."
Ozanus' eyes were closed tight and his face was contorted
with pain. Kenene checked each limb for broken bones. He
searched in his saddle bag for anything he could use as
bandages. He grumbled to himself at the craziness of it all.
He wished he had brought others with him so they could fly
together as protection. He felt sure the monstrous dragon
wouldn't have given up. He looked to Nimib, *"Nimib, I
need you to fly back to the Valley and bring back help. I
need to try and stitch the worst of the wounds and I don't
dare move him."*

"Are you going to be alright on your own?"

*"I'm armed and Eciplso isn't as tired as you are. We'll
look after him. Go, go now."*

"Be safe." Nimib said before heading skyward and
towards the Valley.

It wasn't hard to miss the fighting going on above
their heads. The whole encampment was out, necks craned
upwards or peering out from watchtowers. For many it was
the first time they had seen their dragon overlords and
watching them fighting was frightening.

As it appeared to come to an end many broke off
from watching and rubbed sore necks to go about their
daily routines and discuss what they had witnessed. One
group remained watching. They had come up against the
Suwars before and the fact one was hovering near by
suggested to them it hadn't come to an end yet. They
guessed the Suwar was waiting for something. There was
only one rider but two dragons so somewhere up there was
another rider and no one had fallen from the sky apart from
five dragons.

They saw a serpentine dragon appear from the
clouds. They watched as the dragon changed to a human
and the two dragons descend to the ground. The leader of

the group turned to the others, "there is a dragon hiding in a human! We have to get them and bring them back for our lord."

"They'll be gone by the time we get out there and there is another rider as well."

"There are more of us than them." Another pointed out, eager to get on the good side of the group's leader.

"And imagine the rewards if we bring them to our new lord." The leader grinned.
The thought of money, women and anything else they could imagine was enough to create a group of nodding heads and exclamations of, "let's do this!"

"Great, now quickly, we need weapons and horses before anyone else comes up with the same idea and beats us to it."

"Hey! Hey! There's a dragon taking off." Someone shouted, pointing in the direction where they had seen them land.

"Can you see anyone on it?" The leader asked.

"No."

"This is even better then. Come on, let's get moving."

Soon after they were all on horseback, thrashing their horses to gallop across the plain towards the distant shape of the grounded dragon. They were armed with hooked pikes, spears, bows and swords. They weren't going to take any chances.

Eciplso sniffed the air and then turned her body and saw the group of riders heading their way, *"Kenene, we have company."*

"Good or bad?" He asked as he snapped a thread with his teeth. He paused in rethreading the needle and glanced up at Eciplso.

"They are coming from the camp below the castle. Can we get him up?"

"I've not finished yet. I need to get these wounds stitched up otherwise he will bleed out." Kenene frowned and looking down at the bloodstained ground around Ozanus' deathly still body. The only sign he was still alive was the fact his chest rose up and down. He looked back up to the dragon and said, *"can you keep them busy?"*

"I can try. Where's your sword?"
Kenene pulled it from its sheath and lay it beside him, *"I'll keep going if you keep them busy for as long as possible."* He answered with urgency.

She nodded and promised, *"I won't let either of you die."*

"Thanks." He smiled grimly at her, *"now, go."*
Eciplso rose into the air.

Kenene briefly covered Ozanus' body with his to keep the dust off the wounds. He sighed as he looked at Ozanus' torn body. Along with the re-opened wounds from the night he now had jagged claw marks on his chest and back from where War had been injured. His clothes were torn to pieces and the breastplate was useless now. His knife had somehow managed to stay put in his belt.

With tongue sticking out in concentration he threaded the needle and prayed that Nimib would be back with help soon but he doubted she would as it was a good two hours flying to be done along with getting dragons saddled up.

There were more of them than she thought and they had come prepared. As she flew down low in the hope of terrifying the horses she noted the abundance of weapons. She swooped round and came down low again and reached for a man and horse with her claws. As she began to lift her victim she felt something grab her other foot and tug down hard. Her body meant she couldn't quite see but she knew she had been hooked. She twisted upwards, dropping the rider and freeing herself. She roared in pain and frustration.

She was tired, she was carrying an egg and however important Ozanus was Kenene was more so as her rider. She knew Ozanus could fend for himself and there were plenty of others to lead the Suwars and anyway. Wasn't Ioan Nejus now?

She did a few half-hearted fly-bys before turning and headed for Kenene. The riders were already within arrow shooting distance but they were being careful as they didn't know which person they wanted.

Kenene could feel the ground shaking from the thundering hooves. He quickly finished the stitches he was doing and got stiffly to his feet. He grabbed his sword and was ready to take a swing at the first rider who was already throwing himself off his horse. He didn't get a chance as Eciplso flew down and grabbed him. He swore at her as she pushed him up towards her back and his saddle, *"what the hell are you doing?! Get back there now! We can't just leave Ozanus!"*

"I'm sorry Kenene, but your life and the one I carry are more important." She responded grimly.

He swore again, *"you bitch!"* Never had he felt so angry with her. If he could have survived the fall he would have made a jump for it and fought to his own death trying to protect his lord.

"We have to tell them what happened." She protested weakly.

"Nimib can do that." He exclaimed and looked back to where Ozanus' body was now surrounded by the riders and feared the worst. Reluctantly he turned to face towards the Valley and face the fact his dragon had betrayed them.

They met up with reinforcements with the Valley still in sight. Gaerwn was leading them and spotting Kenene on Eciplso he hallooed. "you got away then." He noted the dragon shifted uncomfortably and frowned and rephrased the question, "what happened?"

Kenene shook his head and unwrapped his scarf to speak, "he's been captured or he's dead."
That quickly went through the group. One asked, "what do we do now sir?"
Another shouted, "we have to go get him."
Kenene and Gaerwn looked at each other. Even the distance couldn't hide Kenene's pained expression. They would talk later. Gaerwn ordered, "head back to the Valley Kenene and we'll talk later."
Head bowed from tiredness and drained adrenalin reserves Kenene said to Eciplso, *"back to the Valley."*
She briefly thought about apologising but felt it would be rejected and she didn't regret what she had done. For once preservation was more important.

For the rest of the group Gaerwn raised his hand in the air and ordered, *"we go forward!"*
He needed to determine if Ozanus was still alive even if it wasn't possible to rescue him. Though he wanted to he couldn't blame Kenene until he knew the full story. Ozanus was too independent and it could well have happened even without Kenene there.

There was a brief discussion over Ozanus' body, "is he alive?"
"How do we get him back?"
"We sure this is the one who fell out of the sky?"
"Well he looks half dead so must have been."
"Hey, his chest is still rising so he's alive."
"Quiet!" Their leader ordered, hands on hips. He nudged Ozanus' body with the bottom of his spear while studying the stitched wounds. The men around him fell silent and shifted uncomfortably as they felt his eyes glaring at them. He went on, "he's very important. I would have left him to die but the rider was stitching him up. Make a stretcher out of spears and belts. Hurry!"

The men quickly worked together to make an improvised stretcher and then carefully lifted Ozanus on to it. Someone quietly slipped the knife from the body's belt and slipped it into his belt with a small smile of satisfaction.

It took them a few hours to get up to the castle as the horses were tired from the gallop over. They skirted round the encampment so that no one could try to take their prize. They were watched by wary eyed children who fled when one of the group shouted and mock charged them.

Reaching the gates of the castle they demanded entry. The two guards, dressed in black and holding hooked spears glared at them, "why should we?"
The leader of the group clicked his fingers and the group parted to reveal their prize. He grinned, revealing surprisingly good teeth, "I think our Lord would like to see what we have."
There was a roar though no obvious source, "let them enter and take them to the Hall."
One of the guards raised an arm and the gates were opened enough to let them through. They didn't bother showing the group the way.

Strife was studying one of his wounds when he had sensed the presence of War, weak but still alive. He smirked to himself. He bet War hadn't planned for this. He had never thought a Valley dragon would have abandoned its human protector so easily with just a little nudge. He hoped that nudge would grow into something bigger within the Valley and then he could take it over. But first he would enjoy the moment.

Sat on his throne, dressed in black, he watched the group from the camp nervously enter the otherwise empty Hall. They froze at the far end, wary of the black skinned man sitting at the other end radiating power that was forcing their spines to shrink. He beckoned them forward with his one hand.

They shuffled forward till they stood at the foot of the dais looking up at the low wide throne and the man cross legged on it. One arm with no hand leant on an arm rest. He wasn't going to let them know he knew who they had and how keen he was. He clicked his fingers and the group parted to reveal the improvised stretcher. He sneered, "a body, so what? What do you expect me to do with it?" The leader stepped forward and declared, "this is not just any body sir, this is a God."

"A god?"

"We witnessed him fall from the sky as a dragon and become a man. The fact he still lives suggests he is immortal. We thought of you when we saw him." The man looked hopeful.

"And what do you want in return?" Strife asked suspiciously though already contemplating eating them all, "no, let me guess." He held up his hand as the man before him opened his mouth. Strife smirked, "money, women and a place in my new world?"

"Yes." The man stood his ground.

"And if I refuse?" Strife asked, standing up and stepping down from the dais revealing his giant size.
The man backed up nervously.

"Thank you for your gift but I have no use for you, any of you."

They were all frozen to the spot as Strife grew and grew, taking over the room in his immortal form. His coils encircled the group gathering them together as his wide mouth filled with two rows of teeth came towards them. Their mouths opened in silent screams as Strife crunched on their bones and then swallowed them.

His wounds from War healed as he shrank back down to his human form. He bent over the stretcher and smiled, *"welcome back my son. Look at you…"*

He ran his hand over some of the wounds and then up to
Ozanus' face. He closed his eyes as he concentrated on
Ozanus' mind. He found the man's anger which had drawn
War to him. A smile danced on his lips. The anger may
have mellowed but it wouldn't take much to rise that back
to the surface, but first the body needed to heal.

Twenty-Eight

Gaerwn found Kenene on the cliffs by the entrance of the Valley. He approached carefully while brushing sweat off his forehead. He called out, "Kenene?"

Kenene briefly turned to see who had called before returning to stare out. His life as a Suwar was over and he didn't know if it was worth living now. His dragon had let him down badly and he didn't know if he could ever trust her again.

With anyone else Gaerwn would have been going in hard but he could already see that Kenene was feeling guilty from the hunched shoulders and crossed arms. It had taken a while but he had grown to like the man and could see what Ozanus saw in the man who was a lot older than them. Another time and place he would have made a good candidate for Chieftain.

He came up alongside the man, "you want to talk?" Kenene's arms remained folded across his chest and he continued to stare out.

Gaerwn reached out, "what happened Kenene?"

"Everything that could go wrong did."

"Don't blame yourself."

"Who else can I blame? I swore to protect our Nejus all those years ago, just like you and I haven't." Kenene pointed out bitterly. He glanced at Gaerwn, "my dragon let us down. How many know?"

"No one knows what happened. Only you do." Gaerwn
replied though he knew rumours were already spreading.

"Good." Kenene muttered.

"What happened?"

"I honestly don't know. I arrived too late to stop it.
War…." He turned and looked at Gaerwn, "War is actually
inside him."
Gaerwn stared at Kenene's wide eyes and knew the man
was speaking the truth.

"And now… Now we don't know if he's alive or dead
again. He could be back in Strife's control, and I don't
think it will end well." Kenene turned to look out on to the
plains again.

Gaerwn did the same and they stood there in silence
for a bit until Gaerwn patted his friend on the shoulder and
left to arrange a meeting to discuss the next steps to get
Ozanus back and protect the Valley.

Ozanus was placed in a bed by Strife's own hands
as a shaking doctor was brought in. Strife looked up at the
man, "clean and stitch up his wounds and then force this
down his throat."
Strife ripped open the veins in his wrist with his teeth and
allowed the blood to pulse into a cup. He handed the cup to
the wide eyed doctor before pinching the wound shut to
make it heal. The doctor nodded and hurried to tend to his
patient.

Strife, his wound healed, demanded, "where are
those two girls?"
A guard threw them both to the floor in front of him. They
didn't dare look up but held tight to each other's hand.
Strife stared down at the sisters and tried to work out what
Bloodlust saw in them. With a frown he said, "you are no
longer Bloodlust's playthings, you are now mine. You will
take care of this man. If he's hungry you will feed him. If

he wants sex let him have it. If he wants blood give it to him."

One of them dared to look up, the healthier one. The other looked half dead as if Bloodlust had drunk from her too much. The new girl exclaimed, "blood?!"

"Ssh Lhateso!" Aerrana pulled her sister's face down as she saw Strife's eyes flash with anger.

Strife demanded, "do you understand?"

"Yes sir." Aerrana said to the floor.

"Good. I will be back in the morning and if he dies you all die." Strife stalked from the room.

The girls stayed where they were knelt staring at the bed wondering who it was. The doctor turned and glared at them, "come on, unless you want to die, I need some cloths and clean water. Find him some clothes as well."

"Lhateso, you stay here, I know this place better than you."

Lhateso just nodded as Aerrana hurried from the room.

"Get his clothes off." The doctor ordered and then commented quietly to himself, "looks like someone has started sewing up some of these wounds."

Reluctantly Lhateso got up and approached the bed. She stared in disbelief at Ozanus lying so still on the bed. She murmured, "I know him."

"I don't know about you but I want to keep my life. Get on with it girl." The doctor snapped.

She blinked, coming out of her trance.

She began to undress Ozanus, trying not to touch him as she didn't know how she felt about him. He had refused to help her when she had asked and now here he was, looking like he was going to die, and she was going to have to rescue him. She couldn't understand why he was so important. She felt sure there were others who would be just as good at leading as him.

Aerrana came back with supplies and as soon as she

had put them down Lhateso dragged her into a corner of the room and in a whisper exclaimed, "do you know who that is?"

"Who?" Aerrana hadn't had a chance to look.

"It's Ozanus, the Nejus Nuna sent us to find, who refused to come rescue you."

Aerrana looked across to the bed, "do you think he killed Bloodlust?"

"I don't know. You'll have to ask him. This is bad. We have to get him out of here." Lhateso exclaimed though a part of her thought he was better off in the castle and left to rot.

"No we can't." Aerrana frowned, "that will make Strife mad."

"I came here to get you away, not to keep you company. Bloodlust is dead. We can leave him here if that's easier and just escape ourselves. Go somewhere far away where nobody knows us. This isn't our fight. Let them kill themselves." Lhateso pointed out angrily.

"Help me." The doctor demanded and reluctantly the pair returned to him.

They helped him finish sewing up wounds and wrapping others in bandages. Then one of them carefully poured Strife's warm blood into Ozanus' mouth while the doctor propped him up. The doctor left with a sigh of relief and they made themselves a bed on the floor to share and prayed he would survive the night.

Strife strode in, startling the sisters wrapped in their cocoon of blankets, "how is the patient? Is he alive? Has he had anymore to drink?"

Aerrana grabbed Lhateso's arm and squeezed it hard in warning to stop her speaking for she could tell Strife wasn't expecting an answer as he already knew the answers.

They watched him in silence as he placed a hand on

Ozanus' forehead, fingers sprayed across it, and muttered something inaudible. Ozanus' body appeared to respond to his touch, a hand clenched into a fist for a few seconds and the muscles in his arm twitched. Strife looked thoughtful before turning on the sisters and shouting, "get out!"
Still clutching the blankets they ran out the door.

"Hmpfh." He slammed the door shut with a wave of his hand.

Looking down at Ozanus Strife wondered why he had even bothered with Bloodlust considering before him was a fully trained killer. He wondered whether he should have tried harder when they were up in the mountains but Ozanus was fit and strong willed then. His patience for War was long gone and he wanted him now. Starving him out of the man hadn't worked. But now both were in a weak state and easy prey for Strife.

He placed his hand on Ozanus' forehead again and sent himself deep into Ozanus' mind; just as Ozanus had done with his son two nights previously. But unlike Ozanus Strife was out to cause mischief and strife.

The world he stepped into was curiously barren and he wondered whether War was involved. Standing still he used all of his senses to try and detect some sign of life. He had nothing else to do and had plenty of time to wait.

An hour later he heard the sound of metal on metal and headed towards it. In an earth bound arena he was surprised to find a boy practicing with an almost faceless adult. The only identifying mark was a scar from where the eye would be to where the mouth would have been.

A wicked smile spread across Strife's face, was he really going to be able to change Ozanus' memories from such an early age? He laughed, he couldn't help himself, making the boy stop and look. The boy demanded, "who are you?"

"Hello child." Strife stepped closer, "I could be your

worst nightmare or your greatest ally."

"Step back." The boy challenged warily, "I am armed."

"I can see that."

"You are not hurting my father. I can kill you."
Strife looked contemplative then as he felt sure if Ozanus
put his mind to it he probably could, which is why he
needed the man on his side. He remarked, "you certainly
become a young man to fear in the future."

"I do?" The boy asked with wide eyes.

"Oh yes, but I'm not here to talk about that."

"You aren't?"

"Yes. Your father betrays you, you know." Strife said
softly, "he doesn't love you."

"Yes he does." Ozanus exclaimed.

"You have no mother or father. The Dragon Lord," Strife
spat the last two words out, "none of them love you." He
flicked a wrist and the scene behind Ozanus changed. He
pointed behind the boy, "see."
Ozanus turned and saw his mother and father lying dead
with the shape of a god standing over them. Behind him
Strife went on, "see, he takes your parents away from you,
just as he takes your closest friend Diego too. And what
about your son? Your so-called wife keeps taking him
away. And don't forget your brother, he wants your son as
well."
At every new point he made Strife flicked his wrist and a
new scene was shown to Ozanus. Diego falling into the
sinkhole in the mountain; him and Miryama arguing and
she taking Shaprour away; Ioan sitting with Shaprour and
putting an arm round him as they studied a book on the
table together.

He smiled as he saw the boy's shoulders shudder
and knew he had got to him. He placed a hand on the boy's
shoulder and said, "but I won't leave you."
Ozanus' tear-stained face looked up, "you won't?"

Strife shook his head, "never. I can help you get your son back and make him love you."

"You can?" Now it was the grown Ozanus in front of him. The one who knew he was failing as a father, who struggled to be a father to his son.

Strife smiled, "yes I can, but first you need to heal. I will be back soon."

Strife faded away leaving the Ozanus in the dream looking forlorn.

Back in the room he felt the fever that was there. With surprising tenderness he dampened a cloth with cool water and placed it on Ozanus' forehead. One of his fingers became a claw and he carefully opened one of his veins on the handless wrist. He held Ozanus' mouth open and let his blood drip in. Some of the more superficial cuts were already healing.

Satisfied he left the room and found the sisters standing outside. He snapped, "get back in there and get him well. Remember what I said last night, that remains the same."

"Yes sir." Aerrana meekly responded and pushed her sister ahead of her, back into the room. Once in she said, "stay with him and I'll get us some food."

"What does Strife want with him?" Lhateso asked, staying where her sister had pushed her and staring at the bed.

Aerrana sighed, "I don't know and don't really care. I am just working on staying alive. Stay here and don't do anything foolish while I find some food."

Every day he came to Ozanus' room, twice a day to visit the man's mind and feed him a little more of his own blood. Soon the body was responding as much as the mind.

Lhateso dared to open the door and peer through the

crack and saw Strife's hand on Ozanus and the body
twitching and the face grimacing. She wondered what
Strife was doing to the man.

Inside Ozanus' mind Strife continued to tinker with
memories and torture Ozanus' thoughts. He didn't always
come across Ozanus as the boy. Sometimes he was a
teenager and sometimes he was an adult. As the early
memories became corrupted so did the future ones making
it even easier for Strife to target his taunts and bring
Ozanus one step closer to his side.

The Dragon Lord tried to make his presence known
to protect his man but with little success. The sky turned
golden and Strife just laughed, *"you can't get him. I'm in
control now."*
Ozanus asked, "who are you talking to?"
 "No one important. I'm the most important thing to you."
The boy Ozanus just nodded.

Strife put the troubled relationship with Ioan to
good use especially once the memories were so warped that
Ozanus couldn't remember anything good about him.
Whispering in his ear Strife told the adult Ozanus as they
watched the scene, "look at your brother. He took your title
from you, he just needs you dead now so he has everyone's
respect. He's been spreading rumours and no one trusts you
anymore. With you dead he can marry Miryama and take
your son as his own. If you go back to the Valley you won't
be allowed to live. Stay with me and have a whole new
army to lead."
Ozanus turned away from the scene, "I still have the
Suwars."
 "They've lost faith in you. You were left by your second.
He left you for dead. If it wasn't for me you would be
dead."
Ozanus frowned as he tried to remember who Kenene was

to him and how they had been together.

"What will you do?" Strife carefully asked to see how well he was doing in turning Ozanus.

"I'll destroy them all." Ozanus calmly said, hand on his knife.

Strife smiled, "and soon you can but we also need some of them. You can't lead without an elite group to obey your every command."

Ozanus smirked, "oh, I can sort that out."

Strife nodded, still smiling, "I'm sure you can." He placed his hand on the man's shoulder and squeezed it before fading away.

As for Miryama he found the memories of her rejecting him and exclaimed, "why did you even marry her? Look how she ignores you. Look how she takes your son away."

Ozanus tried to remember why she had departed so suddenly but his memories felt all screwed up. He felt sure there had been some happy times but couldn't remember any of them.

Strife flicked his wrist and they were in a tent, in the dark, before the fight with Timijin. He remarked, "she used you every step of the way, stole your masculinity. You should have been in control the whole time. Because of her you lost the battle with Timijin. Your riders lost faith in you then."

Ozanus' hands were fists as Strife fed his memory with images of him fighting for his life in the arena with some other Suwars and two Daughters of Scyth. Surrounding them in their seats was an audience shouting, "death! Death! Death!"

"Enough." Ozanus roared.

Strife looked at him, head on one side.

"I'll destroy them all." Ozanus growled. A sword

appeared in his hand and Strife knew his work was done. Strife remarked, "my work is done."

Twenty-Nine

Ozanus woke with a start. His body ached and was stiff from lack of use. He had no idea how long he had been unconscious. He tried to remember how he had even ended up unconscious but couldn't. His mouth felt dry. He carefully propped himself up on his elbows and looked around and spotted the two sisters staring at him. He licked his dry lips, "I'm thirsty. Where am I? Who are you?" Aerrana cautiously approached and asked, "can you not remember me?"

He frowned at her, "just get me something to drink."
Aerrana bowed her head and nodded.

"Not water." His nostrils twitched and he could sense her pulse.

A tear rolled from her eye and she moved her arm into view.

Lhateso stared in horror and grabbed her sister and dragged her back, "no, no you don't."

"What did Strife say." Aerrana calmly replied.

"Let me then." Lhateso stood up straight, "you've only just got your strength back."

She crossed to the bed and held her arm out and stiffly said, "here."

She closed her eyes to the claw that Ozanus grew and used to cut into her wrist. He sucked on it till his thirst was sated and then he lay back and went back to sleep.

Aerrana crossed and wrapped a bandage around her sister's wrist as she said, "thank you, but you didn't have to."

"I left you, I owe you."

"I told you to go and it hasn't been all bad. He sort of loved me in his own way." Aerrana smiled to herself.

"I could kill him. I could kill him now." Lhateso showed her older sister the knife she still had.

"Hide that, quick and don't even think about it. Either one of them could kill us." Aerrana hissed and then added, "he's different now." She glanced back to the bed as Ozanus rolled over, "this is just the beginning of our trials with him. He's not going to be placid this time round."

"Placid?" Lhateso looked at her sister as she couldn't think of Ozanus as placid from what she had seen of him in the Valley. If he was different now and possibly dangerous wasn't killing him the right thing to do before he grew too strong? She would have to wait till her sister left the room and do it then.

"Let's get that sewn up." Aerrana said, changing the subject to distract her sister.

The opportunity came a few hours later. Aerrana left to get them food. Lhateso looked out the door to check she was really gone before crossing over to the bed. She stood beside it looking down at the sleeping Ozanus, finding the courage that she had had earlier.

She told herself she couldn't chicken out now. She pulled out the knife and looked at it. It had once been owned by the man lying in the bed. She barely knew him but what she was seeing now she knew the world wouldn't be safe. She took a deep breath and then murmured, "I'm sorry Miryama, but this needs to be done."

She braced herself and then before anything else could stop her she stabbed him in the back, glad to not be able to see his face. She thought if she stabbed him enough and then lie him on his back no one would notice.

She managed two deep stabs before her whole body was frozen. However hard she tried she couldn't move her arm. Strife's voice filled the room, "what do you think you are doing little girl?"

She couldn't even open her mouth to scream as she felt claws tighten around her throat. Her eyes slowly turned to the side and she saw Strife standing behind her, his head close to hers, his mouth full of sharp teeth at her ear. He hissed in her ear, "do you want to die that much?"

He released her throat long enough to let her answer. Hoarsely she answered, "you can't be allow to win."

"Ha! Too late for that." His grip tightened on her throat again until it was so tight she couldn't draw in a breath. She couldn't even try to defend herself. He released her and her body dropped to the floor like a sack of flour.

He sneered at it before stepping over it and checking on Ozanus. He had sensed Ozanus' brief wakening earlier. He placed a hand on the man's shoulder, "wake up my son."

Ozanus stirred, a new ache coming from his back, and rolled over. His eyes widened briefly, flashed red and then settled.

"Are you ready?"

Ozanus carefully sat up and frowned at the body on the floor. He looked back to Strife, "food, a wash and then I will be."

"Excellent." Strife remarked with a smile.

Aerrana returned then and dropped her dish on the floor in shock. She stared at her sister on the floor and then at Strife. She screamed her anger and threw herself at Strife though she didn't know how she would kill him. He swung out his arm and she went flying against the wall. She slumped to the floor with a groan. Without touching her

Strife lifted her into the air, her head slumped forward.
Once closer he lifted her head with a hand, "you have one
more job to do."
She tired not to look at him.
He growled, "answer me."
  "Yes sir." She answered meekly.
  "Wash him and get him in some clean clothes and then
give him your lifeblood."
Her mouth opened to protest but she didn't have the
strength to object.

She wished that time could go back to when she
was happy in the palace being served and being told stories
by Nuna. She didn't have any worries apart from whether
she would marry and who that would be. She couldn't
remember how she had become Bloodlust's mistress but at
least he had protected her. He had been infatuated with her
and Strife had ignored her until now. Her sister and lover
were dead and now she had no reason to live.

He dropped her on the floor and she didn't even try
to sit up. He strolled from the room without a backwards
glance.

Ozanus slowly pushed back the covers and swung
his legs over the side. He bent down and helped her up. He
swayed a little and she said with concern, "you shouldn't
be up. Get back in bed and I'll get you some food. I'll
organise hot water for you."
She helped him sit down and left him looking confused.
She paused at the door and looked back to see he was
frowning at the scars on one of his arms. She felt a little
sorry for him. Strife had done something to his mind and he
was veering between arrogance and confusion. She would
have to go carefully around him to survive.

While other silent servants filled a large wooden tub
with water in the adjourning room under Aerrana's
guidance Ozanus ate. He watched as two men came and

took the dead girl away and realised his back ached from where she had stabbed him.

A part of him wanted to go back to sleep but he knew he couldn't remain sleeping. He knew he needed to gather his elite group of Suwars together and then prepared to destroy the Valley that no longer wanted him.

He frowned at Aerrana when she came and stood by his side. He felt sure he knew who she was. She softly remarked, "a bath will help you wake up and ease some of your aches." She held out a hand and he took it.
On stiff legs he let her lead him to the next room. She removed the bloodstained tunic and his trousers. She fought the sudden urge to stroke some of the scars. Some were still red from the rapid healing process they had gone through. She wondered if they still hurt.

He stepped up and into the tub of scented water. Aerrana had added ginger and peppermint oil to the water. He sank into the hot water with a sigh and felt it starting to relax tense muscles and tight skin.

Aerrana reached for a small cloth and began to wipe his skin. He lay back in the tub and her hands came down his chest. He hissed as the rough cloth caught a stitch that still held. She froze. His eyes were closed when he said, "don't stop."
She dipped the cloth in the water and started from his neck again and washed downwards.

"Mmm." He turned his head to look at her and saw her swallow and lick her lips. He could sense her heart beating just a little bit quicker than it should be.

He caught her eye and they stared at each other waiting to see who would make the next move. He lifted an arm and put it round her shoulders and drew her head closer. She didn't dare breath until she found him kissing her. He broke off long enough to say, "get in with me."
She nodded and without even taking off her dress she

slipped into the tub. She told herself she was doing this to protect herself. Hopefully he would be better than the fumbling motions of Bloodlust.

She knelt opposite him and began to run fingers along the scars on his chest. He found himself catching his own breath. He saw her dark nipples showing through her wet dress that clung to her thin body.

He drew her closer to him so she straddled him. He kissed her again as his hands found her breasts and gave them a squeeze. She held the edge of the tub until he took one of her hands and put it between them. She could feel him swelling up.

His hands ran down her back and pulled up the skirt of her dress so he could grab her buttocks. A hand found the cleft between her buttocks and followed it between her legs to where his erection waited. He drew her closer to him so he could explore her opening with his fingers. She gasped and clung to him as he pushed in with his thumb. Her fingers dug into his back and the pain he felt in the new wound woke him up.

He scooped her up and turned her around, pressing her against the side of the tub. He spread her legs with his knees, felt for her sex with rough fingers and then shoved himself in. She cried out in shock and pain as she was pressed against the wood, her hands clinging to the edge. One of his arms was wrapped round her waist keeping her hips against his while the other held on to the tub.

As he pressed deep within her his breath became faster and she could feel him panting into her neck. He let out a roar as he came, half deafening her. He felt in control and powerful.

He stepped away, letting her sink slowly into the water. He cocked his head as if listening to something only he could hear. He considered whether he should kill her and drain her of blood but that voice told him not to. It was soft and warm and quietly asked him to obey compared to Strife's loud demanding voice. It lulled him, soothed him in a way he didn't understand.

He reached for the cloth floating in the water and wiped himself over before getting out of the bath feeling alive and ready to take on the world. He didn't need her blood, that was too easy and wouldn't taste like the adrenalin and fear he wanted. Strife had fed him enough to sustain him for the moment.

He stretched his arms and back before reaching for the towel. He paused to study his new scars and ran a hand over some of them. He turned and challenged, "am I terrifying?"

Aerrana huddled in the bath, her arms wrapped around herself. She couldn't find her voice for fear of making him angry and nodded.

"Good." He smirked. He wrapped the towel around himself and left the room.

Strife was in the bedroom waiting for him. He sat in a chair with a pile of folded clothes beside him. He smiled, "did you enjoy your bath?"

Ozanus studied the god through lowered eyelids. Strife maybe his Overlord but he didn't need to know everything. Strife stood up, "now you are up, let us move this fight on." Ozanus smiled, "with pleasure."

"I think you will be needing these." Strife gestured to the pile of clothes.

Ozanus strolled over and pulled on the shirt which was embroidered with copper thread and trousers. He didn't need a coat, War's presence was keeping him hot. He pulled on the wrist guards noticing his left hand had lost its shake and smiled to himself. Strife offered the man the copper breastplate, "I think you will need this."

Ozanus grunted his approval and pulled it on and allowed Strife to buckle him in. As he pulled on boots he remarked stiffly, "I need a dragon."

"That can be organised."

"And the leaders of the camp. I want them on the move by this evening. We have no time to waste."
Strife smiled again. Why hadn't he done this earlier? He added, "of course."

"Hmpfh." Ozanus shoved the thick leather gloves temporarily in his belt. Spotting a dragon headed knife on the floor he picked it up, noting the blood on the blade and handle. Sneering he wiped it clean on the stained bedsheets and tucked it into his belt as well. He was ready now.

Thirty

Within the hour a group of men and a woman stood in the Hall of the castle looking nervous as the guards stayed close to them, eyeing them up. They turned as a door opened and Ozanus walked in and up on to the dais. Their eyes went wide as they couldn't understand why Ozanus was there. Had Strife lost? Or had the most well known Suwar in the known world changed sides? There was something different about him. His eyes were red and there was shimmer of power around him.

He glared down at them from the dais, "nothing has happened this past year. All you have done is grow fat on the land and our Overlord's benevolence. Now that is about to change. I want the whole camp armed and moving by tonight. You'll camp a mile from the Valley and be prepared to attack as soon as I give the command. This fight for supremacy is coming to an end and I will ensure we will win!"

He didn't expect cheering as they were all out for themselves but he would have liked an acknowledgement of some sort. They were not scared enough. He pulled out his knife and threw it at his chosen target without appearing to aim at them.

The thin man scrambled at the knife now sticking out of this throat while staring at the handle. He gurgled and blood bubbled up out of his mouth. He dropped to the ground and twitched.

The rest stared down at him and then at Ozanus who had stepped down from the dais and was approaching them all. They parted as he drew near and asked, "anyone else want to die?"

They hastily shook their heads.

"Then get going." Ozanus snarled.

They turned and fled as a guard was coming in. He pressed himself against the door. Once they had gone he approached Ozanus and saluted him. Ozanus was crouched pulling his knife out and wiping the blood off on the dead man. He glanced up and growled, "what?"

"Sir, the dragons are here to be looked at."

"Good."

Out on the road leading from the castle stood a black scaled dragon with silver tips to the scales that looked familiar. Ozanus frowned, "I thought you said dragons?"

"I did sir, there were four of them." The guard replied in confusion.

"My lord. I am Savan, at your service." The dragon bowed its head.

"And where are the others?" Ozanus demanded.

"They weren't worthy to be considered so I have chased them off."

Ozanus smiled, *"let's go then. We need to head for the Valley."*

"And destroy it?"

"Not yet." Ozanus replied as he climbed on to the dragon's back.

At the sight of a dragon turning and revealing a rider on its back the youths hanging out in one of the watchtowers got excited, believing it was Ozanus returning. One slid down the ladder and ran off to let the Valley floor know. They all froze at the roar they heard. It wasn't a roar of celebration. It sounded sinister.

Those left in the watchtower watched as the dragon rose higher into the air and turned to dive, folding in its wings to punch through the barrier. They watched in horror as the rider pulled back its bow and while the dragon was still in its dive, shot their friend in the back. The young man stumbled, tripped and then went sliding down the path and saw himself flying off the edge.

With a sound that sounded like a crack of lightening the barrier protecting the Valley disappeared as Ozanus flew through it on his new dragon. Everyone who was outside looked upwards at the sound and their hearts were filled with dread. Then they saw the dragon and wondered who it was that had broken the barrier.

Miryama ran out of the house followed by Gaerwn and Ozanus' siblings. She hoped it was Ozanus but they all caught their breaths at the sight of the black dragon that glided in low and the copper dressed rider glowing golden red in the sunlight. Didn't Kenene say that Bloodlust was dead?

Above the Valley floor Ozanus called out for the dragons and Suwars, *"I am making a new army to rule this world. Come all those who have become disillusioned, who have been snubbed, who had realised you will not win. Come to me those who now see it will be safer for you on the new winning side, my side! This Valley should never have ignored me, revenge will be mine! I am going to take back what is rightfully mine. For I am Ozanus, true heir to the title which has been stolen from me by my brother."*

Amongst those who heard there was confusion. Some heeded his call and decided to join him. Others who had always carried the suspicion that Ioan had stolen the title from his brother also decided to change sides. However, the majority weren't sure. They headed to the house for answers as Ozanus flew off, not waiting to see who would join him.

Lylya, Ioan and Miryama looked at each other with fear. Ioan exclaimed, "what is he playing at?! Now is not the time to be splitting us!" He threw his arms in the air in exasperation and stomped back inside.

"I'm going to have to sort this mess out. There are some that are definitely going to be leaving us." Gaerwn sighed heavily.

"How many do you think?" Lylya asked.

"I don't know. Hopefully I can talk some of them out of leaving."

"And Ozanus' old team?" Miryama asked.

"Depends which side Kenene decides on. He is being ostracised at the moment for not getting Ozanus back to us."

"I'll go talk to him." Miryama replied and hurried down the steps with Gaerwn. She would deal with the personal side of it later, somehow.

She found Kenene heading towards the cliffs where the dragon nests were. Ahead of them on the cliffs the dragons were talking amongst themselves. A few had abandoned their riders and gone. Some had lost their riders by refusing to leave. She shouted, "Kenene, stop, wait up!" He glanced back with a frown and adjusted the bow he had hooked over his shoulder and grumbled, "can't."
She picked up her pace and reached for him. She forced him to stop and look at her. He was old but the last week had aged him even more. No one was talking to him and he blamed himself for not ensuring Ozanus came back and not having better control of his dragon.

She challenged him, "where do you think you are going?"

"To join him." Kenene replied without emotion.

"Why? It's not your fault you couldn't get him back." She protested.

"I'm not wanted here anymore."

"We need your experience more than ever. How many are following you?" She asked with concern.

"I haven't encouraged any of them, so you don't need to worry about that." He turned away and continued walking. She couldn't think of anything else to say to persuade him to stay because even a part of her disliked him for abandoning Ozanus, even if he hadn't planned to.

She turned away and returned to the house, slowly. Her mind was in turmoil. What had happened to Ozanus? What had Strife done to him? How was she going to get him back? Was history going to repeat itself with Shaprour?

She inwardly told herself to stop. She needed to concentrate on protecting both the Valley and Shaprour to ensure he had somewhere to grow up in and rule. She didn't even want to think of a life without Ozanus. She would try her best to bring him back to her side.

Ioan had demanded a meeting when they heard that Strife's whole army was on the move. A map of the Valley and its surrounding area was on the table. Gathered around it was Lylya, Miryama and the leader of the Daughters of Scyth; Gaerwn and his deputy and the Mayor and leader of the guard of Linyee as well as the head of the Valley's village with his son. Ioan fought down fear as this was the sort of thing Ozanus was good at.

He looked at everyone around the table and all the experience they had and hoped they could all manage to work together. He looked to Gaerwn and hoped the older man would take the hint. Gaerwn gave the barest of nods and spoke up, "thank you to everyone for coming."

"Is it true that the Nejus has changed sides?" The Mayor of Linyee asked with worry.

"We don't really know what is going on." Lylya said

sternly, cowering the man.

"Ssh Lylya." Ioan warned.

"We've lost about ten riders and their dragons." Gaerwn informed everyone.

"And Kenene." Miryama added.

"No one is missing him though." Gaerwn's deputy muttered to his leader.

Gaerwn ignored the man as he went on, "and another six dragons on their own and four Suwars."

"That's not too horrendous then." Ioan remarked with relief.

"Except they have a bigger army than us. We have a small group from Linyee and the same again from the Village. We rely heavily on the Suwars." Gaerwn remarked.

"Don't forget us." The leader of the Daughters of Scyth remarked with a frown, "we might not be riders but there are about one hundred of us who can fight on foot."

"Good to hear, thanks." Gaerwn answered gruffly.

"Soooo… what's the next step then?" Ioan asked.

"Two choices, we can fight in the Valley or we can fight them on the plain. We need to catch them unprepared. We can't let them get themselves organised. They aren't organised like us."

"But they have a God." The Mayor of Linyee exclaimed. Gaerwn sighed as he didn't have an answer to that.

"We can't plan for that." Miryama pointed out, "not even Ozanus could have."

"We'll have to kill this rogue rider." The Daughter of Scyth remarked.

Miryama stood and left the table. She didn't leave the room but she didn't want to hear every disparaging word that was likely to be uttered.

Back at the table they didn't acknowledge Miryama who had stepped away. Gaerwn's deputy remarked, "it's

going to be hard to get to him if it is Ozanus as I'm sure
Kenene will be right there with him."
There were a few nods from those who remembered the
early days of Ozanus' reign.
"We'll have to organise a separate group to deal with
him." Gaerwn sighed. He turned, "Miryama?"
She reluctantly turned back to the table, "yes?"
"I think it would be best if you lead. You can confirm if it
is Ozanus and maybe you'll get through to him. Will you?"
She nodded, "sure."
"Thank you."
She left the room then.
        She had to think and hard. She had to make the
decision now on what she did in regards to Ozanus so she
could prepare herself and not change her mind at the last
minute. She wanted to scream and rage but couldn't find
the energy to. She returned to her home and was relieved to
find Shaprour home. She gathered her son into her arms
and held him tight. He squirmed in her arms and pushed her
away. As he broke free she said, "you know I love you."
"Of course mama, don't be silly. Can I go play now?"
She reluctantly let go of his hand and he ran out without a
care. She wished then she could go back to being a child
herself with no adult responsibilities.

        Word reached them that Strife's main army had
arrived and set up camp a mile from the Valley. There were
no dragons present. The Valley became a hive of activity.
Those going on foot gathered outside the main entrance.
The Suwars and dragons gathered by the village.
        Miryama's small group of Suwars stood on the
clifftops. They would not be flying unless the mystery
rogue rider that was possibly Ozanus appeared. The five of
them stood on the edge, hands shielding their eyes from the
sun as they watched the foot soldiers head out to meet the

encamped army. One of them asked, "do you really think it is Ozanus?"

"Can you remember seeing War flying alongside him when we fought Timijin's army here in Keytel?" Another replied.

"Sort of."

"I bet He is involved." The second remarked with confidence.

"Ssh." The Daughter of Scyth in the group said to the others with a glance towards Miryama who was staring out from the cliffs, "have some respect, that might be her husband out there and we have to kill him."

"Here they come!" One of them shouted as a distraction as the Suwars and dragons flew over the Valley with roars to announce their arrival.

"We have surely got to win." Another remarked on the awe-inspiring sight, having not seen anything like it as he hadn't been in Moronland.

"Quiet!" Miryama turned and snapped, "this must be taken seriously. You aren't going up against foot soldiers, you will be going up against your equals and at least one of them is known to be one of the best. If they come today your job is to distract the others and I'll go for the rogue." Silence returned to the group.

Miryama returned to looking out. In the distance a large dust cloud was rising into the air as the fighting began. It had been discussed at length round the table but they all knew Strife and the rogue wouldn't show on the first day. Today was about getting rid of weaknesses and seeing how strong the Valley was in numbers. Tomorrow would be the big one, dragon against dragon, Suwar against Suwar while ducking around anything coming from any war machines that would have been hastily built overnight. But it was better to be prepared. She wondered if Ozanus was watching somewhere on the other side of the fighting or was it War.

Everyone who survived came back exhilarated, exhausted and mournful. Villagers and Linyee's refugees headed out with carts and their own armed guard to gather up as many of the wounded as they could.

Ioan stood at the entrance of the Valley with his sisters watching the carts return. This was the first time in a long time that he had ventured out. He stood stiffly as Shiang quietly wept and Lylya, a witness to fighting before, tried to comfort her. This was the closest to war either of her siblings had ever got. She could only hope it didn't stretch on and on and that Ozanus would come back to them.

As the last cart was pulled through the entrance they headed back in behind it. Ioan remarked, with a bitter note, "we are getting too many mounds of the dead. Timijin, that plague, and now this."

"This is war Ioan." Lylya retorted with disgust, "none of us want this but it's happened. As a country we have been extremely lucky that we haven't had more battles and invasions. We should probably get everyone together and make the plan for tomorrow."

"We should all go and give an offering to the Dragon Lord." Shiang remarked firmly.

"She's right." Ioan replied, anything to not hear the dead and wounded list, names that would mean nothing to him. It was too uncomfortable for him. He knew he needed to show the Dragon Lord that he was just as capable as his brother and the Valley was worth saving, "I'll go with Shiang. You plan tomorrow."

"You should be there. You are the Nejus." Lylya retorted in frustration.

"This isn't my skill, that's why we have Gaerwn." He answered stiffly,

Lylya huffed and walked on ahead.

Thirty-One

The dead were being dealt with and the wounded looked after as with the dawn everyone fit enough to fight prepared themselves. They all felt sure the day would be the big one. Even the Gods were alert to it all. Dark grey clouds hung low in the sky. The wind spun dust devils high into the sky. Lightening flashed within the clouds making the atmosphere charged with electricity that sparked off tails, spears and rocks. Thunder was silent for the moment. There was no sign of the Dragon Lord which was ominous.

Goodbyes were said once again to those staying in the Valley. Those not fighting made their way to the cliffs to watch. They kept their distance from Miryama and her small group as they waited for their moment.

The shout from the watchtowers announced the arrival of the renegade dragons and Suwars. They in turn announced themselves with roars. The Valley's dragons and their riders rose into the air and responded.

The clouds began to turn black as a God swept through them and then dived out with a roar that deafened everyone. With Strife's arrival the dragons on his side were re-invigorated. Valley dragons with no riders turned and flew towards Strife. They would die trying. With a swipe of a claw, a swish of his tail and a few snaps of his jaw it didn't take long to kill them. A few managed to scratch their claws on his scales but didn't cause him to bleed.

Miryama frowned, why was Strife here before the rogue Suwar? She scanned the sky, the rogue had to already be out there. She spotted another black dragon and hissed in frustration that she had missed his arrival. She headed to Spilla as she shouted, *"it's our turn!"*
The others quickly ran for their dragons and climbed into their saddles. They waited for Spilla to rise into the air before joining him. Miryama waved a hand forward, *"let's go!"*

The five dragons roared at the thrill of joining the fight, while their riders held on tight with their thighs as they pulled out scale piercing arrows and placed them to their bows.

As a group they swept into the fighting. Dragons moved around them like they were a rock in a stream, snarling, roaring and fighting. Strife circled them all, chuckling to himself. He tore through if he saw a Suwar fall from their dragon and swallowed them whole. The dragons fought hard, barely remembering the riders on their backs.

A few turned their attention to Strife as he swept through only to find themselves turning on their Valley mates, refreshing Strife's smaller numbers.

Miryama and her small team pushed through, snapping at anyone who got too close. It didn't matter which side they were on.

In the centre of the fighting, just above it, surveying it all, was Ozanus. His mouth was slightly open and his heart was beating fast as if he was being pleasured but it was War within him savouring it all. Kenene was beside him, his eyes constantly on watch to everything going on. The others that had come to Ozanus' call were deep in the fighting.

Ozanus' eyes narrowed as he saw the small group heading their way. He wondered who they had chosen to take him on. He raised a gloved hand and pointed to one side. Kenene turned and looked. Grimly he remarked, "they hope Miryama will get you to change sides."

"Hmpfh, that's wishful thinking. Too many bridges have been burnt."

Kenene frowned. Since changing sides he had spoken briefly to Ozanus but not a lot had made sense when they had spoken. War or Strife had damaged Ozanus somehow. To Kenene it was like his leader's memories had been tampered with.

"I'll take the leader, you the rest." Ozanus directed.

"You sure?"

Ozanus glared at Kenene and the older man took that as his answer.

Miryama unwrapped her headscarf to reveal her face before calling out, "Ozanus? Is that you?"

His posture was Ozanus' but she still wasn't sure since he seemed to have become the enemy.

His red eyes narrowed and he put an arrow to his bow. He muttered under his breath, "prepare to die bitch!" He released the arrow and if it wasn't for Spilla it would have hit Miryama in the chest and probably killed her. He rose up so the arrow bounced off his scales. Spilla called out, *that has to be him. I don't think I know of anyone else just as good. He would have killed you.*

"Something has happened to him." She frowned with concern and then shouted down to Ozanus, "it's me, Miryama! Your wife!"

"You are no wife to me!" He shouted up at her as he put another arrow to his bowstring. He ordered his dragon, *"take them out."*

Spilla saw it coming and quickly retreated. He shouted, with a look behind him, *"hold on tight."*

He banked round in an attempt to throw Ozanus' dragon off his tail and then went in to headbutt the black dragon. The dragon twisted round at the last moment and whacked

Spilla with her tail. Ozanus released his arrow and it narrowly missed Miryama who had leant down in her saddle to keep herself in it as Spilla was thrown back.

Spilla's wings missed a beat and he began to fall but quickly recovered. He flew under the black dragon and twisted round as he shouted, *"you have to take him out!"*

"No! No, I can't do that." She exclaimed.

"It's kill him or be killed ourselves." He snarled as he used his rear claws to scratch at his opponent's snapping jaw.

"Let me try something else first."

"Hurry, because I can't keep going like this."

"Hold steady, just for a minute please." She called in desperation.

"I'll try." Spilla hit the other dragon in the head with his tail, briefly dazing it. It shook its head and snarled in anger. Ozanus was putting another arrow to his bow, looking unfazed by his dragon's erratic flying.

Miryama took a deep breath, trying to calm herself so she sounded commanding rather than desperate. She felt her hand rest on her dragon headed knife and smiled, she knew she could do this. Seven years ago Ozanus believed in her. She looked Ozanus in his glaring red eyes and demanded, *"WAR! You fickle bastard! Come out now! You owe me this!"*

Nothing happened. With reluctance she pulled an arrow from her quiver and put it to her own bow string. She wasn't as good as Ozanus on the back of a dragon but she had to drive War into revealing himself. She released her arrow. She shocked herself when it skimmed past Ozanus' arm, cutting through his sleeve and marking his skin. He stared in surprise and muttered, "lucky shot."

Miryama shouted, *"Spilla, move now!"* She could see Ozanus getting ready to shoot another arrow in their direction.

"We are just going round in circles Miryama. We aren't going to win." Spilla remarked as he flew up to get out of the way of Ozanus on his dragon.

"War is in him, I know he is. We've got to draw him out. Charge him Spilla. Go for Ozanus, not the dragon." She ordered, hiding her fear in the stern tone of her voice.

Spilla glanced round to check Miryama meant it. He swallowed and thought it was mad. With reluctance he did as he was ordered. He turned to face Ozanus and his dragon.

Plan made he headed straight at Ozanus' dragon. At the last moment he adjusted his position and grabbed Ozanus in his mouth and lifted him off his dragon. He could have bitten down and killed the man in an instant but he couldn't do that to his Nejus.

Strife witnessed the attack and twisted round. He charged through the fighting, dragons sent scattering like skittles being hit by a ball. There were screams from the men and women thrown off their dragons who found themselves falling to the ground.

He charged at Spilla with a roar and head butted the dragon. Spilla dropped Ozanus as he flew sideways. Ozanus began falling.

Ozanus didn't stay human for long. He stretched and grew bigger and with a roar of his own War joined the melee. As if they had been waiting for this moment the thunder rolled out of the clouds and lightening forked downwards narrowly missing several dragons. The rain started as well.

He didn't stop growing either. Fueled on the anger Strife had fed Ozanus and two days of fighting he soon became the same size as Strife, his burnished copper scales glistening in the rain.

Those who witnessed the change couldn't believe

what they were seeing. At the size of the God the dragons decided it was time to retreat. The rain had dampened their desire to keep fighting and the lightening was making it too dangerous to keep flying.

Neither God cared what was going on with the mortals around them. They only had eyes for each other. Strife called out, *"ready to rule this world with me?"*

"This is my world." War answered with a snarl. Strife frowned as he circled War.

War went on, *"you are obsolete. No one knows who you are, no one fears you. The new Gods have reigned supreme longer than you ever did."*

"Where are they then?" Strife sneered. He turned and flew at War, head butting him. War went flying but quickly recovered. He flew along the length of Strife's back, his claws dragging through the Basilisk's scales.

Strife roared in pain. He spun round and opened his mouth wide to grab War by the trunk of his body, pushing him up through the clouds. Lightening stretched out to hit the ancient dragon.

The cloud was thick all around them, but the Dragon Lord's glow was strong enough to be seen as he came roaring through and raked his own claws along the Basilisk's back. War bucked and squirmed until Strife released him. Strife called out, "Death! I know you are out there. You have not abandoned me I hope."

The day grew darker as if the light and life was being sucked from it. Out of the blackness emerged a bloated Death. He weaved towards where War and Strife fought and chuckled. Strife realised that his last ally, if he still was, was going to be of no help. Death seemed to be unable to bear his own weight as he slipped down into the cloud cover.

The golden Dragon Lord and War teamed up and held tight to Strife. Out of the cloud cover Death emerged again, coming straight up, mouth wide open and full of rows of sharp teeth. Strife was determined not to give up without a fight. None of this was what he had planned. He had truly underestimated the immortals who had been biding their time till the right moment. He wouldn't give them the satisfaction of knowing they had won as Death bit deep into his thick trunk, before retreating and coming in for another bite.

Other Gods started to appear to take their own bites from the ancient god and even the Dragon Lord and War had their share. The Dragon Lord broke through Strife's ribs and grabbed at the huge black beating heart of the Basilisk and flew off with it before any other god could protest.

With no beating heart and so many bites taken out of him there was nothing to keep the Basilisk's body in the sky. The gods retreated and let the body begin its long fall to the ground where, once the scavengers had been at it, would leave the skeleton as an eternal memory of the long year that had been Strife's return.

Under the clouds the rain had cooled everyone's fire. They could hear the fighting happening above them and in flashes of lightening see the huge bodies clashing. Gaerwn shouted to his second in command, "get everyone to the ground. It's not safe up here, we need to regroup."

"And the others?"

"Them as well. It's not us versus them anymore. This is man against God. We have no idea who is going to win up there." Gaerwn glanced upwards as there was a roar and a golden light streaked through the clouds. He needed to find Miryama.

As word spread to go down only Gaerwn, Miryama and Kenene remained in the air, looking fearfully up into the sky. Gaerwn asked as they waited, "what happened to

Ozanus?”

"He was trying to kill me." Miryama exclaimed.
Kenene was wrapping an arm wound up as he replied with
a frown, "I really don't know. We barely spoke but his
memories seem off."

"His memories?"

"What we briefly discussed was definitely not how I
remember them."

"Look out, something's coming!" Spilla called out in
alarm.

The three dragons flew out of the way as to their right the
remains of Strife fell past them.

"Well, that's one issue dealt with." Gaerwn remarked
grimly.

"What about Ozanus?" Miryama exclaimed.
No one could give them an answer.

Above them, in the clouds, the winds were calming
and the clouds were growing lighter. Death remarked, *"I'm
going to sleep well."*

"Thank you." War said back.

*"Now, are you going to free yourself from that poor sod.
He's going to be of no use to anyone now, not even you."*

"He served his purpose." War agreed callously. He
stretched out his body and then it convulsed and he vomited
up Ozanus' body. It slid from his mouth and he let it start to
fall. Without a backwards glance he flew upwards towards
the heavens. Death circled the body a few times and
realised the man was somehow still alive so lost interest in
him.

The three riders waited and hoped, scanning the sky
for either man or dragon. The dragons were getting restless
from circling. Kenene remarked, "I don't think we are
going to see him again."

"What's that?" Spilla called out and they all turned to look.

Falling rapidly through the sky was Ozanus, being buffeted by the winds.

"He's not going to survive the fall." Gaerwn exclaimed in horror.

"None of us will be able to catch him." Spilla pointed out.

"We have to try Spilla." Miryama demanded.

He would willingly try but knew it would be impossible. He turned to dive down, tucking his wings in to dive as quickly as possible.

As Spilla turned over to catch Ozanus' falling body in his body, Miryama clinging to her saddle, a thick dart of gold shot down from the sky and wrapped itself around the unconscious body. Spilla pulled himself and watched as the Dragon Lord disappeared heavenward with Ozanus. Between heavy breaths he asked, *"what now?"*

"I don't know." Miryama answered carefully as she sat up from where she had been holding tight. Her thighs ached and her hands shook from the overload of adrenaline and fear.

"Do you think he will come back?"

"How am I supposed to know." She snapped and then quickly apologised, *"I'm sorry Spilla. It's been a long day already and...."* She felt tears welling up, *"I don't know what is happening any more than you."*

"It's alright. Let's head home."

"That sounds like a good idea." She smiled.

Thirty-Two

Reluctantly they headed back to the Valley. Gaerwn flew down to the rest of the Suwars to tell them it was over. He felt sure there would be some fights with the traitors and would have to watch the drinking tonight. It would be a strange evening for there would be those mourning deaths but wanting to celebrate the death of Strife. There would be confusion as well and questions no one could answer in regards to Ozanus.

Ioan and his two sisters stood at the top of the veranda steps. They had been there as soon as the first dragons had announced their return to the Valley. Kenene, Gaerwn and Miryama finally appeared, some of the last to return. They looked exhausted and not in the mood to celebrate. Ioan, trying to contain his excitement cautiously asked, "well?"

"Keytel and Moronland are now safe." Gaerwn grimly replied.

"And Ozanus?" Lylya asked hopefully.
The three on the lawn glanced at each other before looking up. Gaerwn answered, "we aren't really sure."

"Kenene? Should I be welcoming you back or locking you up?" Ioan glared at the man.

"He is a Suwar and I will deal with him and the others." Gaerwn retorted, not in the mood for Ioan trying to show he was just as good as Ozanus with the riders."

"They need some sort of punishment for deserting us."

"And I will decide that. You deal with the leftovers of Strife's soldiers. I'm sure the town of Linyee will help you there." Gaerwn rubbed his forehead where a headache was forming as he hadn't eaten all day and walked away, "Kenene, come on, before he locks you up."

Kenene stared up at Ioan and wondered whether it was worth the stress to remain a Suwar. He wondered whether he should do what Ozanus had done and just disappear with his family. Ioan was not Ozanus and would never be so. He knew Ioan struggled under Ozanus' shadow in a world use to a Nejus that was strong and a fighter rather than a diplomat and an administrator. He walked away then, in silence.

Lylya looked down at Miryama. She could see the woman was battling with a whole range of emotions. She wanted to go to her but she felt Ioan's hand grab her wrist. She looked into her brother's face and realised that with Ozanus gone, as far as he was concerned, he was now going to make sure he was properly respected as Nejus. Keytel would have to rely on him and Miryama was not part of the plan. She wondered if he was going to take Shaprour as well. She would actually be glad to go back to Moronland, away from her brother's threatening tyranny.

On the lawn Miryama blinked a few times. She was still in a daze over what she had witnessed and the fact Ozanus now apparently hated her. She walked away as the desire to embrace Shaprour grew too strong. He could have lost both parents today but thankfully he hadn't.

After holding Shaprour so tight that he protested she found some bread and cheese and ate it. She didn't give herself anytime to get changed or wash before heading up to the temple. She stood in front of the altar and stared out past it to the sky which was now clear, not a cloud in it. It

266

turned orange and yellow as the sun began to set.

She cut open her palm and let the blood drip into the water filled bowl and sent up a prayer, *"please give me a sign, anything. I just need to know if I will get him back."* There was no answer or sign.

Wrapping her hand up she sank to the floor and leant against the altar to wait. She wasn't going anywhere till He gave her a hint of what her future would be.

Lylya found her friend, head slumped forward and asleep, her bandage soaked with blood. She crouched down, "Miryama, Miryama, wake up you can't sleep here."

"Is Ozanus back?" Miryama asked sleepily.

"No."

"Has there been anything from the Dragon Lord?"

"Nothing that I am aware of."

"What's going to happen to the dead that we couldn't bring back? That's meant to be Ozanus' role. I should go out and do it." Miryama made to stand up but her legs nearly gave up underneath her and she had to grab Lylya's arm.

"I think you are going to bed. We will worry about the dead tomorrow. Gaerwn can look after that in the morning, he is next in command after Ozanus."

"I can do it, I'm Ozanus' partner. I can ride Nimib, I know she can breath fire."

"No, sleep. You have had a long hard day." Miryama shook her head, "I can't go anywhere. The Dragon Lord might bring him back here."

"Do you think he will be brought back dead or alive?" Lylya asked and then instantly regretted speaking the question out loud.

Miryama glared at her, "I don't want to think about it. Last time, when he was in the mountains I felt sure he was alive. This time I don't feel a thing." The tears began to roll down her cheeks, "I am staying here until his body is returned either dead or alive.”

“I’ll stay with you then.” Lylya offered.

“I don’t expect or need you too.”

“I am going to get us some blankets and food and some warmed ale.”

“Go down and join the others.” She could smell the rancid smoke of the large burning pyre.

“I think tonight you are more important. I am here as your friend as well as Ozanus’ sister. I am just as worried as I don’t know what I will do without him either. This world won’t be the same if he never comes back. What do you think happened up there?”
They both looked upwards where the moon was shining down. Lylya added, “do you think She is with him?”

“You believe in the healing moon more than me.” Miryama answered stiffly, “and thank you. You can keep me company if you want.” She gave Lylya a tight smile. Lylya returned it as she said, “I’ll be back shortly then.”

She wasn’t sure if time did stand still or if it really was almost a week of waiting and slowly coming to the realisation that Ozanus might be gone. Gaerwn went out on Nimib to burn the dead that had been left on the plain. Then he, Kenene, Arno and Lylya took it in turns keeping Miryama company in her vigil. As day six started Lylya asked as they ate the breakfast Arno had brought for them, “when do we end this?”

There was a flash of golden light and the three of them were forced to retreat to the steps of the temple. The pillars cracked and two fell off the cliff edge as the golden scaled Dragon Lord filled the space. The three of them glanced at each other and then back at the God whose coils were shrinking.

No one moved as Ozanus’ body was revealed, laid out on the paved floor. Lylya finally found her voice,

"Arno, go fetch the others."
She didn't move as she watched Miryama slowly approached the God. His tail twitched and he shook his head to remove his feathery mane from his eyes. She bowed to him, *"noble lord, do I dare ask?"*

"He lives but his memories have been severely tampered with. I have removed what I can but you must lead him to the right ones."

"And War?" She cautiously asked.

"He won't be interfering down here for a long time."

"Thank you. Can you not leave us all alone now?"
The God chuckled as he pushed up into the air.

"You leave my son alone!" She shouted.

"I can't promise anything." He called down as he flew heavenwards.

She knelt down beside Ozanus and touched him to make sure he was real. His clothes were ripped, and he had lost his breastplate, knife and wrist guards. She stared at the scars that now covered his body, half hidden by the torn clothes. She ran a hand over some of them as she whispered, "what did he do to you?"
She wondered what memories had been recovered and what had been lost.

She only looked up when she heard footsteps and heavy breathing. Behind her now stood everyone that mattered, and Arno stood off to one side. Ioan asked cautiously, "well?"

"He's alive." Miryama said staring directly at him, and with bitterness added, "Nejus. Don't worry, you are safe from him."

Ioan shifted uncomfortable and was relieved when everyone's attention was distracted by Ozanus groaning. Lylya ran to him and helped him sit up. He rested against her chest staring at everyone staring at him. He frowned at Miryama and then at Lylya, "who are you?"

Shiang let out a sob.

He blinked and then looked down at his body. In bewilderment he asked, "what happened to me?"

"A lot." Miryama replied, "but let's get you down from here and washed and fed."

"That sounds like a good idea." Ozanus brightened, "and you are?"

She smiled at him though it felt fake, "I am your wife, Miryama." She held out a hand.

He cautiously took it and found his hand felt right in hers. He smiled as he was pulled up and remarked, "I think I remember you."

"One step at a time my friend." Kenene stepped forward. Recognition showed on Ozanus' face, "What are you doing here? How have you managed to get through this unharmed?"

"Not quite." Kenene smiled and patted his injured arm, "but I have fared better than you. You are a crazy fool who needs a crazy old fool to have his back."

"Sounds good to me." Ozanus grinned.

Breaths were released as the others realised Ozanus wasn't completely gone and that some of his memories might be recovered. Maybe it had been a good thing that Kenene had changed sides.

Arno led the group out of the temple and down the steps carved into the cliffs. He hoped nothing more would happen to the Valley and his adopted family during the last of his life at least. Behind the servant Miryama held tight to Ozanus' hand. She wasn't going to lose him again if she could help it. She hoped that they would be able to live as a proper family from now on.

Author's Note:

As an independent author I would like to thank you for purchasing this book and I hope you have enjoyed it. With no support from a big publishing house every purchase and review mean something to me so please spread the word and write a review. You can find me on Instagram as @f_garstang_author and let me know personally what you thought. You'll also see what I am working on and what will be coming out.

I am a multi genre author and I also have the below out:

Historical: The Crusade's Secrets
Historical Fantasy: Kukulcan's Messenger
Historical Romance: Masked
Historical Supernatural: The Dacha in the Forest
Fantasy Series: The Defenders of the Valley
                The Lost God
                The Daughters of Scyth
Romance: Biker Leather and Woolly Sheep.

Thank you